FROM

SWEETGRASS

BRIDGE

Stonehouse Publishing Inc. is an independent
publishing house, incorporated in 2014.

Cover design and layout by Elizabeth Friesen.
Printed in Canada

Stonehouse Publishing would like to thank and acknowledge
the support of the Alberta Government funding for the arts,
through the Alberta Media Fund.

Government

National Library of Canada Cataloguing in Publication Data
Anthony Bidulka
From Sweetgrass Bridge
Novel
ISBN 978-1-988754-54-3
First edition

FROM SWEETGRASS BRIDGE

A NOVEL BY
ANTHONY BIDULKA

FOR HERB

PROLOGUE

Every prairie summer has one. A lucky few know it as it's happening; the fleeting climax of the season, a day so achingly perfect it seems unreal until, someday, you see its reflection in a photograph or flash of memory. It's a day with seemingly endless hours stretching lazily from one unblemished sunlit horizon to the other. Heat permeates the air like popcorn soaking up melted butter, teasing breezes come out to play. The green of grass, lemon yellow of sun, soft lavender of delphiniums, pale pink of crabapple skins harmonize with the pungency of baked earth and maturing fields of flax. Cast aside pool towels, dogs running through sprinklers and drips of ice cream on sizzling sidewalks become the unmistakable scents of nostalgia. As the brilliant palette of a living sky announces the languorous arrival of dusk, Saskatchewanians turn their sun-burnished faces towards the heavens and smile their gratitude, an unexpected tugging at heart strings telling them the flawless day is almost over. Today was that day. Beautiful. Peaceful. Making what came at its end all the more tragic.

Billie Jo didn't know what to expect when she accepted Robby's invitation to accompany him on a late night drive on Saturday night. They'd been dating for several weeks. Her girlfriends told her to expect a play for a full-on hookup. Her sister, Betty Jo (their mother was an avid fan of the 1960's television show *Petticoat Junction*), said if it didn't happen soon, she should assume he probably wasn't interested in her in that way.

With a full moon lighting the way, windows rolled down and

sultry summer air playing in their hair, Robby's car hit cruising speed on the narrow, two-lane highway heading south out of the city. Before long he slowed, turning right onto a grid road.

"Where are we going?" Billie Jo asked, glancing over her shoulder to confirm she could still see the lights of Livingsky.

"You've never been here before?" Robby asked, sounding hopeful.

"I don't think so. Should I have?"

"Cool. It'll be a surprise then."

"A good one?"

He glanced at her. "Of course."

A sharp tap on the brakes threw the couple forward. Billie Jo yelped.

"Sorry, sorry, sorry!" Robby exclaimed, manhandling the steering wheel to make another turn. "I didn't think the turn off was so soon."

"Turn off to what?" She was beginning to feel a bit uneasy. But that was silly. Sure, they'd only been seeing each other for less than two months, but they'd known each other for more than a year. They worked at the same accounting firm, having been hired at the same time as they pursued their CPA designations.

"We're getting close." He snuck another glance in her direction. "I hope you don't think this is too cheesy. If you do, or you don't want to do it, we can leave."

Do it? Do what exactly? "Now you've got me curious. Come on, tell me, where are we?"

Robby pulled the car into what looked like a makeshift parking lot that was really nothing more than a clearing surrounded on three sides by trees. Shifting the car into park, he loosened his seatbelt and said, "They used to call this place *Lover's Lane*. Boomers probably still do. Can you believe it?"

Glad for the dim lighting, Billie Jo felt herself blushing. At twenty! Blushing because a guy she liked was probably going to ask her to have sex with him. *How ridiculous am I?*

"I have another surprise. If you're into it."

"Yes, I'm into it," she replied so quickly she worried she'd sounded a bit too enthusiastic.

"Come on." With that Robby jumped out of the car.

Billie Jo followed him to the rear of the vehicle where he was struggling to open the trunk. She used the cover of darkness to adjust her blouse which had come untucked from her jeans, which were maybe a size too small.

"Can you light me up, please?"

Illuminating the area with her cell phone flashlight, Billie Jo watched with increasing giddiness as Robby finally managed to open the trunk, revealing a picnic basket and blanket.

"You're kidding. A picnic? At midnight? Out here? In the dark?"

"No?" he looked at her for permission or refusal, adjusting his glasses which had slipped too far down his nose.

"Yes! I love it! Let's do it. Right here, or is there a picnic spot around here? Do you know where to go?"

He gave her a exaggerated look. "You know I'm an accountant, right? I am nothing if not organized and well-researched."

"Oh, I get it," she teased to cover her concern about the answer to what she was about to ask. "You've been to *Lover's Lane* so many times you know the way by heart, huh?"

"Oh yeah, Robby McAllister is a real lothario. They're even considering renaming this place Robby's Lane."

Billie Jo smiled, much wider than was probably necessary. "I'll be the judge of that."

"Promise?" With a wink and lighting the way with his own phone, Robby led them out of the parking lot toward a gently worn path.

Billie Jo was surprised to find the route was on a rather sharp incline and tried her best to control her breathing. She didn't want him to think she was out of shape (which she probably was but he didn't need to know that). With all the trees it was impossible to know where their final destination might be, but instead of focusing on that, she used the beam of her phone to highlight Robby's rather generous rear end. She liked a meaty guy.

"Get ready," he warned a couple of minutes later as they crested a hillock.

Coming to a stop next to Robby, Billie Jo's mouth fell open. "Oh. My. God."

Thick foliage had given way to a small patch of grass and a wide-open dome of starry sky. Taking her hand in his free one, Robby led Billie Jo closer to the furthest edge of the hilltop where it suddenly dropped into a deep gorge. To their left, gracefully suspended above the river valley as if perfectly placed there by a landscape painter, was a truss bridge, bathing luxuriously in the glow of a moon at the zenith of its fullness.

"What is this place?" Billie Jo whispered reverentially.

"Down there is the South Saskatchewan River. Well, actually it's a tributary than joins back up with the main river a couple of miles from here. And that," he pointed up, "is Sweetgrass Bridge."

"It's beautiful."

"Yeah. And really old. It's been around forever."

"I didn't even know it existed and it's only a few kilometers out of the city."

"Close enough to get to in a jiffy, but far enough from prying eyes if you want a little privacy," he said in what he hoped was a seductive voice.

Billie Jo, however, wasn't quite ready for seduction. "Can you drive on it?"

"I guess so."

"Where does it go?"

"I'm not sure. There are probably faster ways to get wherever it takes you, so it probably doesn't get used much anymore." Robby surmised.

"That's sad."

Not wanting *sad* to become a thing, Robby decided it was time to get the mood back on track. "Come on." Grabbing Billie Jo's hand again, he pulled her to the centre of the opening, where the grass was thickest and smelled the sweetest.

The generous moon provided more than enough light, allowing the couple to extinguish their phones. While Robby was busy laying

out the blanket and unloading wine, candles, watermelon slices and
bottles of water from the basket, Billie Jo found herself pulled back
to the magnificent view of Sweetgrass Bridge. Although she wasn't
afraid of heights, her stomach trilled with butterflies as she inched
closer to the cliff's edge. Leaning forward, she peered down into the
vale and could just make out the snaking stream far below. Suddenly, she jerked back.

What the hell is that?

An unexpected sound had disrupted the idyllic scene. It had
come from—as all unexpected sounds usually do—somewhere in
the darkness.

Behind her? In front? Did it come from the gorge? The bridge?
The woods?

Looking back, she saw Robbie still busily working on setting up
their picnic. Obviously he hadn't heard the noise, or maybe he had
and knew it was nothing to be bothered by. Taking a deep breath
she settled her nerves and told herself that there were probably all
sorts of late-night woodland noises she hadn't heard before. She was
a city girl not used to the country. It was a bit creepy, but not unusual and certainly nothing to be afraid of. Her gaze shifted back to the
Classic-movie visage of Sweetgrass Bridge. All that was missing was
a soaring orchestral soundtrack. She sighed and felt herself falling
a little in love. With the bridge? With Robby for bringing her here?

"Ready," Robby called out, disrupting Billie Jo's musings.

She turned to see her date kneeling on the blanket, lighting candles. She didn't have the heart to suggest it was too warm for candles.
Even this late at night the temperature hovered in the mid-twenties.
Instead, she smiled, approached the dreamy setting like a leading
lady and graciously lowered herself next to Robby.

In short order they were settled, candles flickering, wine poured
and sipped, bites of gloriously sweet and juicy watermelon taken.
With flushed faces awash in mellow moonlight, set against the perfect backdrop of Sweetgrass Bridge, Billie Jo knew in her heart that
this was going to be the night. There wasn't even a single mosquito
to mar their special evening. It was perfect.

Then it wasn't.

At pretty much the exact same time, both Robby and Billie Jo ran out of superlatives to describe the bridge, the wine, the flawless summer night. Suddenly, there was nothing left to say. Silence encircled them. It was time. Right now. Why was nothing happening? Billie Jo did her best to look open to a kiss, a touch, anything really, but Robby seemed oblivious, disinterested even.

In a flash of instinct, Billie Jo knew her girlfriends had been wrong about Robby McAllister. He hadn't brought her here to have sex. If he had, he'd have tried something by now. Betty Jo's warning echoed in her head. Robby wasn't trying anything because he wasn't into her. *Why not?* Did he only see her as a colleague, a good sport willing to go on a late-night adventure? And here she'd bought new underwear and shaved where she typically didn't.

Abruptly, thankfully, the unbearable silence was broken. "Billie Jo," Robby started. "I wanted to ask you something…"

If it's an accounting question, I am outta here! her inside voice shrieked as she shifted on the blanket to face her date…friend?… co-worker? Her movement caused the blanket to bunch up and send one then two candles toppling.

Turned out, the fresh-from-its-packaging blanket was highly flammable. Billie Jo screamed as a wave of shockingly aggressive flames leapt toward the frilly lace of her blouse.

Robby swore—quite colourfully for an accountant—jumped up, and grabbed both bottles of water. He twisted off the caps and simultaneously stomped out the burning blanket with his feet and doused Billie Jo. She squawked as cold water hit her overheated face, her hair and the bare skin of her chest. It was a rude shock, but Robby's quick thinking did the job. The whole thing was over in a matter of seconds, leaving the couple staring at one another, first in terror, then disbelief. Then, as if rehearsed, they both began to howl with laughter at the ridiculous turn of events.

"I am *so* sorry about this," Robby proclaimed when the laughter subsided and Billie Jo had proclaimed herself unharmed (the same could not be said for her hair and blouse).

Tossing aside the lightly charred, still-smoking blanket, they sat cross-legged on the soft grass, facing each other.

"Look!" Billie Jo held aloft the wine bottle. "Not a drop spilled."

"Well, it was the first thing I saved," Robby quipped. "You were more of an afterthought."

Strangely, the idiotic comment made Billie Jo's heart melt. Her eyes welled with tears as she reached over and hugged the surprised young man.

"What was that for?"

"This could have been so bad, Robby, like really bad, but you're making everything okay just by...by being stupid, silly you."

With a mock frown, he asked, "Should I take that as a compliment?"

"It doesn't even matter that you don't want to have sex with me. This, tonight, all of it, it's just so wonderful." Realizing what she'd just said, Billie Jo quickly shifted her body away from Robbie and attempted to distract him by gesturing towards the majesty of Sweetgrass Bridge. "I mean, just look at that. It's magical. Who gets to drink wine by candlelight and stare at that?"

"Billie Jo."

She shot a peek over her shoulder. He hadn't hightailed it out of there. That was a good sign.

"You want to have sex?"

"No. Maybe. Well, do you?"

Who was he to turn down an invitation like that? He reached over and pulled her towards him. Nuzzling her neck, he whispered, "I think your top got a little burned. You should probably take it off."

Billie Jo smiled. Girlfriends for the win. Her sister was an idiot. She unbuttoned her blouse and slipped out of it while watching Robbie pull his shirt over his head, buttons be damned. Dad bod. She was into it. She considered taking off her bra too but decided to save it for later. She moved in a way that invited him to embrace her.

"What was that?" Robbie's back straightened to attention, the abrupt motion pushing Billie Jo away.

"Wh..."

"Shhhh."

Don't shush me!

After a count of ten, he said, "You didn't hear that?"

"No." The word came out sounding like an accusation.

"It was like…"

"Like what?" Didn't he know the countryside was filled with weird country sounds? Even she'd figured that one out and if she could get used to it, so could he.

"Who's out there?" he shouted.

Billie Jo's body tensed at the harshness of the demanding words. He sounded different, his voice was loud, deep, it sounded…scared. Her skin began to crawl. *What's going on?* She moved further away from him. "Ro…"

"You didn't hear that?" He was kneeling, about to get up, reaching for his shirt.

"No, I didn't." *Shit.* He *really* doesn't want to do this. She'd asked for sex, he felt obligated, and now he was trying to get out of it by making up a boogeyman in the woods.

Robby rose to his feet, pulling on his shirt. "It sounded like somebody yelling, maybe calling for help or something. You didn't hear it?"

Making his way to the edge of the landing, Robbie scanned the blackened landscape, his gaze eventually landing on the bridge. Nothing had changed. It was just as magnificent, just as peaceful and silent as when they'd first arrived. He moved closer to the drop off. A shiver zagged up his spine as he felt the ground, softer at the brink, begin to give way. He hastily stepped back for safety. He stared deeper into the abyss, listening for something more. He extended the top half of his torso forward, ears at full alert. A few seconds later he heard something. Or were his ears playing tricks on him? Maybe they had been all along? His feet inched closer to the bank's end. There! A noise! Behind him this time. He turned too quickly, almost losing his footing. He scanned the shadows. Billie Jo was gone.

CHAPTER 1

Friday night and Merry Bell was where she knew she shouldn't be. At work. Well, calling it work was laughable, seeing as she had none. Tonight was Livingsky Sharpe Investigations' (LSI, for short) six-month anniversary. Half a year ago she'd pulled the plug on what was supposed to be her dream life in glorious Vancouver, British Columbia, packed up her meagre belongings (which may or may not have included a collection of hair scrunchies and a pair of Christian Louboutin boots that cost more than what she currently paid in monthly rent), and skedaddled it back to Saskatchewan, specifically her hometown of Livingsky. She was desperately broke, and a changed person, in more ways than one. She needed to start over.

Someone should have told her starting over was bloody hard.

Merry Bell arrived in Livingsky with a new dream: to get back to Vancouver as soon as possible. She knew it wasn't going to happen overnight. She was going to have to earn her way back, and she had a plan. The moment she stepped foot in Livingsky, where the cost of living was considerably less than on the west coast, she rented a small office at 222 Craving Lane and started her own P.I. firm. She figured it would take a year to eighteen months to earn enough cash to hightail it out of the prairies and back to the land of magical mountainscapes, ocean mist, and the freedom to live life the way she wanted to.

But as someone—probably some monk sitting on top of one of those glorious British Columbia mountains—once said: *life does not always go according to plan.* Sitting at her worn-out desk in a cramped office with a view of a graffitied back alley, Merry wondered if the only good thing to come out of the past six months was currently sitting next to her desk: a minibar fridge. She'd found it cheap on Kijiji and it was worth every penny. She had her work neighbour, Brenda Brown of Designs by Brenda, to thank for the idea. Brenda kept hers stocked with Sauvignon blanc. Merry preferred chalky chardonnay and peaty scotch, but the best she could afford these days was swill in a box. Tonight, in disputable honour of her anniversary, she'd splurged for a not-horrible bottle of Prosecco and a small charcuterie platter from a surprisingly good deli in Livingsky's version of the wrong side of the tracks, Alphabet City, where Merry currently resided.

As she poured herself a second glass of bubbly and topped an artisanal cracker with a mound of unpronounceable cheese and a dollop of red pepper jelly, Merry fought off—not very successfully—the out-of-work-P.I. blues. In the early, heady days of her career after she first moved to Vancouver, celebrating involved hanging out with friends in whatever the latest hotspot was; the more pretentious the better as she'd dance until the wee hours of the morning, downing too many Alabama Slammers. How far she'd fallen. Here she was on a Friday night in her office, which was at best *downtown-adjacent*, drinking barely passable bubbles, broke, alone, about to turn thirty, and marking a passage of time that seemed more millstone than milestone. True, she was much younger back then, immature, still trying to figure out exactly who she was. Calling people she hung out with back then *friends* was probably a stretch, but who cared? At least she had people. People to go out with, laugh with, be silly with, talk to, cry with. In Livingsky, she had no one.

Six months into her eighteen-month plan and her goal of leaving Livingsky seemed no closer than it did the day she arrived. Despite what she thought was a kickass website (which, admittedly, piggybacked on the website and reputation of her former boss, Nathan Sharpe), paying clients had been few and far between. Her first job was an arson case that ended up being considerably more complicated and political than she'd counted on. She'd prevailed and proved her client (an oddball property owner named Gerald Drover, who also became her landlord) innocent, but since then she'd had little luck finding more work. Was it because she'd ruffled a few too many feathers at City Hall in the course of the Drover case? Maybe it was her affiliation, more perceived than actual, with Drover himself? Or was Livingsky simply too small a city for an investigator to make a living? She was barely scraping by, working jobs that were more private security than private eye.

By glass number three, Merry's mood turned from blue to cloudy grey. Sliding open the bottom drawer of her desk, she dug beneath a stack of empty file folders that should have been filled with client records and pulled out two well-worn sheets of paper. They were identical except for the message scrawled on each one. The first read: "I know it's you" and the second: "I still know it's you". Note one was mysteriously slipped under her door at 222 Craving Lane not long after she first arrived in Livingsky; note two, several days later. Then nothing. Six months had passed and not a single word or attempt at follow-up communication from whoever sent them.

At first, Merry suspected her too-friendly, too-bossy, too-nosy, too-intrusive, too-everything neighbour, the ever-prissy Brenda of Designs by Brenda, a business that Merry suspected was more of a front to give Brenda reason to get out of the house than an actual service to paying clients, which she, not unlike Merry, seemed to have a hard time attracting. But when Merry eventually confronted her, Brenda denied it, a denial Merry felt compelled to accept.

The only remaining possibility that made any sense was that the note-writer was someone from her past. Whoever it was, Merry preferred to leave them there. Once a month she pulled the notes from the drawer fully intent on shredding them to pieces, relegating them to nothing more than a bad memory. Yet every time, after staring at them for ninety seconds, she'd change her mind and bury them deeper in the same drawer until next month. Tonight was no different. She stared at the words she knew by heart with the faint hope she'd see something new, some hidden message, something that would tell her who wrote them and why. She'd tell herself how lucky it was that the messages stopped when they did, so she didn't have to deal with it; the who and why not really mattering anymore. But in the depths of her being she wished the opposite was true. She wished the sender would persist, send more messages, push harder and, eventually, show themselves and proclaim their position as someone who... What...? Someone who knew her? Someone who gave a shit? Not knowing the answer, Merry would stash the notes away again, out of sight, but not out of mind.

Just as she was shoving the papers back into the drawer, an unfamiliar high-pitched ping drew her eyes to the computer screen where a small box had appeared at the bottom right-hand corner.

Email! I have an email!

Of course Merry had received emails before, but her excitement was warranted because this one was different, this one was momentous, this one originated from the LSI website and did not appear to be an offer for a low interest business loan or an overture from a lady who was both busty and lusty. With a subject line that read: Investigation Inquiry, the message appeared to be from an actual real person, one who was potentially interested in hiring a detective, one who'd presumably reviewed the website, one who understood LSI's standard fee was $100 per hour plus out-of-pocket incidentals and hadn't been scared off.

Almost too nervous to click on the email in fear of her high hopes being dashed, Merry spread a dab of pâté on a crust of bread, topped it with a dry sliver of Pecorino, and took her time savouring the lovely taste combination that exploded in her mouth. She topped up her Prosecco, took a sip, then another, and only then did she hit the icon that would reveal the email's content.

Hello,

I am interested in hiring an investigator. This is a private matter. Can we meet in person to discuss? The sooner the better.

Ruth-Anne Delorme

Merry jumped up and did the air pump thing usually reserved for bros watching football at a sports bar, and shouted "yes!" to her reflection in the office window. It was certainly not what her former boss and mentor Nathan Sharpe would have done, but screw it. She followed this up with an off-tune, made-up chorus of "I'm gonna get a client, I'm gonna get a client."

Once her exuberance was exhausted, she returned to her seat, closed her eyes to collect her thoughts, then typed out a response, suggesting a meeting the next day, Saturday. She was about to hit send, then stopped. Did she sound too desperate? Did she sound inebriated? How many glasses of Prosecco had she drunk? Should she wait a couple of hours to respond or, better yet, wait until Monday morning so it wouldn't look like she was some sad sack sitting in her office on a Friday night with nothing better to do? Screw that too! She *was* desperate. She *was* a sad sack. She hit send.

—

"Is there a party going on in here I wasn't invited to?"

Merry, startled, responded with: "Nope. No party in here."

Brenda made no effort to hide her pointed surveillance of Merry's desktop littered with charcuterie remains and a nearly empty bottle of Prosecco. Brenda Brown was no stranger to hiding hurt feelings with a bright smile, and although her words sounded like jest, she meant them in all seriousness. She'd tried for months to entice Merry Bell into some kind of sisterhood/officemates/Gossip-Girl type of relationship, but to no avail. How many times had she opened her wine fridge and offered Merry Bell a glass of Sauvignon blanc, just to be rebuked with some flimsy excuse? The P.I. obviously had *someone* over for a Friday after-work drinkie-poo and chinwag. Why wasn't it her?

"I must commend you and whoever you had over, you certainly kept things quiet. I didn't hear a peep, even though I'm right on the other side of this wall. Alvin always says these old houses are made of good bones. I guess he's right."

Alvin Smallinsky was the owner of 222 Craving Lane, having purchased the wartime house and successfully converted it into multiple rentable business spaces over three floors.

"No party. Just me."

"Oh. Well, that's too bad. Friday night drinkies are one of my favourite things." Brenda smiled sweetly. *Is she lying to me?* Brenda preferred to believe she wasn't. It meant she hadn't been excluded. Besides, it wasn't entirely surprising that Merry had been drinking alone. Despite the small amount of time she'd managed to spend with the woman, she knew a lonely soul when she saw one. In the six months since Merry Bell moved to Livingsky and hung her shingle out at 222 Craving Lane, where Brenda made it her business to get to know all her fellow tenants—because that's what good neighbours did—there'd been no evidence that she'd made even one friend. This fact made Brenda feel a little better about her own lack of success in befriending the private investigator, emphasis on the *private*.

At first, she'd thought things were heading in the right direction. She'd invited Merry to her home for a makeover (which Brenda could see was clearly in need of a refresher). This had led to a burgeoning apprenticeship-thingy-relationship between Merry and Brenda's husband Roger, who himself was an amateur sleuth, and then Merry shared her status as a transgender woman. After all of that, who wouldn't think a girl's day at the spa and a Winners shopping spree weren't in the future? But no. Merry Bell had resolutely kept her distance.

"I love Prosecco," Brenda cooed, taking a baby step into the office.

"I'd offer you some but it looks like I drank more than I thought I did." Merry sighed. "I guess you might say I *was* having a party, sort of. Today is six-months since I opened LSI."

Brenda danced fully into the room and flounced herself down in the chair across from Merry. "Oh my goodness! Congratulations! How silly of me to forget. You should have said something, you silly goose. I would have gotten you something; a card, bouquet of Gerberas maybe. I love Gerberas! The colour choices are so wonderful, don't you think?" She pulled out her phone. "I'm entering the date on my calendar right now so I won't forget again. For your one-year anniversary I'll make sure to have an extra special bottle of Sauvignon blanc chilled and ready!" Didn't hurt to keep trying.

"You don't have to do that." Merry said in a way that made Brenda wonder if she'd even be here in six more months.

"It's my pleasure. It really, really is. I'm just sorry I forgot about today. You have to let me make it up to you."

"That's not necessary. It's really not a big deal."

"I just decided. Roger and I are having a pool party tomorrow night. You have to come. Seven work for you?"

"You have a pool? Like, in your yard?"

"Mm-hmm. I guess the last time you were at the house it was winter so you wouldn't have seen the back yard. So, seven then?"

Merry shook her head. "I don't think so but thank you."

Brenda sat up straighter in her chair. "Merry, you know I'm always going to be straight with you." She reached across the desk, picked up the Prosecco bottle, raised it to her mouth and downed the last few drops. She smirked at Merry's response to the unexpected action, something beyond surprise and closer to appreciative amusement. Small steps. "Merry Bell, you need to get out more. You need to spend time with people instead of always holing up at work, always alone. It's not good for you. It's not good for anybody. Six months of LSI? More like six months of being a hermit."

Merry sputtered. "How do you know what I do when I'm not here. Maybe I have tons of friends and go out all the time."

"Is that true?" Brenda asked, sincerely.

"No," Merry whispered.

"It'll just be a few friends and neighbours, nothing fancy. The weather looks like it's going to be perfect. You'll have a swim, eat finger foods, have a cocktail or two, it'll be fun. Seven, then?"

"I…no."

Why is she resisting me? "Oh my gosh!" The colour behind Brenda's artfully applied makeup drained away as realization struck. "I'm so sorry. I get it now. I didn't even think about that!"

Merry gaped, clueless. "Think about what?"

"Why you wouldn't want to attend a pool party. I'll think of something else. What about a barbecue? Or we could go bowling!"

"What are you talking about? Why wouldn't I want to go to a pool party?"

"Because you're transgender."

"What does that have to do with anything?"

Brenda winced. She was really screwing this up. Merry was probably regretting telling her and Roger her secret. "Merry, I want you to know that I don't say what I'm about to say to be rude or insensitive. I only want to learn and educate myself so I can be a better friend to you. I…well, gosh now, how do I put this? Do transgender people go to pool parties? Do you wear swimsuits?"

Merry's eyes widened. Then she laughed, big, bellowing guffaws.

Brenda stared, not quite certain what was happening. Was that a "you're so silly, Brenda" kind of laugh, or a "you're an idiot, get out of my office" kind of laugh.

"Transgender people can go anywhere you can go," Merry eventually answered. "We do go to pool parties. We do wear swimsuits. Transgender women have all the same choices. Like any woman, we can wear suits that show off the parts of our body we want to show off or hide the parts we want to hide. Some transgender women may have a vagina just like yours and wear a swimsuit as revealing as one you would wear, or not, depending on her personal preference. Some transgender women may not have a vagina and still wear a revealing swimsuit if she wants by tucking."

"I know about that!" Brenda crowed. "I know tucking! I've seen every episode of RuPaul's Drag Race, both the U.S. and Canadian versions. They talk about tucking all of the time."

"What about Roger?"

For a moment Brenda was speechless. So few people in their world knew about her husband's affinity for dressing in womenswear it was shocking to hear someone refer to it in such a casual manner. Fast on the heels of this first shock, another overwhelmed her: she didn't know the answer to Merry's question. They'd been married for seven years, dated for two before that. He'd told her about his crossdressing as soon as the relationship became serious, so she'd known for nearly ten years. Still, she had no idea whether he tucked when he dressed up. How could that be? Was it that she didn't think to ask, didn't care to know, or didn't want to know? Did she not really look at him when he was dressed as a woman? Whether he tucked or not was something that was likely pretty obvious if you looked in the right places. Was there something about her husband tucking his genitalia away in order to be this other version of himself that made her uneasy?

Never one to be comfortable in silence, Brenda opened her mouth to say something but, try as she might, nothing came out.

She was saved by an insistent ping coming from Merry's computer.

Merry read the new email then looked up, flushed. "I'm sorry, Brenda, that was a message from a client. Looks like I'll be working tomorrow and won't be able to make the pool party. Maybe another time."

Brenda knew a convenient excuse when she heard one. Merry Bell was a "tough nut to crack," a saying her mother often used. She rose to leave. When she reached the door she stopped, turned, and said, "Well, if your plans change, you're welcome to join us. Anytime after seven."

Merry nodded but was noticeably distracted by something on her screen.

"Is everything okay?" Brenda asked, noting how the colour in the other woman's face had fallen away with remarkable speed.

Merry didn't seem to hear her.

Brenda raised an eyebrow and left.

CHAPTER 2

LOCAL HERO MISSING: LPS AND RCMP ASK PUBLIC FOR HELP

Saskatchewan Roughriders' quarterback Dustin Thomson was last seen in Livingsky at approximately 4:00 p.m. on Saturday, July 13.

Police Chief Jay Cuthbert said search teams are scouring the city and surrounding areas by air and land. Cuthbert added that drones will assist search efforts.

"We are working in concert with the RCMP and pursuing every avenue to find Dustin Thomson," Cuthbert said.

He added that police officers have found no indication of foul play, though the investigation is ongoing.

"It's not just about someone not showing up one day," FSIN Vice-Chief Sherry Little said. "As Indigenous people, too many times we have (had) our missing people not investigated properly. We're not going to allow that to happen here." 25-year-old Thomson is a member of the Little Turtle Lake First Nation.

Riders' head coach, Robert Calder, said the team's players and management are "shattered" by the disappearance of its quarterback, who Calder has referred to as the organization's most valuable asset on and off the field. Thomson went missing during the team's July bye week.

Along with LPS and local RCMP detachments, Police Dog Services and Search and Rescue teams are searching for Thomson. They're joined by Livingsky Police Air Services, the Civilian Air Search and Rescue Association, the Saskatchewan Public Safety Agency and the Search and Rescue Saskatchewan Association of Volunteers. LPS and

RCMP are asking any members of the public with information on Thomson's whereabouts to contact their local police.

Thomson is described as weighing 215 lbs (98 kg) and is 6 ft 2 in (188 cm) with dark hair and brown eyes. He was last seen wearing blue jeans and a green and white Saskatchewan Roughriders jersey.

Like everyone else in Saskatchewan, and quite possibly Canada and beyond, Merry had heard about the shocking disappearance of the quarterback long before reading the Livingsky Tribune article Ruth-Anne Delorme sent her the previous evening. Except for curiosity's sake, Merry hadn't paid the matter much attention. She was not a football fan and her lack of blind adulation for the province's CFL team was reason enough for her to have escaped Livingsky all those years ago. But the news story had her attention now. Delorme sending her the article had to mean the reason she was interested in hiring a P.I. had something to do with Dustin Thomson, which made the football player Merry's new obsession.

She arrived at the office the next morning with a couple of hours to spare before her meeting with Delorme. She wanted time to dig through the internet to learn what she could about Thomson... and football. She was pretty sure that was the one with tight pants, touchdowns and tailgate parties.

It didn't take long for Merry to learn a couple of important things about Dustin Thomson. The first was that he was extraordinarily popular, not only with fans in Livingsky and Saskatchewan, but throughout the world of football. The second was that his popularity stemmed from much more than the fact that he was a beloved football team's current starting QB. Turned out, Thomson was a bit of a unicorn. Not since the early 1950s, with a player named Ron Adam, did the Saskatchewan Roughriders have a quarterback born and raised in the province. Even at that, Adam was in a back-up position, whereas Thomson was #1. Furthermore, although the team had recruited Indigenous players before, never one in the quarterback position.

There was no doubt Thomson was special, but even Merry knew

that no one, hometown boy or not, Indigenous or not, made it to starting quarterback position without having the goods to back it up. According to media reports, Thomson had the goods and then some. In an article penned by William Selnes, a local journalist renowned for his decades-long no-nonsense coverage of the Roughies (a pet name bestowed upon the team by the fan base), he described his take on what makes a perfect quarterback. He claimed the person in that role needed to be quick and coordinated, have a strong arm, be smart, be accurate, be able to process visual information faster than it came at him. Most of all, the quarterback needed to be the team's undisputed leader. According to Selnes' ranking of all active CFL quarterbacks in the running at the time, the player who topped his list was Dustin Thomson.

Searching beyond the sports pages, Merry was surprised to find a whole other side of the footballer. From the glossy pages of a Livingsky lifestyle magazine—Merry was also surprised to learn Livingsky had one of those—she read about a man described as a gentle giant, dedicated community advocate and handsome eligible bachelor. A series of photos, a few of which Merry magnified to get a better look, confirmed some of that. In off season, Thomson called Livingsky home. He spent much of his time at a local youth centre he'd raised funds for that promoted life skills education, career training and diversity awareness. He was a sought-after public speaker not only at Roughrider rallies but at schools and community fundraisers. For all of this, he was lauded as one of the team's most outstanding ambassadors. Merry had no choice but to conclude the guy certainly seemed to have everything going for him. Until now.

A sharp rap on her outer office door shortly after 10:00 a.m. roused Merry from her deep dive. She looked up to find a slender woman with dark hair cut in a no fuss style wearing a plain pantsuit over a white t-shirt and simple jewelry.

"I'm here to see the detective," the woman said.

Merry got up and greeted the woman with a handshake. "I'm Merry Bell, private investigator. You must be Ruth-Anne?"

"Yeah, that's me. I sent you an email," she said in a way that made it sound like a question. Wide-eyed, the woman scanned the room.

Merry closed the door. "Yes. Please have a seat and we can talk about things."

Once they were seated on appropriate sides of the desk, Merry poised a pen above a ready pad of paper and asked, "Do you mind if I take notes while we talk?"

"I guess not." Ruth-Anne reached into her purse with one hand and left it there.

"Good," Merry said, noticing how nervous the woman was, which was nothing unusual in a first meeting with a detective. Rarely was it something joyful that led people to seek out the assistance of an investigator. The hand in the purse thing was a little strange though.

The woman must have noticed Merry's attention on her purse because she pulled out her hand to reveal a fidget spinner. "I know these things aren't so popular anymore, but I'm addicted to mine. Have been for years. I suppose lots of people who come here are stressed out or anxious about something? Probably why they come to see you in the first place."

"There's no need to be nervous. We can take this one step at a time. Maybe we can start by talking about the article you sent me, the one about Dustin Thomson?"

"Yes," the woman jumped on the idea. "I want you to find out what happened to him."

Merry's heart sank a little. Thomson's disappearance was an active police matter. She doubted her one-person detective agency could compete with the investigative powers of the Livingsky Police Service. Then again, even the police weren't infallible. "Can you tell me a little more about what you mean by that? What do you think may have happened to him?"

The woman huffed and puffed a little. "Have you been reading the papers the last few days? Or the stuff online?"

Having only been contacted by Delorme the day before, Merry only had time to research the meat, not the gravy. Gravy was important. "I know the facts about his disappearance," she said, "at least the facts as they've been reported to the public. He was last seen a week ago, this past Saturday afternoon, at a Livingsky youth centre where he volunteers. He told people at the centre he was going home, but his roommate said he never got there, at least not before he left for work as a night shift janitor. It wasn't until the next day, late Sunday afternoon, that people…maybe you?…began to worry and called the police. I also know a little about who Dustin is, his career…"

"That's not what I mean," Ruth-Anne interrupted. "I'm talking about the rumours the cops are starting to spread. It's total crap."

Merry highly doubted the police would knowingly spread rumours, but she said nothing.

"They're saying because there's no evidence of foul play that maybe it was some kind of accident or—and this is the really fucked up part—that maybe Dustin committed suicide. There's no way Dustin killed himself."

"I'm sorry," Merry said gently, "I should have asked you this to begin with. What is your relationship to Mr. Thomson? Are you a friend? Relative?"

"Both. I'm his cousin. Probably his closest relative in town. Most of his family still live on the reserve."

"I see. And do they feel as you do, about what the police are saying?"

"Of course. Everyone who knows Dustin thinks the same thing. He wouldn't have just gone off without telling anybody. He wouldn't have killed himself. No way. It's just not the kind of man he is. He isn't missing because he wants to be missing. Something bad's happened to him. I know it. We all know it. Except the cops. I don't think they're even looking for him. They're just waiting for him to show up in a dumpster or something."

That didn't seem to be the case, from what Merry read in the papers, but she could understand Ruth-Anne's anxiety and suspicions. Indigenous peoples and the police had a long fraught history in Canada. Mistakes were made, grievous ones, some were intentional, judgements were passed, trust was lost. Reconciliation had begun across the country but the process was far from making significant inroads into healing wounds still raw and gaping. That would take generations. "How can I help you, Ruth-Anne?"

To Merry's surprise, the woman reached into her purse with her free hand and pulled out a thick stack of bills secured by an elastic band. Ruth-Anne laid the money on the desk and pushed it with a chipped fingernail in Merry's direction.

"I want you to do what the police should be doing. I want you to look where the police aren't looking. I want you to do what you'd do if Dustin was your cousin and you knew in your heart he didn't just take a walk somewhere and forget to come back, if you knew he wouldn't take his own life. I want you to act like something bad happened to Dustin and you have to find him and bring him home before it becomes permanent."

Merry nodded. The instructions couldn't be clearer. She had no way of knowing whether Ruth-Anne Delorme was accurate in her assessment of what the LPS was or wasn't doing to find out what happened to Dustin Thomson, but neither was that knowledge a necessity in taking the case. This woman had needs, LSI was going to fulfill them.

"That's twenty-five hundred right there," Ruth-Anne said indicating the pile of cash. "Is that enough to get you started?"

With a charge out rate of $100/hour (although $70 was the best she'd done so far), it was more than she would have asked for as a retainer. "Yes it is, thank you." From a desk drawer she pulled out a blank contract she'd cribbed from the one used by her former employer, Sharpe Investigations. As she handed the document to Delorme, a thrill tingled through her. *A new client. Finally.*

"Is this thing really necessary?" Ruth-Anne asked, flipping through the pages. "I already paid you, so do we need to do this?"

"Well," Merry began, surprised by the woman's hesitation, "it's a professional thing. Having our agreement in writing protects both of us."

"Whatever." Ruth-Anne shrugged. "I'll need a pen."

Merry was glad the resistance was short-lived. She gave the woman a pen, saying, "Once you've signed the contract, I'll need to ask you a few more questions about Dustin."

"Can you get started right away?"

Merry debated her answer. She didn't want to come off as some kind of down-on-her-luck P.I. waiting around for work, even though that was pretty much the truth. She smiled and said, "Missing person cases are extremely time sensitive. I promise you, Ruth-Anne, this case will be one of LSI's top priorities."

CHAPTER 3

A good detective never presumes their client knows the truth or tells the truth. Ruth-Anne Delorme had hired LSI to disprove what she believed were inaccurate assumptions by the police about why Dustin Thomson was missing. If the quarterback disappeared on purpose, as the cops seemed to suspect, Merry needed to find out why, and the best place to start was his apartment.

Pulling up to the building where Dustin Thomson lived in her new (to her) clunker named Doreen, Merry knew the swanky apartment high-rise commanded top dollar. When she'd first arrived in Livingsky looking for both office space and a place to live, she'd undertaken an exhaustive search into the Livingsky real estate market. With LSI taking priority, after leasing 222 Craving Lane there was little more than a pittance left to spend which, pitifully, resulted in her taking up residence in a part of Livingsky most residents avoided if they could. Alphabet City was like a city within a city, a sprawling multi-block area directly adjacent to downtown but incontrovertibly separated from it by the steel beams of a CP Rail line, as well as a number of less visible but just as rigid cultural and economic barriers, leading many to call it "the wrong side of the tracks".

Defenseless against powerful self-fulfilling prophecy, Alphabet City, beginning with A Street hugging the rail line, and ending at a freeway that sliced through the city's west end at Z Street, was debatably the least desirable place to live or do business in Livingsky. Efforts to gentrify or resuscitate pockets of the neighbourhood, especially those closest to downtown, historically experienced questionable degrees of success. Over time the worst areas, those least visible pockets that many considered beyond help, descended into near slum conditions. Rundown tenement buildings and deteriorating houses were overcrowded, inhabited by people who came from other countries, from First Nations reserves, abandoned rural communities, and others who'd fallen on hard times and couldn't find their way out. Turned out, Merry was one of those people. No one was more surprised than her.

Stepping into the building's glitzy foyer Merry guessed that the lease on Dustin Thomson's suite was probably shared disproportionately between the Roughrider football star and his night janitor roommate. She ascended in a glass elevator which seemed to be bragging as it unabashedly showed off brilliant views of trendy Connecticut Avenue. The busy street was a Livingsky mainstay of chic restaurants and fashionably casual pubs, independently-owned shops and art galleries, an artsy cinema and too many coffee shops. She got off on the fourth floor, fighting off pangs of depression at the thought of her own home, a place she'd nicknamed "the Junk House" because of its unusual location within the gated compound of an abandoned scrap metal yard smack dab in the middle of Alphabet City. It was the only place she could afford, likely for the foreseeable future.

In a flash of self-pity, she wondered why fate hadn't been as kind to her as it had been to Dustin Thomson. Why hadn't she been granted the fairy tale of growing up the kind of boy who was obsessed with football and eventually became a highly-paid, highly-respected sports star? Instead, she'd grown up the kind of boy who was obsessed with girls and eventually became one. One of those fairy tales seemed immeasurably easier to navigate than the other.

By the time Merry reached her destination and knocked on the apartment door she managed to nip the woe-is-me-ing in the bud, knowing from extensive experience it never did any good.

The man who answered the door was roughly the same age as

Dustin Thomson. He was also about the same height but that was where the similarities between the two men ended. Whereas Thomson was leanly muscled and darkly handsome, Calvin Wochiewski was a pleasant-looking sandy blonde with a sad smile, lanky in the way of someone whose idea of exercise was multiple sets of lifting a gamer's handheld console.

Invited in, Merry was greeted by another unexpected inhabitant of the apartment. One with a wet nose and thick, curly hair, both the colour of brown sugar.

"Who's this sweet guy?" Merry asked, crouching down to say hello and bury her fingers in the dog's soft, thick mane.

"I don't know what made Dustin think he could have a pet when he's away so much. He says it's his dog, but I kinda wonder if he really got him to keep me company."

There'd always been a dog around when Merry was growing up. This brown furball with golden eyes and perfectly pert snout was an unexpected reminder of how much she missed that. "He's adorable. What's his name?"

"Marco."

"That's an unusual name for a dog. I like it."

"It's cuz he's Italian."

After a quick final rub down, enthusiastically appreciated by Marco, Merry rose to face Dustin's roommate. "The dog is Italian? What breed?" He looked a little like a small labradoodle.

Calvin rolled his eyes. "I hate when people ask that question. It's embarrassing."

Merry laughed. "Really? Why?"

With a special emphasis on rolling the "r"s and attempting, poorly, an Italian accent, he declared: "Marco is a Lagotto Romagnolo." Seeing the blank look on Merry's face, he added, "Never heard of it, right?"

"No, I have not."

"Every time someone asks me what kind of dog he is, I've got to say he's a Lagotto Romagnolo. It's a mouthful. Sounds super pretentious. Why couldn't he have just gotten a German Shepherd or a poodle?"

She glanced down at the dog who was looking up at her with a curious smile. "I'm sure he must really miss Dustin."

"Yeah," Calvin agreed, critically eyeing the dog, "I think you're right."

Merry followed Calvin into the living room which boasted yet another enviable floor-to-ceiling Connecticut Avenue vista. A quick survey revealed high-end furniture littered with low-end clothing, take-out containers, beer cans and other detritus strewn about the place. The place was clean, but messy.

"Sorry about all this crap," Calvin apologized, picking up an insignificant portion of the debris in a half-hearted effort to clean up. "I usually keep it neater, especially when Dustin's in town, but, well, this past week's been...hard."

"Please," Merry quickly responded, "don't worry about it. Leave everything where it is. I know how difficult this must be for you. I get it. Tidiness is not a priority."

Calvin looked at the woman with something akin to surprise mixed with gratitude. "I know this sounds petty, but ever since Dustin disappeared, no one seems to get that this is hard on me too. Dustin was my best friend."

Merry moved a stack of gamer magazines from the centre cushion of a couch to the coffee table, making room for two. She took a seat. "Let's just sit here and talk." Marco settled himself at her feet.

"Can I get you something to drink, a beer, or water?"

"I'm good, thanks, I already had a few too many brewskies this morning."

"Really?"

Merry smiled. "Sorry, sometimes my weird sense of humour comes out at the most inappropriate times."

Calvin grinned. "Don't be sorry. I could use a good laugh right about now."

"I'll try harder next time to say something that's actually funny."

Calvin sat. "You're probably wondering how a guy like me ends up living in a place like this? It's even nicer when it's not so messy."

She thought she knew the answer, but when it came to interviews like this one, except for a few verbal directional nudges here and there, it was always best to let the other person talk as much as possible.

"Dustin and I were best buds in school."

"I thought Dustin grew up on Little Turtle Lake Reserve. Didn't he go to school there?"

"He did, until Grade 6 when his mom decided to move to Livingsky. I didn't know it at first, but she was pretty sick and needed to be near a big city hospital. She died the same year we graduated. It was a really sad time. Dustin and I got pretty close over that cuz my dad died early too. And because we were both into football."

"I didn't know you played." She didn't add that his physique didn't suggest it either.

"I wasn't anywhere as good as Dustin. I only got to play because at our kind of school—you know, it's what they call an inner-city school—most guys are more into doing drugs, skipping class, and getting tail than playing sports. I really liked football, but I wasn't any good at it. Not built for it, I guess. I got hurt a lot," he said with a nervous laugh. "But Dustin, that dude was made to play football. Our coach and teachers knew it too. They helped him a lot, but he hardly needed it. He was good at football and good at school stuff too. A guy like that, growing up the way we did, it's pretty special."

Merry nodded, admiring the young man's willingness to appreciate a friend's abilities, despite his own shortcomings. "Yes, it is. It sounds like he had a very good friend in you."

Calvin shrugged. "I suppose. It was easy. He was a really good guy. It was his idea that we get a place together after we graduated from high school, even though our lives were moving in such different directions. He got into university and then all the football stuff started to happen. I tried university too, but it just wasn't my thing. He didn't seem to care about that though."

"University didn't work out for me either." Merry allowed herself the white lie. She would have loved to have gone to university, but life had other plans for her. The education she most needed was the kind that helped her figure out who the hell she really was.

"Our first place was pretty gross, this dump in Alphabet City, but when he started making good money with football, he got this place. I just figured that was it for our roommate days, but he had different ideas. He was away so much, especially during the season, but he still really wanted to have a place to call home in Livingsky. There's no way I could ever afford to live in a place like this, but Dustin said I was doing him a favour. He said he was lucky to have me to look after it, and Marco, whenever he was gone."

"Calvin, I know you've already gone over this with the police, but like I told you on the phone, Dustin's family wants me to take a closer look at things. Would you mind telling me about the last time you saw Dustin?"

"Yeah, of course, anything I can do to help. I work nights, cleaning offices at Realtech. I'm not exactly sure what they do there, some high tech-y stuff, I think. Anyway, even when he is in town I don't get to see Dustin a lot because I work at night and sleep in the day, but the day before he disappeared, Friday, we hung out here a bit before I went to work. That was...," he stopped to clear his throat, "the last time I saw him."

"I know this is hard to talk about." Merry looked down at Marco who also appeared to have a disturbed look on his face. "You alright?"

"Yeah, sure." Calvin jumped up and headed toward the glassy shiny kitchen area. "I'm just gonna get a drink of water. Sure I can't get you anything?"

"No, thanks."

When Calvin returned, Merry resumed her questioning. "So you worked your night shift Friday night, got home sometime Saturday morning, but you didn't see him at all that day, the day he disappeared, is that right?"

"When I get home from a night shift I'm pretty knackered and usually go straight to bed. By the time I got up on Saturday, Dustin was already gone for the day."

"People at the centre where Dustin was volunteering that day said that he'd told everyone he was going home when he was done for the day."

"Yeah. He may have come back, but it wasn't before I left for work."

"What time was that?"

"What?"

"What time did you leave for work on Saturday night?"

He thought for a moment. "About nine-thirty, I'd say."

"Dustin left the youth centre around 4:00 p.m. on Saturday afternoon. Since he didn't come home between then and 9:30 when you left for work, do you have any idea where he might have been for five hours? Would he have gone to visit friends, see a girlfriend?"

"He doesn't have a girlfriend right now, as far as I know. I used to kid him about it, but he always said he's too busy with football and all the other stuff he did to have a relationship."

"What about friends, or maybe buddies he played football with? Could he have been with them?"

"I suppose. I don't really know his other friends, or his football buddies; that's not really my scene anymore."

"The football scene?"

"I don't really do the friend thing," he looked away as if sheepish to make the admission to someone he just met, "other than Dustin. I'm into gaming and Dungeons and Dragons and that sort of shit, y'know. Most of the people I know live in here." He indicated his phone, then pointed to his bedroom door. "Or in there." He sniggered, "Not actually in my bedroom, but I've got a pretty sweet set up in there, big-ass monitors, high-end speakers, shit like that. You know what I mean?"

"Sure." She did. He was a loner. He worked nights. Merry remembered a friend she once had, Brad, a baker who plied his trade from sun down to sun up so people could have their fresh pastries and breads first thing in the morning. It's tough to make friends when your world happened when everyone else was asleep. Calvin's dad was dead, no mention of a mother or other family, his only friend was a celebrity quarterback who was hardly ever home. Calvin Wochiewski—she was taken aback to admit— was not unlike who she'd become since moving back to Livingsky. She wasn't—yet—a gamer nerd, but she was pretty much a loner with no one to rely on but herself.

The young man looked miserable, his eyes were rimmed with red and deep lines furrowed his forehead.

"Are you okay, Calvin?"

"I should have checked on him when I came home Sunday morning. I shouldda looked in his bedroom to make sure he was there. If I did, maybe the police would have started looking for him sooner. Maybe they could have…could have…"

"Calvin," Merry said tenderly, "did you typically look in on him when you got home from work?"

He sniffed away a half-hearted laugh. "No, of course not. We're grown-ass men. It's not like he was my kid or something."

"Exactly. So there was no reason for you to do it that morning either, right?"

"I guess not."

"Was there anything going on that weekend, anything unusual, something that should have made you think to look in on him?"

"No."

"Then you shouldn't blame yourself. You did what you always do. You came home from work and you went to bed. Sounds completely reasonable to me."

Calvin let out a massive blast of pent-up air, as if it had been building up inside of him for days. Then, quietly, he said, "Thank you."

"You're welcome." Merry readjusted herself on the couch to get a better look at the man. Marco did not approve, as the movement of her feet disrupted his nap. "That being said, Calvin, can you think of anything going on in Dustin's life, big or small, anything out of the ordinary, that might have had an impact on whatever happened to him that night?"

"I've thought about it, a lot, but nothing comes to mind. Like I said, these days I don't spend much time with him even when he is in town. So, if there was something, I might not know about it."

"What about other people in his life? You said he didn't have a girlfriend, but were there other people around him, maybe old friends who suddenly showed up, or new friends, anyone who visited him here, someone you hadn't seen before?"

Calvin shook his head.

Merry sighed. Her exchange with Thomson's roommate was producing less information than she'd hoped. There had to be something. Wochiewski might know something he didn't even know he knew, but the only way she'd find out was if she asked the right question. "You said the two of you hung out a little on the Friday night before he disappeared. What did you talk about?"

"Oh, you know, guy shit. Mostly football, how excited he was with how well the team was doing this year. He talked a bit about the youth centre, he played with Marco, but that's about it. When guys talk it's not usually about feelings or any of the stuff girls talk about."

Despite herself, Merry grinned at the stereotyped characterization.

"Calvin, would it be okay with you if I took a look around Dustin's room?"

He shrugged. "The cops have already been in there, so I guess one more person snooping around won't make a difference."

Merry was glad Calvin did not feel it was necessary to follow her into Dustin's room. She did her best work when no one was looking. Marco did not extend her the same courtesy however, although he remained a polite and quiet onlooker. Half an hour later she'd turned up nothing, no smoking gun pointing at a potential reason for the Saskatchewan Roughriders' star quarterback to have disappeared off the face of the earth. Maybe there was nothing to find, or maybe the cops had already found it.

Overall, the room was neat and tidy, the bed was made, clothes were neatly hung up in the closet or arranged in drawers. Merry guessed the same could not be said for Calvin's room down the hall.

She also noted there was no "sweet" gamer set-up like the one Calvin claimed to have, but there was a computer with a large screen monitor sitting on a desk. Merry had already asked Calvin if he had the password to unlock it. He did not. Sitting at the desk, she tried some obvious ones, like 1-2-3-4-5-6-7-8-9 and Dustin spelled backwards, but quickly gave up the guessing game. She found it interesting the cops hadn't bothered to take away the hard drive. Maybe Ruth-Anne Delorme wasn't so far off-base depicting police efforts as lackadaisical.

Debating whether to bring her search to an end, Merry sat idly at the desk watching the steady stream of images of Dustin's screen-saver slide across the screen, each photo hesitating for the count of five before moving on. The pictures, likely downloaded from Dustin's camera, depicted his teammates, coaching team and what Merry guessed were youth he mentored at the centre. Most were candid, fun, sweet. Until the one that stole her breath away.

CHAPTER 4

After Merry came up empty in Dustin's bedroom, she asked Calvin's permission to search his truck. It was a late model Cadillac XT5, matte black with custom matte black grill and rims and Roughrider-green running boards. Very sharp looking, she thought. She scoured every inch of the vehicle but, other than some loose change, dried up Listerine Breath Strips, receipts for groceries and lotto, scratch lists, and a stash of random papers in the glove compartment box, she found nothing of note. Despite having discovered little of tangible worth, Merry felt something she hadn't felt in a long time. Excitement. Merry Bell, P.I., was back in action.

During her time working for Nathan Sharpe in Vancouver, pre-transition, Merry had become a damn fine detective. Those days were gone. And so was that investigator. Merry Bell, P.I., was someone new and it was taking time to find her footing, rebuild her confidence, trust her abilities. But it was happening. Right now. *I can do this.*

Leaving everything where she found it except for the chits and bits which she stuffed in her purse, Merry locked up, jumped into Doreen and headed for her next appointment at Love Stadium. It was named after a local entrepreneur and die-hard football fan who'd made a fortune in the global telecommunications market and donated several million to its construction. Although not quite big enough or tricked out enough with jumbotron screens and multiple merchandise concession stands required for CFL games, the Livingsky facility was a Saskatchewan Roughriders' favourite for practices between game days and on bye weeks. As a youngster, Merry could never have imagined a situation where she would have cause to willingly enter the players' clubroom at a football team's workout camp, but that was exactly where she was headed. Head coach, Robert Calder, had been unexpectedly accommodating when Merry called to request an opportunity to speak with the team on behalf of Dustin Thomson's family. She left out the part about her not actually being a member of the family.

On the drive from Connecticut Avenue to Love Stadium, Merry fought an overwhelming urge to cancel the meeting. All she could think about was the photo that had scrolled across Dustin's home computer, shocking to her, but otherwise unremarkable. The image was a group shot, obviously taken in a locker room. *Could it be Love Stadium?* Based on the triumphant, beaming faces Merry guessed it was meant to capture the elation following a winning game. Dustin Thomson was in the frame, but it was another face in the photograph that caused Merry's heart to be replaced by a conga drum. He wasn't a player and didn't have enough prominence in the photo to be a coach. Maybe an assistant coach? A locker room attendant? Journalist? Maybe he was nothing more than a lucky fan who managed a photo bomb. Why he was there didn't matter anyway. What did matter was the man himself...and a face Merry recognized.

While Merry couldn't be one hundred percent certain, because she hadn't seen him in years, the man in the picture looked like her cousin Preston. Seeing the familiar happy face, caught by the camera in a moment of communal joy, was like an electric jolt, an unexpected reminder that she was in the city of her birth, a place where she'd be a fool not to think she wouldn't, at some point, run into someone she knew or, in this case, a family member. For the millionth time since she'd made the move from Vancouver, she asked herself: *Why the hell did I come back here?*

She'd had no choice, she told herself. She'd run out of money, in part due to the exorbitant costs associated with transitioning, in part due to the fact that even when she was physically cleared to return to work as an investigator with Sharpe Investigations, she was nowhere near ready to take on the mental commitment the job demanded. By the time she was ready, it was too late. She'd dug herself into a financial hole so deep that no version of living in Vancouver other than setting up a tent on East Hastings was going to get her out. She had to leave. She had to find a less expensive world to live in, one where she could save money and eventually return to her life on the west coast where she belonged.

Merry could have picked a great many other cities to live in other than her hometown of Livingsky, Saskatchewan. So why had she? The simple answer was that it was easy. She knew the city, knew how it worked, and hoped that familiarity would give her a leg up when it came to starting a new business. The sooner that business succeeded, and she amassed a healthy nest egg, the sooner she could leave. The not-so simple answer was one she hadn't quite figured out yet.

Maneuvering through traffic Merry did her best to convince herself that the chances of running into her cousin at Love Stadium were minimal. Just because he was in one photograph didn't mean he was a permanent fixture with the team. Or maybe her eyes had deceived her. The guy in the picture could be anyone. On the off chance he *was* her relative and he *was* at the stadium, was that really a problem? No one had changed more than Merry over the past several years, so it was doubtful a distant relative would even recognize her. By the time she pulled into the stadium's parking lot, Merry was feeling less concerned and refocused on the case.

"I'm glad you're here," the team's head coach said as he directed Merry down a set of labyrinthine corridors and into his office.

"Thank you for agreeing to this, Mr. Calder," Merry replied.

"Call me Bob, everyone does."

Merry smiled and nodded. Bob Calder, well into his fifties but still holding on to an impressive former football player's physique, had a disarming face for someone in charge of a team of men whose job—from what Merry could tell given her minimal knowledge of the game—was to smash into one another. His cheeks were Santa-rosy and his smile was wide, which was going to make it all the more difficult to admit her duplicity.

"We've talked with the police, and of course the media, but the men haven't had the opportunity to speak with Dustin's family since all of this happened. It's still so fresh and sudden, and I'm no psychologist, but I believe some of them are in shock. They walk around here like zombies; on the field too. They show up to practice but you can hardly call it that. They're just going through the motions. It's the not knowing where he is or what's happened to him that's the hardest. They act tough, like they think they're supposed to, but I know they're confused, and hurting, and they need to get it out. I'm sure the family is going through the same and worse. It'll help them to remember that, to know that what they're feeling is normal and they're not alone in this. So, Ms. Bell, I greatly appreciate your visit."

"Merry is fine."

"Merry, then. My wife is a big fan of those Mary Tyler Moore show reruns, so I end up watching a lot of them too," he said with a generous chuckle. "You remind me of her a little."

Merry smiled. "Except I'm Merry with an 'e.'"

"Oh. Like Merry Christmas?"

"The same."

"Humph. I like that. I don't think I've heard that name before. It's festive, like my wife's. Her name is Holly."

Little did he know the name had been chosen, not given. "Thank you. I like your wife's name too." There seemed no better time than during a pleasant exchange about names to bring up the unpleasant matter of her lie. "Bob, there's something I should clear up with you."

"Okay, shoot."

"I'm a private investigator. I was hired by Dustin's family. I'm sorry if I didn't make that clear when we spoke on the phone."

"Oh," he said, visibly surprised by the revelation. "I didn't know they'd hired a private detective. Can you tell me why they did that?"

"As you can imagine, the family is very concerned about Dustin. Now that it's been a week since he disappeared, they want to do whatever they can to help the police find him." Inwardly, Merry winced. Yet again she was telling the head coach of the Saskatchewan Roughriders a half-truth. Ruth-Anne Delorme wanted her cousin found, but her motivation had little to do with helping the cops. *Oh well*, she reminded herself, *little white lies here and there are useful tools of the trade*. So, she told another one. "They thought it might be helpful if I could speak with his teammates to get a sense of what was happening with Dustin right before he disappeared."

"Of course, of course," Calder mumbled, studying his guest as if trying to decide whether to trust her. "Are you a Rider fan, Merry?"

Nearly blanching, Merry wielded the tool once more. "Isn't everybody?" She made a note to get herself one of those green and white t-shirts she saw everyone wearing on game days.

Jumping to his feet, Calder clapped his hands together as if an important deal had been struck to his liking. "Well then, let's take you in to meet the guys!"

Merry remained seated. "Maybe I could start with you?"

Calder's smile and the rose on his cheeks faded ever so slightly as he returned to his seat behind the desk. "Of course. What can I tell you?"

Merry wondered if the man's diminished cheeriness was because she'd taken the lead in their meeting when he was used to being the one in control, or because he didn't want to be questioned. "Were you and Dustin close?"

"Well, ma'am, I'm not sure if I know what you mean by close. We're as close as head coach and quarterback should be. As I'm sure you might surmise, our successes are as tied together as Wheaties and star athletes. A bad coach can mess up a good quarterback and a bad quarterback can end the career of a good coach. Out on the field, Dustin is an extension of me, both in how he plays and how he leads the team.

"Now if you're asking whether we hang out after hours or get invited to each other's birthday parties, that's a hard no. And—I think the guys would back me up on this—Dustin is the same when it comes to his relationship with them. In the locker room and on the field, he is the leader, no question. He's respected, he is liked as a person, but when it comes to socializing away from the game, he doesn't do it a whole lot. And believe me, that's not always the case with QBs."

"How do you mean?"

"Let me put it this way: there've been plenty of teams that have had to deal with quarterbacks who've been, shall we say, a little less responsible when it comes to their non-game activities. Not Dustin. He's something special. If he keeps going like he is now, if he doesn't get derailed by…something or someone…I guarantee you he will go down as one of the CFL's best. Right up there with Calvillo, Flutie and Moon."

Merry had no idea who any of those other people were, but the firm nod of her head indicated otherwise. The more interesting thing to her was Calder's comment about the possibility of Dustin being derailed. "Do you have concerns about Dustin being derailed by something or someone?"

"Of course I do. I'd be foolish not to. It happens, not all of the time, but it happens. Best you can do is stay vigilant and stay ahead of it if it does."

"Any specific concerns you can tell me about? Was Dustin seeing anyone romantically, for instance?"

"Not to my knowledge."

"Did he have a best friend, or someone he spent a lot of time with away from the team?"

"I think there's a roommate, but other than that, not to my knowledge."

Eyeing up the coach, Merry sensed the Santa vibe waning. She needed to dig fast before she got a lump of coal thrown at her.

"I don't know a lot about what happens in locker rooms, but I would guess, especially during the season, that emotions and tensions between players might run high. It would be unreasonable to expect everyone to get along. To your knowledge, did any of the other players or members of the coaching staff clash with Dustin recently, even in an insignificant way?" Last night she'd indulged in a mini-binge-watch of *Friday Night Lights* which, aside from teaching her a thing or two about football both on and off the field (influencing today's questioning strategy), she'd thoroughly enjoyed.

Calder's broad forehead rippled with…concern? Irritation? "Are you suggesting one of my men out there might have had something to do with Dustin's disappearance?"

Having anticipated the reaction, Merry was ready. "I'm not suggesting anything. I'm only trying to get an accurate lay of the land, a complete picture of what was happening in Dustin's life prior to last Saturday. Having a fight or disagreement with someone would influence his state of mind. When it comes to missing person cases, knowledge of state of mind can be vital information when it comes to figuring out what happened."

"Yes, I see. I suppose that makes sense. To answer your question, to my knowledge, there were no such clashes, big or small…personally. Professionally, I'd be lying if I said there weren't skirmishes over game play, but that, frankly, is part of the game. It's not unexpected."

"Thank you for your honesty. One last question, if I may. In the days and weeks leading up to Dustin's disappearance, did anything in terms of his performance or behaviour stand out to you as unusual?"

The coach took a moment to consider the question. "As you know, it was a bye week. Because of that I didn't see Dustin as regularly as I do otherwise. That being said, from what I did see, from the interactions we did have, I would have to say the answer to your question is no. I…" His words faded away.

"What is it?" Merry asked.

"I would like to believe, as his coach and someone who's known Dustin for a while, that if there was something seriously wrong going on in his life, I'd know about it."

Merry thought Calder's response was interesting, given that he'd made the point earlier that the two weren't on buddy-buddy terms. She debated pushing him on the matter but decided against it for now.

"Ready to meet the guys?" Calder asked, edging up from his seat just short of standing up.

Merry nodded.

—

The team's clubhouse was more dad-man-cave than virile-sports-men-hangout. The room was generous in size with pockets of soft-seating sitting areas, some arranged around TV screens, others meant as quiet corners for reading or private conversations. One side of the room was lined with arcade games, the other held tables for pool and ping pong. As soon as Calder and Merry entered, the men assembled in the centre of the room where most of the couches were. Some took seats, others remained standing, all were fully attentive. What most surprised Merry was the difference in the players' sizes. There were 300-pound behemoths, who in this environment looked like gentle gorillas, but whose job it was to mow down opposing gorillas to clear the way for cheetah-like runners and pass catchers who might hit 200 soaking wet. Ironically, for someone who'd at times struggled to sit comfortably in her femininity in the company of others, in this place of testosterone and male meatiness, where she'd expected to feel out of place, Merry had never felt more a woman.

"Men," Calder began in a booming voice, much different than the one he'd been using in his office, "I'd like you to meet Merry Bell, the visitor I told you about. Merry tells me she's a big Roughrider fan, so we'll dispense with individual introductions, as I'm sure she recognizes most of you."

Merry choked a bit but covered it with a small cough. *What have I gotten myself into?*

"Turns out I was mistaken when I told you Merry was a relative of Dustin's. She's actually a private investigator. She was hired by Dustin's family to help the police find some answers." This was met with little more than idle curiosity.

Merry tried for an open, friendly smile. At the same time, she scanned the faces and was grateful to see that the one she'd hoped would be missing, her cousin Preston, was indeed not present.

"This has been a tough week for all of us," Calder kept on. "Everyone is concerned and rightly so. Some of you are closer to Dustin than others, but I know you all love him. Each of us deals with stress and worry in our own way. But I can tell you one thing for certain," he said, coming to a full stop. Merry's eyes widened as she, along with the players, was drawn in by the *Ted-Lasso*-worthy speech and the man delivering it, the healthy pause designed to underline the importance of what he was about to say. "Talking about what you're feeling, answering whatever questions Ms. Bell might have for you, will help. You hear me?"

"Yes, coach," came a resounding chorus of agreement.

Calder tuned to Merry and asked, "You good?"

Merry nodded, wondering if there was any way Robert Calder could give a speech every time she planned to interview a room full of people.

CHAPTER 5

Head coach Robert Calder had given a rousing speech meant to encourage his players to open up to Merry. Most seemed willing to talk, but what they said gave Merry little more than what she already knew. Although no one claimed to be a best friend or confidante, one thing was clear: everyone liked Dustin Thomson. They respected his role as their leader, in some cases as mentor, and greatly admired his skills as a player. Merry studied the men for signs of jealousy or resentment, but found none.

One after another, as if they'd rehearsed a synchronized response, Dustin's teammates (a) claimed to have no idea what could have happened to Dustin and (b) expressed concern and sympathy for his family. For the most part, they were cordial, polite but, Merry suspected, not entirely forthcoming. She wasn't surprised. She didn't know much about football, but she knew that any elite team, especially one that played at the level of the Saskatchewan Roughriders, survived and thrived by agreeing upon a code to live and die by, one that united them within an impenetrable bond to the exclusion of anything or anyone else who might tear them apart. Which was all very well and good on the football field but did little to help Merry with her case.

Halfway across Love Stadium parking lot, heading to where Doreen was patiently waiting, Merry heard someone calling her name. Turning she saw a large man barrelling in her direction. Friend or foe? The fact that he knew her name lent to the friend side, the fact that he looked like a charging bull with a bad attitude lent to the foe side.

As the man got closer she could see that the face was familiar, he was one of the Roughriders she'd just met and interviewed. Trent? Brent? A linesman? Offensive tackle?

"Thanks for stopping," he huffed and puffed as he pulled up in front of her. Merry was surprised by how out of breath the big man was.

She led with a dangling "Hi…" hoping he'd fill in the name part.

He did not, too used to being readily recognized by adoring fans. Fair enough, the city and province were full of them. Yet again, Merry was in the minority.

"Hi. Sorry to hold you up like this. I'm sure you have places to go."

"No problem. Was there something you wanted to talk about?"

"You forgot this."

Merry looked down and saw that Trent or Brent was holding a telltale green and white t-shirt in his beefy paws, a popular piece of Roughrider merch, probably with his player number emblazoned across the back. She didn't remember asking for one, never mind leaving it behind. She smiled. This guy had something to say he didn't want to say in front of the others. Excellent! Maybe this trip wouldn't be a complete loss after all.

"That's very thoughtful, thank you."

Handing over the shirt, he said, "I hope it's the right size. I bet it is. I'm pretty good at sizing up girls." His grin suggested he'd used this line more than once before, always to good effect.

"It's perfect," Merry said, taking the shirt without checking the size. Then she waited.

"So, uh, thanks for coming by today. I think some of the guys really needed that, to talk about Dustin, connect with his family and all."

Coach Calder had made it clear that Merry had been hired by the family, not part of the family itself, but whatever, maybe Trent/Brent hadn't been listening to that part.

"I know you probably couldn't tell us everything in there," he said, making it sound more like a question than an opinion.

"Oh?" *Come on, guy, gimme what ya got.*

"You're tall," was his next unexpected gambit. "Don't see a lot of tall girls in Saskatchewan."

"Is that so?" Merry doubted it.

"Yeah. Back in Georgia, where I'm from, girls are taller. Maybe it's an American thing."

"Maybe."

"So, about Dustin…"

"Mm-hmm?"

"What do you think really happened to him?"

"I don't know…I'm sorry, I'm blanking on your first name."

He looked surprised, really surprised, maybe even a little hurt. "Trent, Trent Brown."

"Of course. Bad memory." Not true, she'd been close.

"I signed the t-shirt in case you forget again," he said with a chuckle, fully recovered. "Do you think it's something bad?"

"You mean about what happened to Dustin?"

"Yeah."

"Like I said in the clubhouse, I was hired by the family to look into his disappearance. They don't know what happened to him and neither do I. Yet. Do you know something about where Dustin is?"

"Who, me?" He seemed genuinely surprised at the suggestion. "I don't. I wish I did." He pulled in a strangled breath. "I really wish I did." He burst into tears. "I really do." In one move the man shrugged his massive shoulders and fell into Merry's arms.

Yes, she was one of those reportedly rare Saskatchewan tall girls, but even so, Merry had to reach high and wide to embrace the grieving football player. Patting his heaving back she whispered comforting words between his sputtering, unintelligible ones.

"Wait!"

The voice came from somewhere behind Trent's shuddering bulk. If Merry had known the parking lot was such a good source of people who actually wanted to talk to her, she'd have stayed out here instead of bothering with the clubhouse. Merry felt the big man pulling away at the sound of the person approaching.

"Trent? Is that you?"

Trent looked pleadingly at Merry.

While the woman was still several yards away, Merry surreptitiously reached up and with a thumb under each eye wiped away the remains of the footballer's tears. "It's okay," she mouthed when she was done.

Trent turned to face the newcomer. "Cassie, girl, you looking good today!" he bellowed as if nothing had happened.

"Are you the detective woman?" Cassie asked, stepping into their circle and giving Merry a very detailed once over.

Merry froze. She knew girls like this, ultra feminine Barbies but in a militaristic way. In G.I. Barbie's world—which was pretty much all of it as far as she was concerned—she was the ruler of all girl stuff, the one who set and upheld strict standards of girldom with a sparkly smile made of granite. She was Brenda Brown at her worst but without the softening benefit of a few hard knocks and bites of reality. Immediately Merry saw a too-familiar look drift across the woman's face. Whereas Trent saw Merry as nothing more than a tall girl, Cassie saw a tall girl with bits and pieces coloured outside the lines that needed some kind of explanation. Merry hated how she'd suddenly become super aware of her outfit, her makeup, her shoes, how her hair looked. Cassie doubted her membership in the girl's club but, even worse, made Merry doubt it too. Even though she'd barely said a word yet, this chick was really pissing her off.

"I am the detective woman." She'd sorely wanted to emphasize the "woman" part but resisted. Too cheap. "I'm Merry Bell. And you are?"

"This is Cassie," Trent made introductions.

Merry hoped for his sake that only she noticed the puffy eyes. Cassie did not seem to be the kind of gal who appreciated a man who cried, especially outside a football stadium in the middle of the day.

"She's one of the best we got."

"Best…?"

"Cheerleaders."

"I'm a member of the Cheer Team," Cassie elaborated.

"What are you doing here?" he asked.

"Brent texted me."

Ah ha! So there was a Brent.

"He told me about her," she said with a side eye at Merry, "coming to talk to all the players about Dustin. I happened to be on campus and came right over." Focusing her full attention on the man's face, which was a good foot above hers, she asked: "Were you two hugging? Did I interrupt something?"

Merry saw the horrified look on Trent's face. He began to stutter an answer he hadn't thought of yet. She jumped in with: "We *were* hugging. Trent and I go way back. I've been living in Vancouver for several years so we haven't seen each other in a long time." Merry was pleased with herself. The best lies always contain elements of truth.

"Oh," the woman uttered, once again studying Merry in an obvious way. "Way back as in you were dating?"

Thankfully by this point Trent had recovered enough to jump into the awkward exchange. "Cassie, you got to be the snoopiest girl I ever met," he declared with a good-natured laugh. "That ain't none of your business. Next question."

Cassie's smile was a crimson tension rod forcefully stretched from one tan cheek to the other. Repositioning herself to face Merry head on, she said, "Fair enough. Mrs. Bell, don't you think the Cheer Team should have been included in your interrogation? We're as much a part of the team as they are." Her thumb pointed at Trent.

Merry didn't know if the cheer team was considered a part of the football team so she let that one go. What she did know was that Cassie calling her "Mrs." in such an intentional way was saying "I question your womanhood" or "I think you're old." Either way, it was a jab. Referring to her visit with the Roughriders as an interrogation was deliberately inflammatory, plain and simple. This girl was pushing buttons. Merry matched Cassie's tight smile and whispered to herself: *I am a professional.* "Actually, Carrie, I was hoping to talk to you next."

"It's Cassie."

"Oh, I'm sorry, Cassie."

Cassie's eyes slid onto Trent. "Could you give us girls some privacy? Maybe you two can finish your catching-up some other time?"

Trent, looking relieved to be released from the situation, smiled and with a quick "good-bye" lumbered off without a backwards glance.

"So, what did you want to talk about?" Cassie asked, all sweetness, acting as if it was Merry who'd chased her down.

"Seems to me that since you made an effort to come all the way over here, maybe there's something you want to talk to me about?" Merry matched the tone granule of sugar for granule of sugar.

"Oh, well, I just thought it was important for the Cheer Team to be represented in such an important discussion at such an important time."

"I see. Does the Cheer Team spend a lot of time with the players aside from game days?"

"I'm sure you're aware cheerleading is a sport. We are part of the athletic department, we train and adhere to strict schedules and rules, just like the football players."

"You train in the same gym?"

"Well, no."

"Do you socialize with the players?"

Cassie hesitated before saying, "Sometimes."

"I see. Are you aware of anyone on the Cheer Team knowing Dustin outside of the game, socially or otherwise?"

"Of course we spend time together. It's important for us to bond."

For someone who ran all the way over here from the university campus, which was on the other side of a busy street, Cassie seemed to have little to say aside from schooling Merry on the importance of the Cheer Team. Merry dug deeper. "Does anyone on the Cheer Team have a *special* bond with Dustin?"

"Are you asking if anyone was hooking up with him?"

"I'm asking if anyone had a relationship with Dustin beyond the typical Cheerleader-Footballer one; hooking up, friendship, whatever."

A sly smile found its way onto Cassie's pretty face. "I won't lie, there were a couple of girls who tried. He's a very handsome man, as you know."

"And…?"

"Nothing happened with them."

Deeper. "Did you try?" Merry would bet her bank account—which admittedly wasn't major collateral—that this was the real reason the cheerleader hippity-hopped her way over here.

"I don't have to try," Cassie said with a TV-ready wink. "It's the boys who have to try with me."

"Okay. Did Dustin try with you?"

Her chin shifted a bit higher. "Well, no, not really. I think he wanted to, but he was a good guy. He was into somebody else, but if he wasn't, who knows."

This was getting interesting. "Who was this somebody else?"

"I don't know. I never met her. But I know she wasn't good for him, leading him on like that. She had him so confused. He never seemed to know for sure whether they were a couple or not, otherwise something probably would have happened between us. There were a couple nights when, well, you know, things got close."

"But he turned you down?"

Cassie's eyes flashed. "We *both* agreed not to move ahead, out of respect for…whatshername."

"Do you know where Dustin is?"

Instead of acting surprised or offended by the question, Cassie appeared stoic, as if the accusation heightened her importance and was her due. "I do not."

"Cassie," Merry pushed, "anything you can tell me about your friendship with him, no matter how big or small, could be important."

"I really wish I could help. I'm so worried about him." Unlike Trent, the baby tears forming in Cassie's eyes were hard won.

Merry handed over a card, saying, "Please let me know if you think of anything that might help."

Cassie took the card but her eyes were on Merry's face. "I like your shoes," she said in a way that implied the opposite.

—

Roger Brown was glad to have an excuse to take a break from the pool party. Georgia and Lily, four-year-old French bulldogs, sisters, had previously made it abundantly clear that he was at the bottom of the list of family members they preferred to accompany them on walks (this probably had something to do with the fact that he always forgot to bring along treats as rewards for making a piddle or poo), but he volunteered anyway. Roger liked their friends well enough; he enjoyed playing host, sharing food and drinks around the pool on a beautiful summer evening, but after a few hours he needed relief, needed to get away, to recentre himself, to save himself from making a big mistake. Never more than when he was feeling carefree, having fun with friends, and maybe a little drunk, did he suddenly feel the compulsion to come clean about who he really was, reveal the part of himself he otherwise felt bound to keep hidden. Wasn't that what you were supposed to do with close acquaintances? Be real. Be truthful. Be free.

Long ago Brenda requested—and Roger readily agreed—to keep his crossdressing between them. He didn't find it hard to do. Fear, uncertainty, and embarrassment fed his silence, none of which, to his mind, were unfounded or inconsequential. He could always find a million reasons not to tell people about his crossdressing, reasons that only multiplied when they had children. There was comfort and ease in keeping that part of himself private. Yet, increasingly, worryingly, he felt the secret growing heavier, as weighty as it was invisible. *How much longer can I keep this up?*

As a boy Roger lived with confusion, as young people often do when their bodies and minds are telling them things about themselves they don't understand, things that don't jive with the experience of others around them. It all began by mistake one Hallowe'en.

His core group of pre-teen friends accepted a dare to dress as the Spice Girls at the after-school "Spookfest" in the school's gym. The costumes were outrageously bad and they looked a fright, but they were a hit. They'd even choreographed a dance to the song *Spice Invader*. Roger was Posh Spice. He wore a tight black dress with pearls and his mother's heels which just happened to fit perfectly. He didn't know it at the time, but the seminal moment would stay with him forever.

For the next week the quintet was alternately the toast of the school or butt of creatively off-colour jokes that even the teachers smirked at. Then it was over. Everyone moved on to whatever came next, their attention spans as fleeting as a puppy's. Everyone except for Roger. He couldn't stop thinking about it; not how he looked but how he felt wearing a dress, women's shoes and a wig. The sudden obsession worried him, but the memory of the experience felt too good to ignore.

For years Roger replayed those moments over and over again in his mind, but it wasn't until his first year living away from home, on a chilly Saturday in October, that he did something about it. He made a plan and followed it. He went to Value Village to shop for shoes and clothes, then Winners for makeup. If anyone asked—which they didn't—he once again planned to use Hallowe'en as a cover, with a fully rehearsed story about needing the outfit for a costume party. That night he lowered every blind in his apartment and for the first time as an adult dressed his body in women's clothing, right down to the underwear. The result was as bad if not worse than his teenage Posh Spice—especially without the benefit of a wig which he'd forgotten to get—but the feeling was just as good if not better. He spent the entire night dressed, doing his regular things, making and eating dinner, watching TV, drinking beers, playing video games. It was the best night of his young life.

Then came Sunday.

Back in boy clothes, makeup washed off, hungover, Roger's brain kicked in and he miserably asked himself: *What the fuck?*

Fear, judgement and disgust overtook him. He stuffed every

piece of womenswear into a plastic grocery store bag, double knotted the top, and tossed it into the dumpster behind his apartment building. He vowed to eradicate the memory of what he'd done from his fevered brain.

Six months later he did it all over again.

What the fuck?

Am I gay? Am I mentally ill? Am I some kind of pervert? Am I supposed to be a woman? Is there anyone else like me? Over time Roger allowed himself to think about why he was the way he was instead of just ignoring what he did as a shameful aberration. Slowly he began to come up with answers for some of the questions that plagued him. He came to understand a few important things about who he was. He had no doubts about his sexuality—he liked girls, a lot—or his gender identity—he was a guy and he liked being a guy. So then... *What the fuck?*

Some questions were harder to answer than others.

By the time Roger met Brenda, he'd had a reasonable number of past relationships, but only one in which he'd confided to his partner about his crossdressing. It went surprisingly well. The partnership wasn't meant to last, but it did convince him that his crossdressing was an important part of who he was and something he needed to share in his next serious relationship. That next relationship was with Brenda. And now here they were, married ten years with two kids and hosting a pool party in their beautiful backyard.

Earlier in the night Roger had turned to Brenda, who'd been helping him refill drinks for their guests, most of whom were bobbing in the pool, laughing and chattering away, seemingly carefree, and quietly suggested he excuse himself to walk the dogs. She quickly agreed. Brenda's mother, Doris, who lived with them but wasn't attending the party, could just as easily have been recruited to see to the pets' needs, but Brenda understood what her husband was really asking. She also knew that what he needed wouldn't take long. He was reliable that way. He'd be back in five or ten minutes, good as new.

With Georgia and Lily having seen to their business, the trio was returning home when Roger spotted the pale blue 1987 Plymouth Horizon. It was parked across the street, a solitary figure hunched behind the steering wheel, lights off. He knew the vehicle well. It was Doreen. Roger was jealous and a little resentful of Doreen.

As creator of the popular true crime podcast, *The Darkside of Livingsky*, which he hosted as his cross-dressing alter ego, Stella, Roger was obsessed with the investigation of crimes and the professionals who did it for a living. The only private eyes he actually knew were fictional, like Jessica Fletcher and Kinsey Milhone, so it was with immense pleasure when, for his thirty-first birthday, Brenda surprised him by introducing him to a real, live P.I., Merry Bell. He quickly learned that Merry ran her detective agency out of the same building where his wife ran her own business, Designs by Brenda. Brenda saw it as a unique birthday gift. He saw it as an opportunity to learn the tricks of the trade, collect fodder for his podcast, and be a part of a world he loved.

Merry seemed to like him well enough at first but was reluctant to take him up on his offer to join her team as an unpaid intern. Desperate to make it work and knowing Merry was new to the city and without a car, his next offer was to chauffeur her around town whenever his schedule as a self-employed electrician allowed. On occasion, Merry took him up on it, which led to Roger promoting himself to P.I. apprentice.

Then came Doreen.

Suddenly Merry didn't need him any longer and their private-eye-intern relationship dried up. Ever the optimist, Roger was hopeful that might change. Judging by the vehicle's portentous rust-to-metal ratio and the disconcerting sounds and smells that regularly burped up from beneath its hood, he predicted Doreen's days were numbered.

Brenda had shared her concern with Roger that in the months since Merry had arrived in Livingsky, she'd grown increasingly aloof and seemed lonely. What she didn't know was whether this was Merry's preferred natural state or some sort of misguided means of self-protection. Brenda had planned the pool party in the hopes Merry would attend, but like many before it, the invitation had been turned down. Which made it even more curious that Doreen along with the detective was parked on the street, close but out of sight of their house.

He had spotted her, but Roger was quite certain Merry hadn't spotted him. Hiding behind a neighbour's overgrown globe cedar, Roger studied Doreen and its lone occupant. Had she decided to attend the party after all then changed her mind when she arrived? Was she sitting in the dark trying to talk herself into it again? What was the hesitation? What was she afraid of?

Recognition struck Roger like a stroke of lightning. He and Merry Bell were the same. Each of them harboured a secret identity but—unlike superheroes like Clark Kent and Spiderman—the world was nowhere near prepared to celebrate them. So they hid. Not out of a sense of humility, but self-preservation. It didn't matter if you were surrounded by friends at a pool party or debating an invitation to one, hard cold reality was inescapable, and it was in those moments that irrefutable, soul-crushing loneliness threatened to overcome you. So you walked the dogs or took a late night drive.

Merry had made the trip in the hope of escaping her self-imposed isolation, at least for a little while. All that was left to do was get out of the car, walk up the path to the front door, and knock.

Instead, the little blue car sputtered to life and drove away.

In that moment, Roger knew exactly what he needed to do.

CHAPTER 6

Realizing she couldn't pay market price rent on both an office and a home, Merry knew something had to give. Which is how she ended up living in the Junk House. The Junk House was actually a converted storage unit that was once a workspace for the former employees of the scrap metal yard that surrounded it. The business had long ceased operations, but the carcasses of cars and kitchen appliances remained, much of it heaped into towering cenotaphs that, if you squinted really hard and knew nothing about modern art, could be mistaken as avant-garde sculptures. At three hundred dollars a month, she couldn't afford to turn it down. The yard's owner—and now Merry's landlord—Gerald Drover, was as peculiar, vaguely repulsive, yet indescribably alluring as his property.

Inside, the Junk House wasn't much, but it was a vast improvement over its original condition. Drover, powered by an unrequited crush on his new tenant, did his best to spruce it up. There was new paint, light bulbs that actually worked, and kitchen appliances and furniture that didn't smell of rot and desperation. He'd even splurged on new bedding and adorned the walls with a series of arresting black-and-white photographs of Alphabet City's urban landscape that he'd taken himself.

Lounging on a deep brown, doughy leather couch with her Sunday morning coffee, Merry was grateful for the oscillating pedestal fan Drover had brought over at the beginning of the summer when she complained about the lack of AC. Surveying the single room that encompassed the kitchen, living room and dining room, she wondered for about the millionth time since she'd moved in why she'd come to like living in the Junk House as much as she did. Everything had something wrong with it, yet the something wrongs somehow made everything just right. The sofa was too soft, which made it super comfortable to doze on. There was only one window in the place other than a half-moon on the front door, but that window was gloriously oversized, its original purpose to allow salvage yard foremen to keep an eye on customers who thought they might sneak off without paying. The massive pane invited in an abundance of light on sunny days and afforded Merry spectacular views of summer rainstorms, winter blizzards and her very own scrap metal sculpture garden. The kitchen was tiny and impractical with plenty of quirks like a microwave that beeped at random intervals for no apparent reason and a table that wobbled no matter how many times she tried to adjust the legs. Merry liked quirky. Not one piece of furniture, kitchen appliance or piece of silverware matched another, yet all together they seemed ideal. The bedroom in the back was actually a large storage closet, but it was inviting and felt safe, like a cocoon. Merry would never admit it to Drover, but the Junk House, despite its name and original purpose, felt like home; something that none of her apartments in Vancouver ever had.

Pouring herself a second cup of coffee—only in the budget when she was at home and not at the mercy of coffee shop prices—and microwaving the remaining half of a Mama burger from last night's late-night splurge, Merry returned to the sofa. She dipped a corner of the burger into a dollop of ketchup as her mind replayed the previous evening. She'd come home from Love Stadium fatigued. Eliciting useful information from a roomful of football players who'd collectively displayed what she could only describe as jock stoicism in favour of personal opinions or real feelings was challenging, as were her later interactions in the parking lot with a grieving athlete and charged-up cheerleader. Every case started out this way, digging and scratching in what seemed like a barren plot of dirt, but Merry knew from experience that even empty gardens could yield bountiful harvest if you were patient and dug deep enough. Still, all that digging could be exhausting.

Returning to the Junk House, Merry opened a chilled box of passable pinot grigio, took the box, a glass, and a block of aged cheddar to a little area she'd carved out between multiple stacks of twisted metal at the rear of the little house. Beneath a late afternoon sun, a favourite iPhone playlist serenading her, Merry splayed out on a lounger she'd reclaimed from the *I Love Lucy* era part of the junk yard. Half a block and half a box later, she was fast asleep.

She awoke sometime later, unsure of how long she'd been asleep. However long it was, the nap did her good and she felt a second wind overtake her. It was late, but at that time of year the sun didn't set until well after 9:00 p.m. with ambient light hovering at the horizon long past that. She had a decision to make. It was either face another Saturday night alone in the Junk House watching Netflix, or take Brenda Brown up on her pool party invitation. After a bit of cajoling and self-arm-twisting, Merry settled on pool party and headed inside to figure out what to wear.

Not long after they'd first met, Brenda somehow managed to talk Merry into a makeover. The results were transformative. She looked different. Really different. She looked good. Really good. The power of know-how, application skill and quality cosmetics that didn't come from a discount store were undeniable. But there was a problem. Merry couldn't decide whether the new face in the mirror was truly Merry Bell.

Brenda Brown had wisely convinced Merry that their session should be videotaped on her phone, leaving her with an instructional tool she could refer to as she experimented with recreating the look on her own. Some of what Brenda showed her was akin to a magician's trick; you could see it happen in front of your eyes, but you could never figure out how it was done. Some of it was so intricate, so meticulous, so time-consuming, Merry knew she'd never have the patience for it. The basics, however, were sound and an excellent base for Merry to work from as she attempted, over and over again, to find and perfect the real Merry Bell. On a good day she looked a little like Gal Gadot from *Wonder Woman*, on bad ones it was more streetwalker-on-a-bender; mostly she fell somewhere in between. Lately, she'd begun to wonder if the variety was A-OK. Maybe there wasn't just one Merry Bell. The concept was a difficult one for her, having spent so much of her early life in a war against how she looked on the outside.

Thinking back to Brenda's original invitation to the pool party, in truth, the nosy designer was not completely off-base about Merry having reservations about wearing a bathing suit. The worry wasn't because she thought she couldn't pull it off or it wouldn't look good. The worry came from never having tried one on. Merry simply didn't know how her body would look in a woman's swimsuit. A public party in front of strangers was not the time to find out. But she could certainly pull off a sexy summer dress. So, with her dark hair piled into a messy bun that took way more time than the term "messy" implied, a colourful spaghetti strap shift and matching strappy sandals completing the look, Merry hopped into Doreen before she had time to change her mind.

By the time she reached Newton Heights and the gleaming white box the Browns called home, she'd pretty much changed her mind. She parked two houses down, turned off the lights and stewed.

What am I doing? I don't know these people. They're not my friends. It was a pity invite and nothing more. Besides, Merry stoked the fire, *do I really want to go to a pool party hosted by Designs by Brenda?* The weight of the woman's pretentiousness alone was sure to drown Merry even if she didn't go anywhere near the pool. She could see it all now. Everything would be flawless. The food, the décor, the swimwear, the cocktails. Even the bloody weather was perfect, as if Brenda had requested it online a week ago. Had Mother Nature been cowed by Brenda? Quite possibly.

Convinced she'd made a mistake, Merry started the car's engine, which despite its age and penchant for dodgy noises, always turned over. It's why she'd nicknamed the car Doreen, after one of her first landladies in Vancouver. Doreen—the human—was as trustworthy as the day was long, older than the Rocky Mountains, and regularly let loose with whatever noises her bodily functions bestowed upon her. The other nice thing about Doreen—the car—was that she always seemed to know the way to the nearest Dairy Queen. Fast food wasn't usually in the budget or diet, but Merry reasoned that if she kept to one burger and a small Blizzard and reserved part of the burger for breakfast, it made sense, the way all things do late at night.

In the stark, sun-bleached reality of Sunday morning, Merry was faced with the cold, hard truth that once again she'd chosen comfort food over companionship. Popping the last bite of breakfast Mama into her mouth, she fretted the choice could become habit.

—

The Jarvis Oleksyn Youth Centre, named for its two primary benefactors, Mervin Jarvis and Marielle Oleksyn, was better known in the community by its acronym, the JOY Centre. The facility, open seven days a week from 8:00 a.m. to 8:00 p.m., was located in the heart of Alphabet City in a converted bingo hall. Most of its clientele were BIPOC between the ages of 10 and 21. Anyone could wander in to check it out, but loitering was pointedly discouraged.

Upon entering through the front doors off of 20th Avenue, Merry was confronted with a large sign proclaiming the rules of JOY Centre in bold letters: NO VIOLENCE. NO WEAPONS. NO BULLYING. NO FEAR. Smiling at the powerful manifesto, Merry approached the reception desk which was actually an eight-foot-long folding table. Behind it were two young women busily divvying up a dizzying selection of colourful craft materials into two dozen lunch-size paper bags. They looked up with matching welcoming smiles.

"You must be Merry?" one of them asked. Her name tag read "Dawn—She/Her".

"Yes. I called earlier. You two look very organized for so early on a Sunday."

"That's because it's still morning. You should see us by late afternoon. Girl, it's a mess!"

Everyone laughed good-naturedly. Merry immediately liked this place. She could already see why kids would like it too.

"You said something about wanting to talk to some of the kids who knew Dustin?" the one with a nametag that read "Cindi—She/Her" said. "Everyone at JOY is worried about him. It's been over a week now, right?"

"Yes. And thanks for letting me in."

"Oh, it's no problem. We love to get visitors, show off how awesome this place is. Dustin was a big part of that, so we're happy to do anything we can to help."

Merry nodded, noting with a tinge of sadness and wariness how the young woman referred to Dustin in the past tense.

"You're in luck this morning," Dawn added, "because one of our board members is here doing a volunteer shift. He can show you around, answer any questions, introduce you to some of the kids."

"Great, thank you."

"Hey, Sweet Lips!"

At the sound of the highly inappropriate but not unfamiliar greeting, Merry spun around to find her one-time client and current landlord, Gerald Drover leering at her.

"Gerald!" Cindi admonished with a tone usually reserved for kids caught being a little naughty. "This is Merry Bell. She's the detective I told you about, so please behave."

Merry addressed the girls to let them know everything was okay. "Mr. Drover and I know one another." She used "Mr. Drover" because she knew the moniker drove Gerald bonkers as it reminded him of his father whose well-earned reputation as one of Livingsky's most reviled slum landlords followed him around like a skunk's scent.

Gerald Drover was all beanstalk, tall and slender. He favoured heavy metal band t-shirts, skinny jeans that still required the assistance of a belt to stay up, and crusty cowboy boots that were older than his thirty years. More bizarre than the man's wardrobe was everything above the neck. Drover's perfectly oblong head was topped by a full-on mullet, ginger red. His cheeks were puffy, his chin pronounced, his ears and nose were super-sized, a collection of parts that didn't quite go together, but then, in a shocking contradiction that still took Merry by surprise, his eyes and lips were stunning. The eyes were like nothing she'd seen before, the colour of an aquamarine sea sprinkled with specks of sand and rimmed with lashes thick as a puppy's. Like many of his other features, Drover's lips were far too big for his long narrow face, but they were so pleasantly plump, cherry-pink, and perfectly shaped, any pre-injection model would kill for them.

"What are *you* doing here?" Merry asked.

"I've been on the JOY Centre board for years. I volunteer here three or four times a month."

For a moment, Merry was speechless. More than once since she'd known him this insensitive, ridiculous, red-headed flamingo with a gopher-cheeked smile surprised her. By every measurement available, Gerald Drover should be nothing more than a money-grubbing cad and outrageous doofus all rolled into one. But then she'd find out he was an expert photographer, a world traveller, a foodie. And despite that he was renting her a shack in the middle of a junk yard, for cash she was certain never reached his CRA forms, he was a pretty good landlord too.

"Come on," he said, opening a door leading into the rest of the centre. "I'll take you on a tour."

"Uh, okay."

For the next half hour Drover led Merry around the building and described the inner workings of the JOY Centre. With focus firmly placed on education and personal development, it quickly became clear this was much more than a hangout for kids with nothing better to do. If a youth decided they wanted to spend time at JOY they were required to select one of three programming streams: Sports, Arts, Society. Thereafter, whenever an entrant signed in at the front, they were immediately directed to proceed to the part of the building dedicated to that program. Once there, they either attended or helped facilitate workshops, mentored or were mentored, or gathered in literal chat rooms to give or receive guidance or spend time with other like-minded kids.

"Nothing is perfect," Drover explained as he prepared a coffee for Merry in a joint use kitchen. "But the basic structure of what JOY Centre is trying to be is solid. Most of the kids come to respect it, some are assholes, but they don't last long."

"What do you do here?" Merry couldn't help being curious.

"I teach 'em the fine art of swindling renters and how to make a quick buck," Drover quipped, winking one of his lustrously lashed eyelids. "Just as you'd expect."

"I can't think of anyone more qualified," she shot back.

"I appreciate the compliment, ma'am."

"Gerald," she said in a more serious tone, "I have to give it to you. If I've learned anything about you in the past few months since we've known each other, it's that you are consistently inconsistent."

"It's a turn on, right, Honeycakes?"

"Case in point." She accepted the drink. It smelled really good.

"So," he said with a slight scowl, "by consistently inconsistent you mean you never thought I'd be involved in something like this?"

Merry couldn't tell if Drover's feelings were actually hurt or he was pulling her leg. "You don't seem like the kind of guy interested in the well-being of kids, that's all."

"That might be true, although I do want kids one day," he said with a libidinous grin, "so get ready for that. But I am interested in the well-being of my community, and like it or not, kids are part of that community, especially Alphabet City kids. I used to be one of these kids."

"Are all the youth who come here from inner-city neighbourhoods?" Merry asked as they stepped out of the kitchen into a large meeting area reserved for the Sports program kids.

"Nope. I suppose most are, but there are others too, kids having problems at home or at school, or who just don't fit in anywhere else. Everyone fits in at JOY Centre. No matter what kind of weirdo you think you are, chances are you'll find someone just like you to hang out with. That's what I like about this place. Even I would have fit in here when I was a kid, and that's saying something 'cuz I was all kinds of weird." Drover used his coffee cup to point at a girl curled up on one of the couches, engrossed in her phone. "Take Aly over there. She don't live in Alphabet City, but she's here two/three times a week, sometimes more."

"Did she know Dustin Thomson?"

"Yep. That's why I brought you in here. Dawn and Cindi told me you wanted to talk to kids he worked with. She used to be a Society program kid, but then she switched to Sports, which is where Dustin spends most of his time when he's here."

"I get Sports and Arts, but what's the Society Program all about?"

"It's my favourite. It teaches kids about how society works and the different ways they can interact with it, either to fit in or, if you don't like what you see, how to constructively make changes, or at least try to. We get workshop facilitators and mentors from every walk of life, lawyers, politicians, businesspeople. Me too, since you were interested in what I do around here. We spend time with the kids in various formal and informal ways. We tell 'em what we do, how we do it, what's good about it, what's not so good, how we see the world. They call us on our bullshit. They ask questions. It's pretty cool."

"All of this is very impressive," Merry agreed.

"I'm gonna take that as an actual compliment, Sweet Lips."

Merry grinned. "Go for it. Gerald, could you…"

"…take you out for drinks and dinner? Gosh, this is so unexpected, but sure."

"In your dreams."

"Your loss. What can I do you for?"

"Could you introduce me to Aly?"

He eyed her up and slowly nodded. "I wouldn't do this for just anyone y'know. We're pretty serious about protecting our kids around here, especially from adults they don't know."

"Thank you."

"Follow me."

Once assured that Aly and Merry were comfortable with each other, Gerald excused himself so they could talk in private, standing far enough away so he couldn't hear them, but not so far away he couldn't keep an eye on them. This wasn't because he didn't trust Merry. It was because he liked looking at her when she wasn't aware he was doing it.

Although it was clear Aly was not a chit-chat-with-a-stranger kind of girl, Merry began with: "I hear you used to be part of the Society group. Gerald was just telling me all about it. It sounds really cool."

"I guess."

Even though she was scrunched up on the sofa like a buddha, Merry could see the girl was small, under five feet, with a pretty oval face only half visible beneath shafts of straight, dark hair streaked with bright pink.

"Did you learn things about…society?" Merry winced at the stupid question, realizing she might need some practice talking to kids.

"Duh."

"Why did you switch to Sports?"

"Change it up," she said, her low voice further weighed down by sullenness. "I get bored easy, I guess."

"So you're into sports now? That must be fun," Merry suggested, herself having very few fun associations with competitive sports. She preferred the gym where she could do her own thing without anyone keeping score.

"Used to be."

"It's not fun anymore? What changed?"

Aly looked at Merry like she might be the stupidest person on the planet. "Duh, Dustin's gone. He was the whole reas…" She stopped herself there. "He disappeared last weekend. Didn't you know about that? Everyone knows about that. It was on socials and everything."

"Yes, I did hear about that," she said calmly. *This is a child, this is a child,* was her mantra.

"It ruined everything."

It was an odd statement to make, one Merry intended to get to the bottom of. She studied the girl. She was holding her body in a peculiar position. Was she cradling an injury or was this some version of don't get-too-close-to-me body language she hadn't seen before? Teenage girls could be prickly, sometimes downright scary. She tread carefully. "Pretty sad stuff."

"So sad."

"Did you know Dustin very well?"

"Yeah." She somehow gave the word three syllables.

"You must really miss him."

"Yeah." Almost four that time.

"Was he the reason you switched to Sports?"

She shrugged. "He said I could be good at it if I wanted to be. Even though I'm small."

"Did you want to be good at sports?"

She shrugged half a shoulder. It appeared to take Herculean effort.

"Was there a specific sport you wanted to try?"

Nothing.

What now? "Did Dustin *ask* you to switch to the Sports program?"

"Never mind," Aly muttered, shifting in her seat so more of her back was to Merry. "You wouldn't understand."

Aha. What's this? "Try me. I'm a good listener."

"I got nothing to say." Then, as if she couldn't help herself: "Dustin and my relationship is private."

Merry felt the pins-and-needles sensation that came along every time she stumbled upon something she didn't expect. "You and Dustin had a relationship?"

"You said it, I didn't."

Uh, you kinda just did, girlie. "What kind of relationship?" Dustin Thomson was 25, Aly was maybe 16. Merry wondered if she was about to discover a blemish in the otherwise perfect billboard-sized picture of the football hero. She hoped not, but perfection, she knew, was almost never reality.

"Who are you again?" Aly demanded to know, suddenly all court-room-lawyer-ish, as if she'd suddenly woken up and realized she was in conversation with a real live human.

"I'm a private detective. Dustin's family hired me. They want me to find out why he disappeared, where he is. If there's anything you can tell me about that they would really appreciate it. They care about Dustin," she said, then added for good measure, "just like you care about Dustin. They're worried about him, just like you are. Do you know where he is, Aly?"

The girl shook her head and looked down at her phone as if it were transmitting the answers to an upcoming test.

"Aly, you can tell me...you should tell me if you know something. This is very important."

"I know it's important!" she cried out, tears spurting from dark eyes. "But I don't know anything. He didn't tell me nothing. That's why I'm so worried about him. You wouldn't understand. No one understands!"

It was the second time Aly claimed Merry wouldn't understand. So far the statement was accurate. Was the girl trying to tell her she and Dustin were so close that if he had planned to go away, he would have told her about it? Was she hinting at an intimate relationship of some sort? Or was Aly simply being melodramatic, a kid with a hard-on for her Sports program mentor who happened to be a very handsome celebrity, the teenager version of Cassie the cheerleader? Kids were sometimes harder to read than adults because they so believed their own bullshit.

Merry handed the girl a business card. She looked at it as if she'd never seen such a thing before, which was not unlikely.

"Aly, if you think of anything that might help, anything at all, would you please call me? Anytime."

"I know one thing for sure," she managed to say between stifled sobs.

"What is it?"

"Something really bad's happened to Dustin."

—

After leaving the JOY Centre, Merry headed for Livingsky Plaza where she was booked for an eight-hour security guard shift. It wasn't a regular gig, but she got called in fairly regularly to replace full-time employees who'd either called in sick or simply didn't show up for a variety of Gen Z reasons. It wasn't ideal, but a girl's gotta eat chocolate, drink wine and pay rent.

By the time Merry got home Sunday night it was late and she was bone-dead tired from walking up and down mall corridors intimidating mostly harmless troublemakers and answering dumb question about washroom locations—there are signs everywhere—and whether the food court sold groceries. To top it off she got drenched by a passing rainstorm while getting in and out of Doreen to unlock then re-lock the gate that surrounded the Junk House yard. By the time she got inside, nothing was dry. She stripped down in the bathroom, hanging her clothes over the shower rod and slipping into a housecoat. She poured herself the last of the wine she'd started on Saturday afternoon then settled on the couch with her phone.

It behooved a detective to stay abreast of all goings on in her community, so she found the feed for a favourite local news telecast and hit play. If there was little of interest, Tik Tok and Instagram were at the ready. Setting her wineglass on the coffee table and her phone on a stand she'd set up for the purpose, she watched the report while fluff-drying her hair with both hands. Brenda would be scandalized to learn she made no attempt at styling it at the same time, having insisted that going to bed with messy hair was just as bad as going to bed without removing your makeup (two things Merry did regularly). Extricating her fingers from a particularly resistant knot, her ears perked up at the sound of the ominous tone which always preceded a "breaking news" segment. She grabbed her wine and sat back in the chair, looking forward to something juicy.

On screen was Cynthia MacDonald who, according to massive billboards spread across town, was "the most trusted face in local news." Tonight, she looked painfully glum.

"Ladies and gentlemen, we interrupt our regular broadcast for important breaking news that has just come into our station," Cynthia warned viewers.

As the station's logo behind the newscaster faded away, revealing the subject of the big news, Merry's wine glass slipped from her hand and smashed on the floor.

CHAPTER 7

A pall had fallen over the city, the province, the country.

The first thing Merry did when she awoke Monday morning was check Livingsky Tribune's e-paper. A single bold headline confirmed the tragic truth: "A Nation Grieves." The sentiment was not only a heart-wrenching statement of fact, but a play on the well-known term: Rider Nation. Although the Saskatchewan Roughriders was the oldest continuously operating professional football club in western Canada playing in the least populated sports market in the country, the team was most famous for the intensity of their supporters known collectively as "Rider Nation," who kept stadiums full, ticket sales brisk, and beer kegs empty. A quick scan of several news articles revealed the same content: after being reported missing a week earlier, Saskatchewan Roughrider star quarterback Dustin Thomson had been found dead. He'd apparently drowned in the South Saskatchewan River beneath Sweetgrass Bridge located a few kilometers south of Livingsky. In the absence of further details from the authorities, reporters desperate for something to write resorted to lengthy expositions describing Thomson's career and what was known of his personal life.

Sitting at her desk at 222 Craving Lane, Merry impatiently waited for the clock to strike 9:00 a.m., a time she deemed reasonable to start making calls. The first was to her client, Ruth-Anne Delorme. It was a short one. Understandably, Delorme sounded upset and somewhat befuddled. Merry's primary purpose, for now, was to express sympathy and ask if there was anything she could do to help.

Delorme appeared unable to put more than two words together and quickly ended the conversation by telling Merry she'd call back as soon as she could. Delorme had hired her to find out what happened to her cousin. Now they knew. Case closed?

Until she had clear direction from her client that she was officially un-hired, Merry decided to keep doing what she did best: investigate.

The person responsible for giving Merry (before she was Merry) her first big break at being a P.I. was a lantern-jawed he-man named Nathan Sharpe, owner of Sharpe Investigations (SI). When Merry decided to leave Vancouver to rebuild her life in Livingsky, Sharpe agreed to allow Merry to co-opt his name and reputation to start her own firm, and so, Livingsky Sharpe Investigations (LSI) was born. In the years she'd worked and excelled in her role as an investigator with SI, Nathan was more than her employer. He was her teacher, mentor and, eventually, trusted father figure who in his rough and gruff way supported her as best he could when she commenced transitioning. One of the many things he taught her was that even though cops and private eyes might see each other as competition, their end goals were usually very much aligned. The relationships were typically fraught with tension, turf disputes and disagreements over how justice was best served, but there was no denying having an "in" with local police was a good thing.

LSI's first case had involved a suspicious fire. The officer responsible for that investigation was Detective Sergeant Veronica Greyeyes, a buttoned-up, serious as a heart attack, by-the-book cop who looked like she'd just as soon shackle you or tackle you than crack a smile. She'd also arrested Merry for the murder of the Vancouver surgeon who'd performed Merry's gender affirming surgery. Suffice it to say, their relationship was complicated. Despite all of that, Merry had found herself respecting and even liking Greyeyes. With no other ready options at hand, whether Greyeyes wanted it or not, Merry was determined to recruit Greyeyes as her "in" with the Livingsky Police Service (LPS).

"Sergeant Greyeyes, thank you for talking with me." Merry was genuinely surprised her call was put through and answered on the first try.

"I assume this is important?" Greyeyes responded, sounding genuinely interested in what was coming next.

"It is," Merry began, knowing the detective wasn't one for idle chit chat. "I'm sure, like the rest of the world, you've heard about Dustin Thomson's death."

Greyeyes did not comment.

"Prior to yesterday's discovery, I was hired by Thomson's family to look into his disappearance." Merry knew her use of "family" was overreaching. It made it sound as if the entire Thomson clan was on her client roster, but what Greyeyes didn't know couldn't hurt her. Hopefully. The problem was, Greyeyes had the irritating habit of knowing more than you expected her to. That's what made her a good cop and someone Merry needed on her side. "As a profession-al courtesy I was hoping you might be willing to share with me any details the police have uncovered that might be useful in helping the family get through this very sad and difficult time. As you might expect, they are devastated." Had she gone too far? Did it sound like the Thomsons were in her living room waiting with bated breath for anything Merry could learn from the coppers?

Veronica wasn't buying it. "The LPS is also in contact with the Thomson family."

"Yes, I know." *Hmmmm*. New tack. "But I was wondering if there was anything beyond the official confirmation of death that I should know about? I've read enough police statements and been to enough press conferences to know when there's something not being said."

"I'm afraid I don't know what you're getting at, Ms. Bell. And I should tell you: I am not the lead investigator on this case."

Greyeyes sounded irritated. Merry wondered if the reason was because of how easily she'd seen behind the blue veil. Cops were infamous for keeping what they knew to themselves. In a city the size of Livingsky with only one daily newspaper, that wasn't hard to do. Eighty percent of the content in the Livingsky Tribune was copied and pasted directly from the mother ship's newspaper based in Toronto. Local news was either fluff, biased editorial soliloquies, or hastily pieced together articles by an ever-diminishing cadre of journalists who didn't have the time or budget to dig deeper into what LPS spokespeople deigned to reveal at infrequent press conferences.

"As far as I can tell," Merry continued, "the police have only released basic facts. Thomson is dead. He drowned. He was found downriver from Sweetgrass Bridge. There's been no reference to whether this was an accidental death or due to natural causes, which tells me you aren't sure whether either of those things are true."

Silence on the line.

"Was Dustin Thomson's death an accident? Or is there something more going on here?"

Nothing.

Merry rejoiced. Silence from Detective Sergeant Greyeyes meant only one thing: there was something to say and she wasn't sure whether she should say it.

"Veronica." She used the woman's first name sparingly, and only to (a) impress upon her the importance of what she was about to say and (b) strengthen their tentative connection by adding a dab of personalized cement. "You know as well as I do, it seems like half of the country is up in arms over Dustin Thomson's death. He's a celebrity. Everyone wants to know everything and they want to know it now. All eyes are on the LPS. How you handle this, in the eyes of the family, his friends, the mayor, the FSIN, and every Roughrider fan around the world, will either make or break the department's reputation for years to come."

Merry hoped her gambit was not too low a blow. The LPS had a spotty history when it came to reputation, especially in dealing with the significant Indigenous population of the city. The issues and challenges were real, they were numerous and complex and affected the city economically, politically and sociologically in myriad ways. Modern policing in the woke era had improved but still had a long way to go.

"If there really is something more going on here," Merry reasoned, "doesn't it make sense to get as much help as possible to increase your chances of getting this right? We can both admit you and I had a rough start, but we got through it. I know you're someone I can trust to do the right thing. I hope you think the same of me. I'm good at what I do, I can be discrete, and I've got nothing but the family's best interests at heart."

More silence. Merry fretted she'd gone too far. Then, "That's quite the speech, Bell."

"Thank you," Merry replied. "Completely unrehearsed." She hoped her cheek-to-cheek smile translated over the phone line or whatever the hell cell phones transmitted over. She pictured the cop's stern face cracking one too. But probably not.

Merry watched the iPhone count off the seconds as time passed without another word coming from the speaker. She was beginning to wonder if the detective had simply walked away when finally she heard the woman clearing her throat.

"You didn't hear it from me."

Merry held her breath.

"There may be more to this."

Merry sucked in her cheeks. *I knew it! Play it cool, Merry Bell, kick-ass detective.* "Okay," she said, drawing out the word. "How can I help?"

"If I share something with you, Merry, you have to promise me it won't leak to the public. Do you understand?"

Greyeyes was also playing the first-name game. A good sign. Or was it? "If it does leak, you have my word it won't have come from me."

Greyeyes let out a sound that seemed half grunt, half air being blown out of her nose in disdain.

"Once again, let me remind you I am not the lead investigator on this case."

"Got it."

The cop inhaled and exhaled deeply. After a count of ten she said, "Evidence has been uncovered which may indicate Dustin's death was not an accident. This evidence is…pointing LPS in another direction."

"What direction is that?"

"Suicide."

Merry's breath caught. According to Dustin's cousin Ruth-Anne, suicide was not a reasonable possibility. Based on her own recent research into Thomson, Merry tended to agree. By all accounts the star quarterback was a well-adjusted, well-liked young man who was killing it in his career and doing good things in his community. He had everything to live for. Merry knew outward appearances rarely told the whole story. Even the happiest, most accomplished, seemingly well-adjusted and beloved people could be plagued with monstrous demons tearing them apart from the inside out, oftentimes without anyone knowing about it. Was that the case here? What could have convinced the police to believe that was true of Thomson? "What sort of evidence are we talking about?"

"A poem."

Merry wasn't sure she heard correctly. "Did you say a poem?"

"Yes."

"Like *Mary Had a Little Lamb* kind of poem?"

"That's a nursery rhyme, not a poem, but yes, a poem."

"You're going to have to give me a little more than that."

"A poem written by Dustin Thomson was discovered when they searched his apartment."

"Wait," Merry said, "are you saying he left a suicide note? In the form of a poem?"

"Not exactly."

Merry grimaced. Getting information from Greyeyes was like pulling molars with needle nose pliers. Would it help if she asked her questions in iambic pentameter? "How not exactly? Either he left a suicide note or he didn't."

Greyeyes released a frustrated breath. "They found a poem. It isn't clear whether it was meant as a suicide note or was nothing more than a random poem."

"Do they know for sure it was written by Dustin?"

"As sure as they can be, at this point."

"So, what's the poem about? Is it long? Can you recite it to me?"
A part of Merry really wanted to hear Detective Sergeant Veronica
Greyeyes recite a poem to her, preferably in the voice of a pre-pu-
bescent girl.

"That's a no."

"Can you text it to me?"

Greyeyes hesitated, no doubt debating Merry's trustworthiness.

"Veronica, you've gone this far…"

"For your eyes only."

"Of course."

"I mean it."

"Me too."

Merry's phone dinged. A text had appeared.

CHAPTER 8

From Sweetgrass Bridge
    by Dustin Thomson

  I see beginning
  I see end
  From Sweetgrass Bridge I
  see forever

  Swift flow, eddies
  Cool
  Damp air moss lichen river
  stone

  Deepening, darkening
  Unexpected
  From Sweetgrass Bridge
  I see never
  I see end

Greyeyes heard Merry Bell's voice catch as the P.I. read the final three words of Dustin Thomson's poem.

"I can see why this would give you pause," Merry uttered.

"Not me," Greyeyes reminded her. *How many times do I have to tell her this?* "I am not the lead investigator here." It was important Bell remembered this.

"Okay. I understand. But just between you and me, what do you think?"

Dead air. The whole point of this was that she couldn't tell her what she thought, what she knew, she couldn't tell anyone.

"About the poem."

"It's not for me to speculate," Greyeyes finally responded.

"If I took you out for a beer, would you be in a more speculating mood?"

Greyeyes hoped her smile didn't translate into her voice. "No, I would not." It felt good to smile. It had been a while.

"I don't think this proves anything," Merry posited, "and neither will my client."

Good. "That may be so," Greyeyes allowed.

"I suppose if a coroner's examination revealed signs of struggle on the body that would blow your—I mean the police department's—theory of suicide out of the water."

Greyeyes bit her lip. Merry Bell was fishing. Hard. She suddenly had a picture in her mind of the kid's game commonly played at fairs where children blindly tossed a "fishing line" over a barrier (usually a bed sheet on a clothesline) behind which adults waited to attach prizes. You always got something good and if you were lucky something really good. Should she attach something good to Merry's line?

"Soooooooo, did it?"

"You know I can't divulge those kinds of details."

Greyeyes waited to see if Merry tugged on the line.

She did.

"Has the body been examined?"

"Of course."

"If I remember my forensic classes…"

"You took forensic classes?"

"Like I keep telling you, Sergeant, I'm a kick ass detective. I was kind of a hot shot in Vancouver, one of Sharpe Investigations' finest."

"I'll have to take your word on that."

"If I'm not mistaken, determining the approximate time of death for a drowning victim can be tricky. A determination is more likely to be accurate when it involves fresh water, like the South Saskatchewan River where Dustin was found, than, say, saltwater in the ocean."

"That's correct."

"And if the deceased is found not too long after the drowning occurred, say a week or less, it might still be possible to use organ temperature to improve on the accuracy?"

"Yes. Much longer than a week and forensic entomology starts to become more important, such as maggots found on the body."

Raising her voice just a tad, Merry responded with, "Sounds like someone else may have taken a forensics class too."

Greyeyes pursed her lips and thought about hanging up. Yes, she'd been a tad judgmental in her surprise at learning Bell had taken a forensics class but, perhaps unfairly, she didn't care for the civilian detective returning the favour.

Merry pushed on. "Dustin Thomson drowned on Saturday?"

"Mmmm."

"Nine o'clock-ish?"

Nothing.

"Ten?"

Nothing.

"Between nine and midnight?"

Nothing.

"Ten and midnight?"

Dead air.

"Ten and Two?"

Greyeyes hung up. But not before releasing an audible "uh huh" under her breath.

When the phone rang an hour later, Merry was still debating between being pissed off at having been hung up on by a member of the Livingsky Police Service or glad that she'd at least gotten some good intel she didn't have before. The number looked familiar but there was no name assigned to it.

"Hello?"

"It's Ruth-Anne."

"Ruth-Anne, I'm glad you called."

"Sorry I couldn't talk earlier. There was…a lot going on."

"I understand."

"Do you need more money?"

Given her dire financial circumstances, Merry's first instinct was to shout "yes," but then she thought better of it and instead asked for clarification. "More money for what exactly?"

"To keep working on the case. Now that it's a murder investigation, do you need more money?"

"Murder investigation? Who told you that? I know the police have been talking to the family, but is that really what they told you?" Murder was definitely not the direction Greyeyes thought the police were taking on the case.

"No, the stupid shits!" Delorme spit into the phone. "Those idiots think it's a bloody suicide. Can you believe that? They don't know Dustin like I do. There is no friggin' way he'd do a boneheaded thing like that. Frankly, it's offensive that they think so."

Was it possible the family didn't know about the poem? If not, was telling Ruth-Anne about it going back on her promise to Greyeyes not to leak the poem to the public? Ruth-Anne was family. Was family considered the public? Or had Greyeyes tricked her into being the one to break the bad news? Was that why the cop had confided in her in the first place? Had she wanted Merry to smooth the road with the family before the police revealed their suspicion which they knew would be unpopular? "I understand you may think it's offensive, but the poem Dustin wrote does open up the possibility. It goes to his state of mind at the time of his death." All of that sounded a little lawyerly, even to Merry, but it was factual and Ruth-Anne's response would tell her if the family was aware of the poem.

"Fucking poem," Ruth-Anne grumbled.

That settled that.

"What kind of police work is that, letting a fucking riddle decide whether someone killed themselves or not? Dustin was always writing stuff, poems, short stories, shit like that. He loved spoken word artists. We have a lot of those in our community. It's our way of telling stories, holding on to our past. He loved how they'd grab any scrap of paper or a glass coaster and write down whatever was on their mind. Sometimes it was stories an elder told them, sometimes it was just a bunch of tough shit they were going through themselves. There's lots of people going through lots of things, especially at that youth centre Dustin always hung out at. That poem was probably about one of those kids, not him wanting to jump off of Sweetgrass. The police are too stupid to figure that out."

Merry nodded. "I can see how that might be possible." The part about the poem being about a youth from the centre, not the part about the police being stupid, although god knew some of them were.

"More than possible. Everybody's seen the stuff on the news about our young people committing suicide all of the time. It's an epidemic. Especially kids in the reserves up north. They feel trapped, hopeless, living in a country that's supposed to be theirs but it's not. And when they finally figure that out they think there's nothing left to live for. And maybe they're right."

Merry was jolted by the woman's words. Ruth-Anne Delorme was talking about more than her cousin. Reports of suicides by Indigenous youth, sometimes committed in groups, was shocking, unbearable to hear, impossible to understand. Or was it? Where did the fault lie? Where were the solutions? Having experienced her own version of feeling trapped in a body not meant for her and living in a world not built for her, Merry shuddered at the immensity of challenges faced by these youth. It was far too easy to falter beneath the weight of depressingly bleak reality. A place like the JOY Centre, Merry now understood with even greater clarity, was vitally important. A place like that could save lives.

"This wasn't suicide," Ruth-Anne repeated "Dustin might have been one of those kids when he was younger, but not anymore. He was one of the lucky ones. He got out. He made good. Our kids look up to him. They need to see someone like him. To give them hope. To show them it's possible. He knew that. He'd never do this to them."

Merry found herself being convinced by Ruth-Anne's argument. Still the fact remained, Dustin Thomson ended up in the river below Sweetgrass Bridge. "You believe Dustin's drowning was something other than a suicide. What was it then? An accident?" Merry already knew the woman was hellbent on seeing this as a murder, but she needed her to explain how she'd reached that conclusion to the exclusion of all other possibilities.

"Uh uh. Dustin was a shit swimmer. That boy could barely dog paddle. Sure, he might have been on that bridge that night, but he would have been real careful up there. He wouldn't have been hanging off the side like some idiots do and accidentally fell off. If he fell from that bridge, it wasn't suicide and it wasn't an accident. This was murder, plain and simple. Nothing else makes sense."

Merry was familiar with clients who came to her with blind conviction, particularly when it came to loved ones whose actions seemed inexplicable, out of character. Sometimes they were right, sometimes not. People are complex creatures. We do strange shit. We keep secrets, even from those we care most about. Her job as an investigator was to follow her clients' wishes, but at the end of the day the real goal was finding the truth.

"Dustin was on Sweetgrass bridge that night," Merry began as she prepared to toss out another possibility, "for whatever reason. Maybe he needed alone time, who knows, we may never know. Maybe what came next had nothing to do with him being there. Maybe he heard someone struggling in the water, calling out for help. Being the kind of man he was he would have jumped in to save them."

"No way. Didn't you hear what I just said? He didn't know how to swim. He couldn't save anybody. He knew he couldn't. He wasn't stupid. If he jumped in he'd die himself and like I already told you a million times he wouldn't kill himself. He would have called the cops or somebody else to help. Did he? Any record of that?"

She'd have to check on that, but Merry guessed that if there had been a 911 call from Dustin, Greyeyes would have mentioned it.

"Nope there isn't, cuz it didn't happen."

Ruth-Anne was no dummy. She knew her cousin and had thought this through from every angle.

"You should talk to those people."

"People? What people?"

"Those witnesses they got."

There were witnesses? Merry had reviewed every bit of information the police released with a fine-tooth comb. There was no mention of witnesses. "Ruth-Anne, did the police tell the family there were witnesses who saw Dustin jump off the bridge?"

"Nobody saw him jump off the bridge because he didn't jump off no damn bridge!" the woman snarled, obviously frustrated. "I don't know what the hell they saw, but if they saw anything, it was Dustin being pushed."

Merry's heart thrummed wildly in her chest. "Are you sure about there being witnesses? Is that what the police told you?" She was excited, but also more than a little miffed. She'd thought she and Veronica Greyeyes had come to an unspoken agreement, professional to professional, to share information as best they could without crossing ethical lines. Police contacts were supposed to collaborate, not obfuscate facts. Witnesses to Dustin Thomson's death was something Greyeyes might have bothered to mention. Obviously, she and the police detective were far from being on the same page.

"Somebody saw something but nobody's talking about it to us. That's all I know. You need to find out what that is. You need to find out what really happened to Dustin."

Oh, is that all? Maybe she *should* ask for more money. "You wouldn't happen to know the names of those witnesses, would you?"

"Got a pen?"

CHAPTER 9

Roger stared into the mirror. Stella stared back. With every passing second, layers of the anxiety and tension he'd collected and carried like an expanding backpack since the last time Stella appeared began to melt away, along with Roger Brown. A familiar and welcome peace descended over Stella. She took a few deep breaths and whispered the words she always spoke at this moment when the transition was complete: "Mirror, mirror on the wall, who's the fairest of them all." She smiled at her reflection, winked, and answered: "You are, bitch."

In truth, when Stella was fully formed and functioning, as she was now, Roger Brown was not entirely missing in action. There remained a duality that neither Roger nor Stella fully understood. The best way they could think to put it was that both were present to differing degrees at all times. When he was dressed and acting as Roger Brown, his alter ego was a woman named Stella who hosted a true crime podcast. When he was dressed and acting as Stella, his alter ego was a man named Roger, a husband and father of two who worked as an electrician. Pretending one didn't exist when he/she was the other simply did not feel right, did not feel good. What did feel good was being fully invested in being whichever of the two he was dressed as at the moment. For instance, Roger Brown, husband, father, electrician, would never say: "You are, bitch". That just wasn't part of who Roger was. That was all Stella.

Every now and then, Roger as Roger would become aware of the presence of Stella or Stella would feel the presence of Roger. The first few times this happened, it concerned him deeply. He worried he was losing the ability to be one or the other without anyone becoming suspicious. If Roger the electrician suddenly started talking to a client in Stella's voice or if Stella began hosting *Darkside of Livingsky* as Roger, it could quickly become a problem. Over time he'd come to accept these lapses as minor quirks, like winks of recognition between Roger and Stella, little messages of support sent to each other saying: *Hi there, don't worry, I'm still here.* Roger and Stella weren't at war; they were comrades. With some regularity, especially when he was tired or didn't have enough time to make the full transition to Stella (it still boggled his mind how women managed it every day), he was left "wearing" bits of Roger while being Stella. Although he usually preferred the "full Stella," he didn't entirely mind something less, especially if it was just him, no Brenda around, no podcast broadcast to host. Eventually he began to do the same in reverse when out in the world as Roger, sometimes replacing his boxers with female underwear or using a dab of floral perfume instead of Roger's preferred musky cologne.

However, recently Roger had begun to notice the slips happening more often, usually in the presence of Merry Bell. They'd be having a conversation, usually something to do with their shared passion for true crime, she as a detective, he as a true crime podcast host, and suddenly words would spill from his mouth that were definitely more Stella than Roger. He'd catch Merry looking at him in a certain kind of way that told him she'd caught the slip too. It wasn't difficult to figure out why this was happening.

Before Brenda, Roger had told only two people about being a crossdresser. Well, one-and-a-half. The first was a guy named Kyle. Roger and Kyle had gone to the same high school but hadn't really known each other or hung out until they both ended up taking the same post-secondary electrician's course. After making the connection, a natural friendship blossomed with the two young men doing all the crazy, stupid, fun things young adult males do together post-high school when the shackles of age, curfews and parental controls are removed. They drank too much, did too many drugs, stayed out too late on weeknights, made mistakes with too many girls. Although verging on the wild side, neither fully entered the realm of being complete assholes or jerks. They were nice guys testing boundaries and figuring themselves out. Some nights, typically after midnight, usually following a night of heavy imbibing and having struck out in the girl department, Kyle and Roger would find themselves having more drinks or drugs at one of their apartments talking about their worries, their hopes and dreams for the future, getting deep. It was on one of those nights when the boys were particularly high in celebration of the stoner holiday known as 4/20 that Roger let it slip that he liked, on occasion, to wear women's underwear (even in his cannabis-altered state Roger knew enough to understate his desires).

In the moment, Kyle said little more than something along the lines of "that's fucked up, dude." After that it was never spoken of again. They still went out together, but usually with others, they still got drunk, chased women, but the late-night talks stopped. When their training was done, so was the friendship. Kyle accepted a job with a contractor in Edmonton and Roger never heard from him again. He could never be sure whether the friendship simply ran its course or if Kyle was freaked out and pulled away intentionally. Whichever was the case, Roger didn't feel comfortable revealing his proclivity again until he met a girl named Ramona.

The relationship with Ramona was highly sexual; both parties on the same page about trying new things they'd read about on the internet. Most of the positions ended up being impossible or uncomfortable or both, but they had fun trying. More often than not they'd end up laughing their heads off and having sex the old-fashioned way. Emboldened by Ramona's sense of adventure and open-mindedness, Roger began introducing the idea of him wearing women's clothing as part of a role play scenario. She was into it and the more she got into it the more he got into it, introducing more of his still-developing alter ego to their bedroom activities. The word crossdressing was eventually introduced. Ramona shrugged it off. They kept having fun, not always but sometimes with Roger wearing women's clothing. The relationship petered out after nine months and they went their separate ways on mutually good terms.

Years later, when Roger met Brenda Reyes, he immediately knew that the phrase "love at first sight" was a real thing. There was something about her that made him spout a bunch of romance movie cliches to his friends, like how he'd found his person and she completed him and he'd met the mother of his children. Yes, Brenda most definitely had her quirks. Plenty of them. But he loved those too. In a way they made him feel even closer to her because he knew that most of her quirks were part of a façade she'd carefully constructed to face the world in the way she thought the world wanted her to be. With him, over time, she slowly allowed the façade to fall away. Behind it was a person who belonged only to Roger; only he was lucky enough to know and love that person and be loved by them in return.

As soon as Roger knew how strongly he felt for Brenda, he knew he had to tell her about who he really was. Unlike Brenda, his outward facing persona was not a façade. Roger Brown was absolutely Roger Brown, what you saw is what you got. But there were two sides to him, one that needed to be hidden because of how the world was. Yes, Stella hid from the world, but she did not hide behind Roger, she hid alongside him. If he was going to make a life with Brenda Reyes, Brenda needed to know all of him.

The difference in the experience between Ramona and Brenda was that with Brenda the subject came up on its own, completely apart from their sex life. This was an important distinction to Roger because he'd long ago concluded that his desire to cross dress was a personal preference thing, not a sexual preference thing. Sex he had as Roger Brown was just as exciting, just as satisfying as the sex he had when he cross-dressed. It was a complicated thing to understand, never mind explain to someone else. The best way he could describe it to Brenda was that if Stella only existed outside the bedroom, that would be fine with him.

Unlike Ramona, Brenda took the news with considerably more

caution, uncertainty and suspicion. None of those feelings, he assured her, were unexpected or unreasonable. Of course it would have been wonderful if she'd simply cheered him on and dove into the lifestyle—was it a lifestyle?—with him. The important thing was that she did not run away. On that first night and on many, many nights thereafter, she remained by his side, she listened, asked questions, cried some, laughed some. Her first big request was that if they were to stay together, Stella could not be something he did exclusively when he was alone. She needed to be a part of it—exactly how they'd have to figure out—lest his crossdressing became a wedge between them that eventually would tear them apart.

Brenda's second big request was that Stella stay between them, until such time as they both felt comfortable enough—or for some reason it became important enough—to share with other people.

In the years that followed, Roger, at first, did his best to tamp his desires. It was simply easier to pretend it wasn't that important to him. His priority was to build a life with this incredible woman, have children, be happy.

There was happiness. But there was also a growing want, desire, need left unfulfilled. Eventually, even Brenda could sense the pressure building. It was Roger's podcast that changed everything, an unexpected gift of salvation. It was Brenda who came up with the idea that he host the show as Stella, with her taking on the role of Stella's stylist and wardrobe consultant and doing her makeup and hair. Brenda approached it as if the cross-dressed version of her husband was some kind of famous on-air TV personality seen by millions every night. It was a kind of role play for both of them. At first it was awkward, but over time they grew to look forward to the process, spending time together engaging in extracurricular activities they both enjoyed, fashion and makeup consultation for Brenda, true crime podcasting and being Stella for Roger, all within the safety and privacy of their own basement.

Then came Merry Bell. It was Roger who told her about Stella, en route to their first stakeout together. To this day he was unclear whether he made the revelation because he suspected the detective was about to uncover the truth herself, because Merry was trans-gender and somehow that made her a safe confidante and automat-ic ally, or because he'd been bursting to tell someone and she was handy. The conversation with Merry went considerably better than the one that came later when he told Brenda he'd broken their rule about keeping Stella to themselves. Eventually she got over it.

While still working their first case together (not exactly how Merry would put it,) Merry indicated that Stella would be a wel-come substitution for Roger should they ever collaborate in the future. The suggestion took Roger by surprise and was still under consideration.

The designated space where Roger became Stella was a small room accessible through a single door at the rear of the podcast booth where *The Darkside of Livingsky* was recorded in the base-ment of the house he shared with Brenda, their two children, and his mother-in-law. It was a smart setup designed by Brenda to ac-commodate Stella without interfering with family life upstairs. At least until, or if, they ever decided to mix the two.

Pushing back from the makeup mirror, Stella rose and stepped into the final part of the transformation, four-inch stilettos in which she'd perfected walking over many months. Painful but worth every second. Even though she was not recording a podcast today, Roger had decided to undertake a full transformation. Partial transfor-mations were becoming increasingly rare, reserved for days when Roger really needed the salve of Stella but didn't have time for a full changeover. Today was special. He was introducing Stella to a whole new role: assistant private detective (again, likely not how Merry Bell would see it). Stella's first investigation was to determine the identity of Merry Bell's mysterious note-sender.

Roger had come to learn about the note-sender (he'd have to come up with a more imaginative name for his quarry) by happen-stance. The first time he met Merry, he'd slipped her a note meant to convince her he'd make a good P.I. intern. He'd kept the note a secret from Brenda, afraid that if his wife knew of his bold request she would think he was taking advantage of her new friend and talk him out of it. The secret was short-lived however because he and Brenda told each other everything; honesty was the bedrock of their relationship. When he'd admitted all of this to Merry, she'd let it slip that his secret note was not the first one she'd received since returning to Livingsky. Actually it was the third, with the first two mysteriously appearing beneath her office door bearing cryptic messages: "I know it's you" and "I still know it's you."

When Roger spied Merry outside their house the night of the pool party and witnessed her decision not to come in, he became resolute in finding out who'd sent those first two notes. His hope was that the sender did not have harmful intent, but rather was someone who once knew Merry, perhaps when she last lived in Livingsky, perhaps before she transitioned into Merry, and was searching for a way to reconnect. Anonymous notes slipped under a door wouldn't have been Roger's first choice to make contact, but whatever. He was intent on discovering the sender's identity because he recognized in Merry a familiar affliction: loneliness. It must have been hard for her to return home after so many years away, especially when she probably believed she never would, and to come home as someone completely different than who you were when you left added a whole layer of difficulty. From everything Brenda told him about Merry, she'd made no friends since coming home. Intentional? Was Merry Bell a loner or simply lonely? Roger was convinced it was the latter. He knew what it was to feel alone when you aren't who everyone thinks you are.

Finding Merry's note-sender would accomplish two things. The first and most altruistic was the potential of uncovering someone who could help assuage Merry's loneliness. The second, and more self-serving, was that if he and Stella did this right, if they could show Merry how good they were at investigating, she might finally agree to take them on as official P.I. apprentices, a dream result for both.

There was one problem. Brenda. Once again concerned that his wife would not agree with his actions and convince him to stop, he reluctantly decided to undertake the investigation in secrecy. Roger hated the idea of keeping a secret from Brenda; Stella, not so much. And so it only made sense that whenever it was time to act on the investigation, the lead investigator would be Stella. Of course Roger would be fully aware and without plausible deniability, but somehow it made him feel a little better about the whole thing, at least until he finally came clean which he had no doubt would happen sooner or later.

Along with nude-coloured stilettos, Stella wore an off-white button-up silk blouse and pale blue skirt made of this magic material that managed to generously accentuate her subtly padded hips and derriere while still being comfortable. Her wig was a simple dark-blond bob that she tied into a loose pony with a patterned scarf mixing off-white, pale blue and beige, perfectly tying together the outfit in a I'm-a-no-nonsense-career-woman-who's-still-sexy way that she liked. Transition complete, Stella entered the podcast booth and sat behind the desk where she normally recorded the show. She turned on the desk lamp, booted up her laptop and opened a new document she named: The Note-Sender Case. She really needed to come up with something snappier.

Although the only other person to ever come into the basement studio was Brenda, Roger had taken the afternoon off from work to ensure complete privacy for his first official solo foray into playing detective. The booth was soundproofed, but still Stella ticked her head to one side to listen for any noise from Roger's upstairs world. She was confident there wouldn't be any; Brenda was at work, the kids at play dates, and Brenda's mother always spent Monday afternoons playing bridge at the club.

If she'd learned anything from hosting the podcast, Stella knew that the first and most important step in solving a whodunit was to identify the perpetrator's motive; why did the note-sender send the notes? Under a column labelled MOTIVE in the spreadsheet she'd created, Stella quickly typed in the three most likely motive scenarios she could think of. The first involved someone who thought they could blackmail/threaten Merry by revealing her transition. Stella jotted down a list of questions with direct bearing on the strength of this motive: Was Merry's transition a secret? Was blackmail a real possibility? Why would the note-sender want to do that? Money? Transphobia? Definitely a bad guy.

The second possible motive was committed by someone who found out something completely unrelated to Merry's transition and decided to blackmail or threaten her. Another bad guy. The question here was whether there was something in Merry's past aside from her transition which was blackmailable? The third motive, and the one Stella hoped for and thought most likely, hinged on the belief that the wording of the note: "I know it's you" was entirely innocuous and non-threatening. The note-sender—this time a good guy—was someone who knew Merry before she was Merry and was looking to re-establish a connection.

Satisfied with her list of motives, Stella moved on to the second column of her spreadsheet labelled OPPORTUNITY. Who had access to 222 Craving Lane allowing them to go up to the third floor, enter Merry's office's antechamber and slip a note under her door, all without being seen? Had someone seen them doing exactly that but thought nothing of it? The Craving Lane building was open to the public during the day but the notes had been slipped under the door when Merry was not in her office. The most likely scenario was that they were delivered after hours, which meant the evening or on the weekend when the doors were locked. Which meant the prime suspect would have to be someone with after-hours access, like a tenant or maintenance personnel, or someone who outright broke into the building (but that was unlikely since no break-in had been reported).

Using the online directory of 222 Craving Lane tenants, Stella spent the next hour researching, assessing, then calling each business owner. A benefit of doing this in the middle of a workday afternoon was the increased likelihood of reaching each potential suspect. Other than Smallinsky's accounting practice which took up the main floor, there were only six other offices in the building, three per floor. Excluding Merry and Brenda, that meant he only had four calls to make. Some of the prospects were known to Roger by virtue of their working in the same building as his wife, but none of them knew Stella (unless they listened to *The Darkside of Livingsky*).

The calls invariably started out the same, with Stella identifying herself as an employee of OUTLivingsky (a real organization) interested in polling a sample of Livingsky business owners about their awareness, or lack thereof, of the issues facing the transgender population of Livingsky (a white lie). Stella counted on the current climate of overt (some thought rampant) political correctness when it came to gender identity issues in the workplace to keep people from hanging up on her. It worked. Stella knew she couldn't come right out and ask 222 Craving Lane tenants whether they were aware that there was a transgender person working in their building, but how they responded to the survey queries told her a lot about whether they had potential to be a bad guy note-sender.

By late afternoon Stella had reached all of Merry's work-neighbours. None ended up in the new column of Stella's spreadsheet with the wordy header: MIGHT BE NOTE-SENDER/FURTHER INVESTIGATION REQUIRED.

Stella's next call was to Alvin Smallinsky, 222 Craving Lane's owner and majority tenant.

"Smallinsky & Co., how may I direct your call?" a voice that sounded suspiciously like Alvin Smallinsky himself answered on the third ring.

"Hi, may I speak to Alvin please?" Stella asked in Roger's voice.

"May I tell him who's calling?"

"Roger Brown."

"Just one moment."

A full thirty seconds later a very similar voice came on the line. "Roger, this is Alvin Smallinsky. It's been a long time since we've spoken. Is everything alright? Is this about Brenda? I haven't been upstairs recently so I haven't seen her today."

"Thanks for taking my call, Alvin. Everything is fine. I'm sure Brenda is busy as a beaver behind closed doors."

"Oh, that's good to hear. Your wife is a dedicated business owner.

You must be very proud."

Something about the comment struck Stella the wrong way. Roger had never warmed to Alvin, but Brenda seemed to respect him, so he let it pass. "We're proud of each other."

"Wonderful. How can I help you today, Roger?"

"Actually, I was looking for some advice."

"Of course, of course," he responded in the manner of a man who was used to being asked for his expertise. "Is this an accounting matter? I know Smallinsky & Co. is currently not your accountant, but perhaps we can set up a time to meet, with Brenda too of course. It's always wise to include the wife in these types of things, at least at the beginning, and then…"

"No, it's nothing to do with that. I was hoping to ask you about your business."

"Oh?"

Stella knew enough about Smallinsky to know it was always a good idea to butter his bread, heavily, on both sides. "You see, one of my clients owns a business similar in size to yours, similarly successful too. He does very well. Like you, he also made the wise decision to invest in and convert a wartime house from which he runs his business. Long story short, he's looking for a cleaning and maintenance crew and asked if I knew of anyone. Brenda raves like mad about the cleaning company you use at 222 Craving Lane. So, I thought, who better than you to ask for a recommendation?"

A few minutes later, armed with the contact information for the 222 Craving Lane cleaning company, Stella moved on to the second phase of The Note-Sender Case.

CHAPTER 10

Merry swallowed a bitter pill of jealousy as she ascended by glass elevator to the 24th floor of the swanky tower that housed the accounting firm of Sage, Cope, Jaspar & Novakoski. When she returned to Livingsky to start her life over, she'd had big dreams. One of them was opening the offices of Livingsky Sharpe Investigations in one of the gleaming downtown skyscrapers that hugged the banks of the South Saskatchewan, where every office commanded a magnificent river view. She'd wear killer business suits and never show up without her hair blown out and make-up perfect. The harsh reality was that LSI was located several blocks away in an area generously referred to by her landlord Alvin Smallinsky as "downtown adjacent" and, catching her reflection in the stainless-steel elevator door, she confirmed that the rest of the dream was still a work in progress.

As the elevator ferried her higher, Merry couldn't help but admire the urban prairie panorama. The river and its longtime companion, the majestic Truemont Hotel with its chateau inspired architecture, were mainstays of every City of Livingsky picture postcard back when picture postcards were a thing. Her eyes meandered down the shoreline to where…wait, was that a crane? Could it be?

LSI's first case started out as a simple suspicious fire investigation and ended up implicating members of Livingsky's City Management team in a dicey development deal with direct ties to Mayor Carol Durabont and her promise to constituents of "A New City for a New Millennium." She pledged a major downtown revitalization which included the creation of a commercial/residential mecca called Riverside Plaza next to the Truemont Hotel. A consequence of Merry's investigation was an immediate and perhaps indefinite halt to the development. But if the crane's presence and location foretold what Merry thought it did, Mayor Durabont—with an upcoming election riding on its success—had somehow found a way to restart the project.

Merry wondered if she should mention the crane sighting to Gerald Drover. His ownership of and refusal to sell an adjacent property played a big part in the case and he'd narrowly escaped prison time thanks to Merry's efforts. She shuddered and shook her head. Nope. She wanted nothing more to do with Riverside Plaza or the mayor's office. Being on the bad side of a sitting mayor was bad for business and she was already on tenterhooks in that regard because of an ill-advised flirtation with a man who'd turned out to be the mayor's husband. How, Merry questioned, had her life become such a soap opera?

The elevator came to a noiseless, smooth-as-butter stop. Merry stepped off the car and found herself in a magazine-cover-worthy reception area. It even smelled good, like a high-end Las Vegas hotel lobby. The only thing missing was an actual reception desk with someone to talk to. *Where am I supposed to go?* She searched the space and although there were several artful seating arrangements, all of them were empty.

"Hello. Welcome to Sage, Cope, Jaspar & Novakoski. How can I help you today?"

Merry did a half twirl and found herself facing a large screen.

"My name is Alexandria," said an impossibly beautiful face on the screen.

Merry stepped closer. "Are you…real?" She knew she was looking at a screen, but Alexandria was so beautiful Merry thought she might be a digital generation rather than the transmission of a human image.

Alexandria laughed. "I'm here to help you. Forgive me, I don't recognize your face. May I have your name please?"

Merry looked up and spotted at least two miniscule cameras—

at least she thought they were cameras—pointing in her direction. Did Sage, Cope, Jaspar & Novakoski have a database of client images that Alexandria, real or android she wasn't quite sure yet, used to identify whoever entered her domain?

"My name is Merry Bell."

"Nice to meet you, Ms. Bell. I don't see an appointment listed under that name. How can I help you today?"

Was this some kind of Zoom set-up? She'd heard of virtual receptionists being used by firms with more than one office, saving on employee costs by only having to hire one person to cover multiple locations. Or maybe Alexandria was the receptionist for the entire building? Merry felt a little strange talking to the image, but the woman appeared to be looking right at her as if they were in the same room and as if she was human and not just a collection of bits and bytes.

"I'm sorry, I don't have an appointment. I was hoping to speak with Billie Jo O'Connor and Robby McAllister. I'm investigating the recent death of Dustin Thomson which, I'm sure you can imagine, is a time sensitive matter." *Can a machine imagine?*

"I don't see you listed as a representative of the Livingsky Police Service. May I ask who you are with, please?"

Merry felt a chill run down her spine. Alexandria hadn't even made an attempt to make it appear she'd consulted a computer screen or done a quick google search before revealing within microseconds that she knew she wasn't a cop. A robot, Alexandria was definitely a robot. A big fan of the 1970s television shows *The Six Million Dollar Man* and *The Bionic Woman*, Merry imagined Alexandria as one of the show's infamous fembots, deadly, dangerous and with guns in their breasts…or was that the *Austin Power's* version? "I'm with LSI, a national private investigations firm. We've been hired by Mr. Thomson's family to look into his death."

For the first time, Alexandria paused, then, "I understand. Just one moment." The screen went blank, quickly replaced by the tasteful and no doubt costly professionally designed logo for Sage, Cope, Jaspar & Novakoski.

She couldn't be sure it wasn't there before, but Merry noticed a third camera had appeared to join the first two, a miniscule green light flashing on its side. The lighting in the room had noticeably brightened.

"Ms. Bell." Merry startled at the sound of her name. Alexandria had returned. "Regrettably, Ms. O'Connor is out of the office. Mr. McAllister will be available to meet with you in approximately ten minutes. May I get you something to drink while you wait?"

Aha. This should be interesting. "Thank you. A cappuccino would be lovely. Double shot, non-fat milk?"

"Of course. Just one moment." The face once again was replaced with the logo.

Merry turned away from the screen and selected an armchair near a glowing wall that turned out to be a massive saltwater fish tank. She'd barely taken her seat when Alexandria was back.

"Ms. Bell, I have your cappuccino. I hope it's to your liking."

Sitting in an opening in the wall next to Alexandria's screen was a steaming cup of coffee in a mug emblazoned with the accounting firm's logo. *Holy Mother Theresa! This is some Star-Trek-replicator shit going on here!*

Merry got up and retrieved the drink. It was the best coffee she'd had since the last time she could afford Starbucks instead of Tim Horton's.

"Merry Bell?"

Standing in a doorway off to the right of Alexandria was a genial looking young man wearing dark suit pants, shirt and tie but no jacket.

"Yes, hello. Are you Robby McAllister?"

"I am. I understand you wanted to talk with me about Dustin Thomson?"

"Yes. Do you have a few minutes.? It shouldn't take long."

"If you follow me we can talk in a meeting room, just down the hall."

As Merry set out to follow McAllister she turned to say farewell and thanks to Alexandria, but the face was gone…but still watching?

"I was hoping to speak with Billie Jo as well. Do you know when she'll be back in the office?" Merry asked once they were settled in the meeting room with, yes, damnit, another gorgeous view of the Saskatchewan River.

McAllister stuttered a bit, blushed, then said, "I don't. Billie Jo and I...well, we haven't spoken much since that night."

"Oh. From what I'd heard I assumed you two were a couple."

"We were, or at least trying to be. But then I guess I did something stupid and..." McAllister stopped, as if suddenly realizing where he was and who he was speaking to. "Alexandria said you're a private investigator working for the family. Do the police know you're here? I already told them everything I know."

Merry was prepared to lie about what the police did and didn't know, but hoped she wouldn't have to. "Do you happen to know Alvin Smallinsky? He's an accountant too. He works in the same building as my firm, LSI. We've often commented on how what accountants and investigators do is quite similar. Whether he's looking for information to back up audit findings or I'm looking for information to solve a case, we both know the best thing is to get evidence from as many different sources as possible. Not only do you end up with a more accurate picture of the situation, but any discrepancies there might be are easier to spot. I've consulted with the police..." True. Sort of. "...and spoken with other people involved in the case..." Also true. "...but if you're willing, I'd like to hear directly from you your recollection of what happened on Sweetgrass Bridge that night. Does that make sense?"

"Uh, I suppose."

McAllister checked his watch, his not-so-subtle way of telling Merry the clock was ticking. Accountants tracked their hours like lawyers and this time was a dud in terms of being chargeable to a client file.

"Can you tell me exactly what you saw and heard the night Dustin Thomson fell from Sweetgrass Bridge?"

"It was late, probably around eleven at night. I'm not exactly sure because, well, because my mind was on other things."

Merry nodded. The time of death was somewhere between 10:00 p.m. and 2:00 a.m., if Greyeyes grunts could be trusted, so this gave Merry a bit of a tighter timeframe to work with.

"We were kissing and stuff and that's when I heard the noise. It was dark so I couldn't really see anything."

"What did you hear, exactly?" Merry wanted to ask if it was a splash or a scream or maybe someone struggling in the water, but she didn't want to plant ideas in the man's head.

"I wasn't sure. All I knew was that whatever it was it came from far away."

"In what direction?"

"Again, I'm not one hundred percent certain, but if I had to guess it sounded like it might have come from the bridge."

"From the bridge or near the bridge or beneath the bridge?"

Robby gave Merry a pointed look. "I'm not going to keep saying it. Just assume whatever I say I'm not completely sure of."

"Got it."

"If I had to pick one, I'd say the sound was like a yelp, and it was coming from the bridge, not under it. I know everyone wants me to say I heard someone screaming as they fell off the bridge or someone crying out as they were drowning, but it wasn't like that."

"Thank you. That's very helpful."

"It is?"

"At this point, anything you can tell me, even if it's a guess, can be helpful."

He said nothing more.

Merry dug in a bit further. "This yelp, was there one yelp or more than one?"

"One. Maybe two."

"Then nothing?"

"Then nothing I could hear."

"If there were two, is it possible they came from two different people?"

"I really couldn't even guess at that one."

"Male or female?"

"Male, I think."

"Robby, I know this may be stretching how much you could make out from what you heard, but if you had to categorize the sound, would you say it was fearful? Angry? Mournful?"

McAllister thought about this for a few seconds. "No, none of those. If I had to pick a word to describe it, I'd say it sounded more...surprised."

A short time later, Merry entered the glass elevator and hit the button for the main floor, twenty-four stories below. As the doors closed she heard Alexandria's disembodied voice say: "Have a nice day, Merry Bell."

CHAPTER 11

Doreen, Merry's pale blue Plymouth, pulled into Lover's Lane several minutes late. Merry hoped to be in sight of Sweetgrass Bridge no later than 10:00 p.m., the earliest estimate of when Dustin Thomson died in the river below. Robby McAllister had given her the best directions he could given that the spot appeared on no map, still she'd taken a wrong turn and had to double back down a dodgy dirt road. Seeing that it was a Monday night, she was not surprised to find the remote parking lot empty. That was fine with her; lonely, dark places did not easily scare Merry Bell.

Armed with her iPhone flashlight, Merry exited the car. Again thanks to Robby's instructions she quickly found and followed the barely visible, uphill path to the same grassy knoll where Robby McAllister and Billie Jo O'Connor had their tryst. Reaching the summit, Merry was immediately entranced by the haunting beauty of Sweetgrass Bridge. The decades-old span was awash in the light of a summer moon so fat and heavy it looked as if it might lose its grasp on the sky and drop into the river below. The entire scene and intoxicating ambiance were so peaceful and romantic it was hard to believe a life had ended here.

Finding a spot on the grass still warm from the day's sun, probably not far from McAllister and Billie Jo's ill-fated picnic, Merry lowered herself to the ground, sitting cross-legged, and extinguished her flashlight. It took only a minute to get used to the dark and the symphony of nighttime noises common to wooded prairie riverbanks. Through her nose she pulled in drafts of air faintly scented with an intricate assortment of mid-summer offerings: awned wheatgrass, tufted hairgrass, wild rye, sheep fescue, purple oat, sorghastrum, tall manna grass, prairie dropseed and sweetgrass.

Merry, a keen researcher, had looked up the bridge's namesake and found that Sweetgrass was a sacred herb (Weengush) widely used by Indigenous people for cleansing, purification and healing ceremonies and smudging. The plant was indigenous to every Canadian province and got its distinctive scent from coumarin, an anticoagulant. It was used for medicinal tea and widely thought to remove negative forces and bring positive energies of love. Sadly, the latter did not prove true for either Dustin Thomson or Robby and Billie Jo.

From her position on the ground, a distance away from the edge of the clearing that dropped down into the river valley, Merry could understand why McAllister might not have been able to clearly hear a noise coming from the bridge, nor see anything once the day's light had melted away. Robby had told her he'd approached the rim of the embankment in an effort to identify a noise he wasn't sure he'd heard. She did the same now and, like McAllister, quickly backed up when she felt the ground softening at the furthest edge.

Quieting her mind and closing her eyes, Merry focused on the sounds of the river valley, inviting them to make their presence known. Slowly, slowly, they appeared: the rustling of leaves, the burble of water over rock, the scurrying of a fox, the song of a night bird, the creak of an old bridge, then something else…something… unnatural? Something…then it was gone. Merry's eyes shot open. She glared into the darkness and quickly closed her eyes again hoping to find the sound again. But it was gone, if it had ever really been there in the first place. More and more she understood McAllister's reticence to firmly identify what he'd heard. Nighttime plays tricks on people's minds, even more so outdoors in an unfamiliar place.

Returning to her spot on the grass, Merry once again closed her eyes and reconsidered what happened in this place ten days earlier. Now that it seemed certain Dustin Thomson had fallen from Sweetgrass Bridge and drowned in the waters below, Merry's first thoughts went to the possible reasons he'd have come to the bridge in the first place so late on a Saturday night. She could think of four. One, Ruth-Anne Delorme was wrong and her cousin did come here to commit suicide. Two, Dustin was doing the same thing as Billie Jo and Robby, visiting Lover's Lane with a partner, and then something went terribly wrong. Three, Dustin simply went to the bridge to be alone and, again, something went terribly wrong. Four, Dustin was lured, invited or forcibly taken to the bridge by his murderer.

Reasons two and three assumed that what happened to Dustin was not contemplated and the result was possibly accidental. Did he accidentally fall off the bridge? Did he hear someone in distress in the river and jump in hoping to save them? Even though Ruth-Anne insisted Dustin could not swim and would have been very careful around bridges and water, both theories were possible. If he was alone, no one could verify what happened. But what if he was not on the bridge alone. Could there be someone out there who'd witnessed the accident, freaked out, and ran away? Perhaps Robby and Billie Jo were not the only witnesses.

Merry was yanked from her deliberations by another unusual noise, the same as before, not a natural creation of her surroundings, but something man-made.

She wasn't alone.

Staying as still as her rapidly beating heart would allow, Merry did her best to focus her ears just in case the sound repeated. A deliberate 180-degree scan revealed nothing out of the ordinary. Moonlight, it turns out, is good for ambiance but crap for clarity. Slowly rising to her feet, Merry brushed detritus from her pants and tried to calm herself. It could be nothing more than her ears playing tricks on her. Right about then, in every horror movie ever made, Merry's character would call out: "Who's there?" Dumbass move. If there was someone out there with a nefarious purpose, all you've done is given them an audio target.

Convincing herself there was nothing more to learn here, Merry declared it time to go. Moving faster than she should have in the darkness and momentarily disoriented, instead of the path leading to the parking lot, Merry found herself ensnared in a tangle of bush with thorns. "Shit!" she grumbled to herself.

Suddenly, again, the noise.

This time it was different, clearer.

Shuffling?

Someone was definitely out there.

Was the dark shape at the opposite end of the clearing an amorphous shadow or something more? Too big for an animal. A figure? A man? Why is it always a man? A disturbing rumbling palpated Merry's chest. Fear? Was she scared? Never once in her years as an investigator with Sharpe Investigations in Vancouver, pre-Merry, had she felt this. A bit worried, yes, uncomfortable, maybe, but never outright fear. She'd been overly (perhaps foolishly) confident about confronting anyone, man or woman. Was that what was going on here? Now that Merry was Merry, fully female in every way, had she suddenly, without her knowledge or consent, adopted some sort of genetic predisposition to fear men, particularly in situations like this one?

That's bullshit!

Something in the dark caught her eye.

The black shape was definitely moving.

Okay, maybe this has nothing to do with being female or male, Merry thought. Maybe this is just downright scary. It was time to hightail it out of there. Freeing herself from the bush she'd stumbled into and eyeing up what she knew—hoped—was the break in the foliage that marked the beginning of the pathway, Merry charted her course. Fortunately, the he, she, or it on the other side of the clearing was moving in the opposite direction. For now.

Staying close to the periphery, her back to the foliage, Merry inched toward the opening.

Closer.

Closer.

Closer.

Finally, she was at the entrance! Turning onto the path, she took one last look over her shoulder. Nothing. Just black on black. *Where is he*? Not good. She no longer knew where the figure was. Did he know where she was? She'd seen him (sort of) but had he seen her? The trail to the parking lot was all downhill. Should she make a run for it? Or should she sneak as slowly and quietly as possible in an effort to get away without him knowing it? Or was he already on his way? Pulling car keys out of her pants pocket, ready for when she got to Doreen, Merry ran. Hard.

Heart pumping in her ears, Merry powered down the track, picturing herself as the Roadrunner easily escaping Wile E. Coyote, the power of positive thinking hard at work.

There was noise behind her. Or was that the sound of her own frantic footfalls? Maybe it was a deer. Bear? No, there were no bears this far south. Moose? Could be. Whatever it was, she had to be speedy if she was going to get away without a confrontation. But she also had to be careful. The ground was uneven and littered with forest debris and exposed roots that could easily cause her to fall.

Faster.

Faster.

Come on, come on!

Then she was there. The parking lot. Instant relief. And then...

What she saw stole the breath from her throat.

Not a moose. Not a deer.

Another car.

CHAPTER 12

Merry's head exploded with adrenaline. She ran towards her car but it seemed to take forever to get there. There was no way she was going to give them the satisfaction of watching her run away. The plan was to get in the car, lock the doors, roll up the windows, start the engine, and stare them straight in the eyes.

Finally, she reached the vehicle. Her hands trembled wildly as she directed the key to its hole. She swore at defenseless Doreen for being of a vintage prior to push button key fobs. There was nothing but the sound of her own tortured, ragged breath in her ears but Merry knew someone else was there, coming for her. Someone whose car was parked right next to hers. She imagined them maneuvering their way down the same path she'd just taken from the lookout point, spotting her, and rushing towards her. Did they have a weapon? A gun? Was she about to get shot? Sweat poured down her face, getting into her eyes. *Damn this key!*

"Hey!" a man's voice filled the air.

The key ring fell to the ground. *Shit, piss, motherclucker!*

Merry felt a tear form at the corner of her eye and resented it.

There was no escaping the inevitable. She turned, plastering her back against Doreen for support. Her hands formed into fists. *The sonofabitch had better be ready because I am prepared to use these things.* She screamed: "What the fuck do you want?"

First a shadow emerged from the darkness, then a shape emerged from the shadow, and finally a face emerged from the shape. "Ms. Bell, it's me."

"Me who?" Still screaming.

"Me. Robby McAllister."

Merry struggled to wrench her phone out of her pocket then activated the flashlight.

There he was, slowly coming toward her, Robby McAllister. He looked different than he had in the accountant's office. The suit and tie were replaced by a pair of shapeless jeans and a polo shirt, his hair was askew probably due to scurrying about in the dark like some kind of wild animal, scaring the shit out of her. But it was definitely him. *What the hell?*

"Stop right there," she ordered. "Don't come any closer. I just took a photo of you and sent it to my…cop friend," she lied. Her hands were too jittery to do any of those things and she didn't have a cop friend (Veronica Greyeyes was so far proving less than friendly.)

The accountant complied. "Okay, but you don't need to do that," he said. "I'm sorry if I scared you. I didn't mean to."

"Oh really? What did you mean to do? You didn't think sneaking up on someone in the dark would be scary? Why are you here anyway? Did you follow me?"

"No. Not really. It's just that, well, after you left the office today I got to worrying about giving you the directions to get out here. You said you wanted to see the place for yourself, at night, like when Dustin died, so I knew when you'd be here."

Merry felt the kickass P.I. version of herself come rushing back. *About time.* The recent lapse in kickass-ness had been a definite turn-off.

"You called him Dustin." Merry kept her eyes focused on the man, searching for a telltale sign that he was bullshitting her. "Did you know Dustin Thomson?"

Robby shrugged. "I'm a huge Rider fan. I watch all the games and go to every home game if I can. I guess it's silly, but it sometimes feels like I do know him. I think a lot of people in Livingsky feel that way."

Not everybody, Merry thought. "You still haven't explained why you're here."

"I was worried about you. I'd feel really bad if something happened to you. I should have told you not to come out here alone, or at least not at night. It's not safe."

Misogynist much? Poor defenseless woman can't go out by herself after dark, is that what this was all about? "Why isn't it safe?"

"There's something I didn't tell you about this place. I didn't tell Billie Jo either."

Merry narrowed her eyes and grasped her phone tighter. Was this about to become about a serial killer describing to his next victim how he comes here every night to prey on young lovers, like something out of a cheap, cheesy, wonderfully absurd horror movie? The setting and ambiance were about right. So was the timing. Having just recovered from being scared out of her wits after running away from an unknown assailant now revealed to be someone she knew; the perfect climax would of course be the terrifying high note of fear as she—the witless victim—realizes there was a very good reason to be afraid of the person she *thought* she knew.

"Oh yeah?" Not appreciating being cast as the witless victim, Merry kept her voice deep and her stance aggressive. "What's that?"

Robby began. "I told Billie Jo this place used to be known as Lover's Lane in the old days."

By the old days he probably meant 2010. "Yeah, so?"

"That was a bit of a...lie."

Merry furtively glanced about for something she could use as a weapon other than her phone and her fists. "What did you lie about, Robby?"

"This used to be a place couples came to make out. That part was true. They do it now too, but a while back everyone stopped coming here because of what happened."

Merry nodded to indicate she was listening. At the same time she crouched down to retrieve her keys. She might need them.

"I told Billie Jo, and you, that this place is called Lover's Lane. But not that long ago it was known by another name."

Merry didn't get it. What was the big deal about what name a make-out spot was called?

"They called it Lover's Leap," Robby said using his best scary-story-around-a-campfire voice.

Lover's Leap. Didn't sound so bad. Merry envisioned randy couples stripping down to their underwear, or less, and jumping off the cliff's edge, hand in hand, aiming for the river below and a midnight skinny dip. The concept was romantic, albeit not very safe. The river was a long way down.

"It all started back in the nineteen nineties. A young couple, high school kids I think, came out here and jumped off the bridge."

The bridge? That sounded even less safe.

"They committed suicide together."

"That's terrible. Why did they do it?"

"Age old story; their parents refused to let them date or something stupid like that. After that people started calling this place Lover's Leap instead of Lover's Lane. There's been at least two other people who've jumped off Sweetgrass Bridge since then. It killed the romantic atmosphere and people found other places to hook up. But years passed, people forgot about it and started coming back."

"So you knew about the history of the bridge but Billie Jo didn't?"

"I should have told her. Dumbass move, I know."

"I still don't quite get why you followed me here," Merry said. "Did you think I was coming here to jump off of Sweetgrass Bridge?"

"Of course not," he said, squirming a little. "I never really gave the whole Lover's Leap thing a second thought, which is why I didn't say anything to Billie Jo. But with what happened to Dustin, and Billie Jo and I almost catching fire then breaking up that night, I dunno, I just think this place is creepy. Maybe everyone was right to stay away from here. It's got a weird vibe. Like it's cursed or something. It's not a place anyone should go alone. But that's what I did, I sent you here alone. I felt really bad about that. It bugged me all day and stayed with me after I got home from work. I went to bed early, tossed and turned and couldn't sleep so I just got in my car and drove out here. When I got here, I realized I'd left my phone at home charging, so I didn't have a flashlight. I got a bit turned around trying to get up to the clifftop. I knew you were up there because I saw your car. I should have called out or something, but I thought that might scare you and…well, shit, I was stupid. I'm sorry."

Merry was silent. Processing.

"Are you okay? The way you were moving and thrashing around in the bushes I didn't know if you were having a problem or being attacked by mosquitos."

She had a problem alright; him creeping around in the dark like some kind of spook.

"I'm really sorry," he repeated. "I didn't really think this through."

"You saw my car when you got here," Merry said the words out loud, almost trancelike, as an idea dawned on her.

"Uh, yeah. I mean I didn't know it was yours, but I guessed it was. That's a really old car. Is it an antique?"

Could Robby McAllister's story be true? If it was, she was dealing with a sweet and thoughtful young man instead of a blood-thirsty serial killer. Overall a much preferable scenario. Although not entirely convinced, Merry once again began to think of him more as a witness than a threat. More importantly, something he said had ignited a wasp's nest of questions: Why was Dustin's white Cadillac SUV parked outside his apartment? If he came to Sweetgrass Bridge that night, for whatever reason, wouldn't his vehicle still be in the Lover's Lane parking lot? If not, how did he get here? Did he walk? Seemed too far from the city. Did he take a cab or Uber? Maybe, especially if he knew he wasn't going back home, which would support the suicide theory. Or, did his killer bring him here?

"Robby," Merry said, stepping closer to the young man. "I want you to think very carefully about this question before you answer it."

"Of course. What is it?"

"When you and Billie Jo came out here that Saturday night, was there a white Cadillac SUV in the parking lot?"

To his credit, Robby did not immediately answer and did a fine job of appearing to review what he already knew to be the answer before responding with a definite "No."

CHAPTER 13

Little Turtle Lake First Nation reserve was a two-and-a-half-hour drive north of Livingsky. It was from here Merry hoped to get more answers about who Dustin Thomson really was. One of Nathan Sharpe's favourite truisms was: "a good investigator knows criminals, a great one knows their victims." Merry's client, Ruth-Anne Delorme was family, purportedly one of his closest relatives and friends, but perhaps that was the problem. Maybe Ruth-Anne was too close to the situation, so clouded by her love for her cousin and grief over his loss she couldn't see beyond who she thought he was, who she wanted him to be. According to Ruth-Anne, Dustin Thomson could not possibly have committed suicide, despite the poem, despite the lack of evidence suggesting otherwise, despite what everyone else, including the police, seemed to think. Not that Merry blamed her. She understood that type of grief, the kind that provided the safety of wearing blinders so you didn't have to see or deal with anything that wasn't right in front of you. But Ruth-Anne had hired her to find out the truth. Whether she really wanted to know it or not was another matter.

To further her investigation, Merry needed a clear-headed account of who Dustin Thomson truly was beyond the glitz and glamour of being a Saskatchewan Roughrider god, a local hero who'd been foisted upon a pedestal, one that had grown even taller since his disappearance. Merry knew from her online research that before he moved to Livingsky as a youth, Dustin had spent his early life on Little Turtle Lake. Most of his family had long since moved away, but his half-sister, Miranda Poile, remained. It hadn't taken much to reach her on the phone and she'd readily agreed to talk with Merry.

Merry and Doreen set out for the reservation on Tuesday morning. It was one of those strange summer days when although there wasn't a cloud in the sky, the air smelled of rain and the temperature struggled to break 20ºC, unusual for July which was typically the warmest month of the year. Having never travelled this far north before, the second half of the two-hundred-and-fifty-kilometer drive was entirely unfamiliar to Merry. The road was a two-lane highway, mostly in good condition (which Doreen appreciated), but construction on a large segment of the south-bound lane slowed things down considerably. In Saskatchewan, highway construction is as expected in summer as barbecues and sunburns, so Merry had wisely set out early, giving herself an extra half hour for the trip. It was also at about the halfway mark that the scenery took a dramatic shift. Undisturbed views of sky and rolling fields of ripening grains stretching to the horizon's edge were replaced by dense tracks of trees, mostly spruce and pine, lining both sides of the road. It was like travelling through an endless tunnel with dark green walls and solid blue roof. Merry cracked a window, filling the car with verdant freshness.

Roughly twelve percent of Saskatchewan's population are Indigenous. These are the original lands of the Cree, Ojibwe, Saulteaux, Dakota, Nakota, Lakota, and the homeland of the Metis Nation. One half live on reserves, the other in the province's larger cities. Like most non-Indigenous people, Merry had never visited a reserve. She had, however, grown up at a time when the province's education system was actively renovating its pre-kindergarten to Grade 12 curriculum through a partnership with local Indigenous groups. Like others of her generation (at least those who'd paid attention in class) she knew that reserves were tracts of land set aside for Indigenous people by the Canadian government through a system governed by the Indian Act. Several treaties covered the province which represented home for at least seventy Indigenous communities, and Metis, Cree, Dene, Denesuline, Dakota, Nakota, Saulteaux and Ojibwe linguistic groups. Reserves could be large or small tracts of land, mainly in rural or remote areas, mostly in the southern half of the province, unlike Little Turtle Lake which was in the north. Some were used solely for hunting and gathering, while others were home to dwellings and schools.

A highway sign instructed Merry to turn right onto a road that sliced through the tree line to reach Little Turtle Lake, just where Google maps said it would be. The road was loose gravel and Doreen swerved her tail and complained accordingly. A kilometer later the foliage thinned out revealing a random collection of buildings on makeshift streets on the western edge of what Merry guessed to be Little Turtle Lake. The body of water was so vast, its other side was out of sight.

Merry checked her watch. There was no time for a tour of the reserve. Miranda Poile was expecting her at 11:00 a.m. and she didn't want to be late. The directions she'd been given were not as straightforward as a house number and street name. Instead, she was instructed to enter the reserve on the main road, turn left at the new health centre, keep going until she saw a pink double-wide trailer, make a right two trailers later then find the house with a birdhouse and an old red truck parked in front. It took a couple of tries for Merry to find Miranda Poile's home because she never did see a birdhouse, and by the time she successfully guessed which old truck had once been red, Merry was almost five minutes late.

She scurried up to the front door of the small house, a thousand square feet at most, and knocked. While she waited, she looked over her shoulder and noticed how Doreen and the old red truck looked quite comfortable together.

She knocked again. Was she too late? Did Miranda get upset and decide to blow her off?

A third knock finally resulted in a face appearing in the door's window. Merry waved and smiled. The door opened. Miranda Poile appeared older than Merry expected, given that she and Dustin were siblings and Dustin was only 25.

"I'm so sorry I'm late," Merry apologized.

The woman blinked her eyes. "Who are you?"

Merry stepped back, wondering if she'd chosen the wrong red truck. "I'm Merry Bell. I might be at the wrong house. I'm looking for Miranda Poile."

"Oh yeah, Merry Bell." Miranda drew out the last name longer than the four letters required. "I forgot about you. Yeah, so you want to talk today?"

"Uh, yes, if that's alright," Merry stuttered, wondering if she'd made a scheduling error.

"Oh yeah, sure. Come on in then."

Without waiting to see if Merry was following, Miranda made the short trip to the front room, a small living room that managed two full-size couches and two loveseats, along with a large coffee table littered with glasses, bottles, bowls and overflowing ashtrays, and a big screen TV airing a talk show. A single window showcased the street and the strange rainless rainy day.

Seeing Miranda had already taken a seat, Merry followed suit, placing herself directly across.

"You want a drink?"

"A glass of water would be nice."

Miranda's laugh was mirthless. "A *glass* of water? What do you think this is, the big city?" she said, hoisting herself up and heading for the kitchen. She came back a moment later, handing Merry a plastic bottle, the top already off.

"Thank you."

"Water only comes in bottles around here, not in a glass. We've been under a boil water advisory since winter of 2022."

"What does that mean?"

"It means our water's no good. Can't drink the stuff out of the taps. The band office brings in these bottles. We got a brand-new water treatment plant a couple years ago but it doesn't work right. No one seems to know how to fix it."

Merry held back a slew of questions that were likely unanswerable. "I've never been this far north before. You're very lucky to have a house so close to the lake."

"We live on a lake and we got no water. What sense is that, eh?" Another laugh that wasn't one.

"It's beautiful though."

Miranda nodded. "We live on our land, in nature. Even though some of us are too lazy to cut the grass and there're too many junkers in our yards, I couldn't live anywhere else."

"I can see why. Do you live here alone?"

"Now I do. Our kids, they have to move out after grade eight."

"What?" Merry asked, alarmed. "Why?"

"We got no high school here. They got to go live in town. Once they go, they usually don't come back. To visit maybe, but that's all. I don't blame them. I did the same. Except I did come back. I didn't like it in the city. Too much trouble to get into. We got enough trouble here. Drugs especially. Used to just be liquor and the puff-puff but now they got all this prescription stuff out here. That shit is bad for you. But people do it all the time. We're a small community, so we try and help each other if we can. Harder to do in the city. Too many people. Too many drugs, too easy to get. Nobody cares."

"Did Dustin have trouble with drugs?"

"Oh yeah, that's right, I forgot, you wanna talk about Dustin. It's hard for me. I been crying every day all day since I heard about what happened to him. News like that makes you do whatever it takes to forget for a while."

"I'm very sorry for your loss."

"You knew Dustin?"

"I didn't. That's why I wanted to talk with you today. The police are beginning to think it may have been a suicide. I know some of the family disagrees with that. They think something else happened to Dustin. I'm just trying to find out the truth."

"I'm glad. Truth is good, truth is powerful."

Merry was relieved to hear the words. "What about you, Miranda? Do you think it's possible Dustin committed suicide?"

"Our people know a lot about suicide. Young people especially. Friends of mine lost both their kids that way. Barely more than babies."

"Did Dustin have a problem with drugs?" Merry asked again. Nothing like this had shown up in his biographical material, but if he did struggle with substance abuse, it might suggest a cause for suicide or association with other kinds of violence associated with the city's drug culture. Perhaps Dustin Thomson was not as straight and clean as his public image portrayed him to be.

"Nah. He was too smart. And he had too many other things to worry about."

"Oh? Like what?"

"His mother mostly."

Merry recalled what Calvin Wochiewski had told her about Dustin's mother. "They moved to Livingsky so she could be closer to medical care."

"That's right."

"She passed away around the time Dustin graduated from high school."

"Yes she did. That poor boy, to go through so much at such a young age. When you think about it, it's surprising he didn't start using or anything."

"It must have been hard on you too."

Miranda shrugged. "I knew her, but she wasn't my mother. Dustin and I had the same father, different mothers."

"I see."

"Dustin went to university, always kept busy with sports. You could say he was a good kid, but around here that doesn't just happen. He worked hard at being a good kid."

They were back to Dustin the saint. There had to be more. "Miranda, I know this may be hard to talk about, but do you know of anything else, besides the loss of his mother, that Dustin might have been bothered by more recently?"

"I don't think so, not very recently."

Merry's ears perked up. "Was there something else, maybe not recently, but in his past?"

Repositioning herself on the couch, Miranda said, "My brother and me didn't get to see each other too often, especially after things started getting good with him and football. But we talked on the phone, at least once every week or two. That's how we shared our lives, him and me. We stayed close. It's not the same as sitting together like this, but it was something. There was a time, maybe four, five years ago, that he started having a rough time."

"Over what?"

"What do most twenty-year-old boys get sad about? A girl. He liked her a lot. Thought it was love. When it was good it was good, when it was bad it was heartbreak. For him. For her, I don't know. I didn't say so because it wasn't my place, but if you ask me she was stringing him along. Did it for years."

"Who was she?"

Miranda shrugged. "Never met the woman."

Merry's heart fell. "He never told you her name?"

"Nah. He said it was like a secret romance or something like that. He could be a little dramatic about things like that."

Biting her lip, Merry considered the response. Was a different picture of the football hero beginning to emerge? Was Dustin love-sick? A spurned lover? Or was there something more disturbing here? Did Miranda's story somehow tie in to the inferences made by the Roughrider cheerleader and the JOY Centre teenager?

"But like I said," Miranda continued, breaking Merry's theorizing, "Dustin was smart. Too smart to get sidetracked for too long by some break-up. And he was lucky. Imagine making all that money from playing a game. Dustin loved what he was doing, he loved helping the kids at that centre. Maybe he was a bit lonely, but he was a happy person. You asked me if Dustin could have killed himself. He didn't and I know he didn't."

Merry leaned in. "What do you mean?"

"We talked on the phone the day before he died."

Sitting up straighter, Merry knew her long drive was about to pay off.

"He sounded happy."

Merry's hopes dimmed. It was not uncommon for family members to report how happy their loved one seemed immediately prior to ending their lives. What they couldn't have known was that the happiness came from relief; relief at finally having committed to a plan that would end their excruciating internal pain.

But then…

"And he had a secret."

With quickening breaths and a silent scream Merry urged Miranda to continue.

"He told me he had very good news to share. He wanted to wait until he visited to tell me in person. He said he'd come soon. He hasn't been on reserve in probably two years. Nobody sounds so happy, promises to visit to share good news, then kills themselves the next day. That's not how suicide works around here. Those kids who kill themselves, they have no hope, no reason to want to live. Dustin had hope and more reasons to live than most."

As investigations unfurl it was not uncommon for unearthed truths to lead to more unanswered questions. What was the big news Dustin wanted to wait until he saw his sister in person to tell her about? Can someone be happy one day and suicidal the next? Was Dustin happy because he knew he was about to end his life? But would he then make a promise he intended to break? Who was it who broke his heart five years ago and was maybe still breaking it on and off since then? Could it have anything to do with his death? The challenge now was figuring out where to find the answers.

"Miranda, do you think Dustin might have shared his good news with anyone else? A friend? Another member of the family?"

"I don't know about friends. He never talked about having too many of those. As far as close family, we don't really have any left in Saskatchewan. His kôhkom passed away. Most of the others went to Alberta or headed south into the states."

"So, it's just you and Ruth-Anne?"

"Ruth-Anne?"

"Ruth-Anne. Delorme. Your cousin."

"You went to see her too?"

"No. She came to my office. She's the one who hired me."

"I don't think so."

A flurry of feather-winged mud-coloured moths fluttered wildly in Merry's chest. "Say what?"

"Ruth-Anne is ninety-six years old. She doesn't speak English and she lives in Minnesota. I don't know who that woman was in your office, but I know it wasn't Ruth-Anne Delorme."

CHAPTER 14

Leaving Miranda Poile's house, Merry Bell was in shock. And pissed off. Instead of heading for Doreen who seemed happy to stay right where she was next to her new friend, the old, almost-red truck, Merry marched determinedly down a street of packed gravel that led straight to the rocky shore of Little Turtle Lake. She needed time to think.

Once on shore, Merry toed off her shoes, yanked off her ankle socks and gingerly crossed a wide stretch of pebbled sand mixed with scrub grass and the occasional discarded coke can and cigarette butt. She only stopped when she felt the screeching sensation of warm skin touching icy water. How could a lake be so cold in the middle of summer? With her face turned upwards, she stared at the strange metal-hued sky that refused to give up even a single drop of rain. Her current mood called for a deluge. Even the air wasn't playing nice, flaunting waves of July heat run through with occasional threads of artic ice. The lake itself was deathly still but changeable in colour, as if lit from below by a kaleidoscope of dark blues and greys.

Allowing herself to be numbed by the ice water, Merry wondered: *what the hell just happened*? Miranda Poile claimed that Ruth-Anne Delorme, Merry's client and the whole reason she was here, was an old woman who lived south of the border and couldn't possibly have been in her office a few days ago. Her Ruth-Anne was a young woman who spoke perfect English and claimed to be Dustin Thomson's cousin and one of his best friends. The only commonality between the two was that they were both Indigenous women. How was this possible? Someone was lying.

When Merry told Miranda about her Ruth-Anne, the woman described how Indigenous people sometimes refer to close acquaintances as cousins even when they weren't actually blood relatives. But cousin or not, unless there happened to be someone else named Ruth-Anne Delorme in Dustin's life, which seemed highly implausible, she could not explain the woman's appearance in Merry's office.

Gulping in a series of deep breaths of clean crisp lake air helped. Realizing she could no longer feel her toes, Merry backed out of the water. To her left in the far distance she could make out a trio of preschool age children playing a game that involved sticks and stones. Other than that, the beach was empty. Finding no bench or even a picnic table where she could sit, Merry gingerly lowered herself to the rocky ground and spread her feet in front of her allowing an indistinct pale sun to warm and dry them. She pulled out her iPhone, found her client's contact info and hit the button that initiated FaceTime. She wanted to see the woman's face when she confronted her.

"Hello?" Ruth-Anne answered after a couple of rings, looking as if she wasn't aware she'd agreed to a FaceTime connection.

"Ruth-Anne, it's Merry Bell. I wonder if you have a minute to talk."

Ruth-Anne focused more clearly on the screen. "Are you...on a beach?"

"I'm at Little Turtle Lake."

"Oh. What are you doing there?"

There it was. If this woman really was a relative of Dustin's, she'd know his sister lived at Little Turtle Lake reserve.

"I wonder if we could get together to discuss a few things I learned today."

Merry could see the lie forming on the woman's face as clearly as an unwelcome zit. After a few seconds Ruth-Anne went with: "I'm pretty busy right now. Not sure I can get away."

"I'm sure you're planning to be at the vigil tonight. How about we meet there?"

The screen went blank.

"Goddamnit." Merry tried the call again, first with FaceTime, then twice more without. Ruth-Anne was no longer accepting her calls. No big surprise. She thought about whether there was a better way she could have played this, but something told her there wasn't. Even if she managed to confront the woman in person, the likelihood of getting the truth out of her was low, unless she was willing to play rough…which wasn't entirely out of the question.

What the hell is going on here? Sticking her phone back in her pocket, Merry leaned back until her head touched the ground, placing her hands behind it as a cushion. She closed her eyes and let her mind go to work.

It was now clear that Ruth-Anne—or whatever her name was—had lied to her. She'd hired Merry under the false pretense of not only being a close friend and relative of Dustin Thomson, but someone who spoke for the entire family. The cash deposit for her services, a rather large one at that, had been a red flag, but one Merry had been too willing to overlook in favour of finally getting a job that didn't involve putting on an ill-fitting security guard uniform to watch people stream into an events centre then a few hours later watch the same people stream out. At least she'd been paid up front for all of her time, and then some. She was not inclined to refund the excess. It was a windfall but not the feel-good kind. As needy as her bank account was, she did not like the idea of making money for doing nothing and less so for being hoodwinked. There was certainly enough left in the kitty for her to continue investigating Thomson's death. But should she? Merry's natural curiosity, a detective's best friend, said yes.

If Ruth-Anne Delorme wasn't Dustin's cousin, then who was she? Why would someone spend money to hire a P.I. to find out what happened to someone she didn't know? It didn't make sense. Maybe she wasn't a cousin, but it was doubtful she was a complete stranger. How else would she know all the things she knew about Dustin Thomson including that he had a cousin named Ruth-Anne

Delorme. Why else would she be so passionate about him not committing suicide and the plight of youth at the JOY Centre, especially Indigenous youth? She had to be connected to him or the family somehow, or was she nothing more than an actress playing a part?

Even though Merry was convinced Miranda was telling the truth, was it possible Dustin's sister didn't know everything there was to know about her brother? It wouldn't be a big stretch to believe the footballer had kept a few things private from his half-sibling. Like the existence of someone he was close to? Miranda knew about the woman Dustin had had an on-again-off-again relationship with, but she'd never met her. Was the fake Ruth-Anne the woman who'd broken Dustin's heart all those years ago and now, worried for the man she still loved, hired an investigator to find out why he disappeared? Possible. Did she know more than she was letting on? Was that why she was vehement Thomson couldn't possibly have committed suicide even when the police seemed certain he had? Did she know he'd been murdered and wanted the assailant to be brought to justice, if not by the police then by someone outside the police's influence? On top of all these questions was: why pretend to be someone she wasn't?

Merry opened her eyes and just as quickly shut them again. Maneuvering one hand from behind her head to shade her face, she opened them again and was surprised to find the day had morphed into something new. The sun was beaming full force, as yellow as lemon Jell-o, in an impeccably unblemished bright blue sky. She sat up to find the lake surface rippling with a playful summer breeze that beckoned her to come back to the water, jump in for a swim. If she'd had a swimsuit she may have been tempted. Hearing voices she turned to find the children had moved closer, curious about her, but too shy to approach.

Merry reached for her socks and shoes, pulled them on and jumped to her feet. She smiled and waved at the kids playing their game. One of the girls waved back. For a moment she thought about how nice it would be to spend the rest of the afternoon cavorting on the beach, playing with sticks and stones in the sun and water. But if her day at Little Turtle Lake had taught her anything, it was that Miranda Poile was right to suspect that there was more to Dustin Thomson's death than a simple suicide. There was work to be done and she needed to get back to Livingsky. She hoped Doreen was in the mood to drive fast.

—

Between completing the install of a LED lighting system in a man cave and a service call at an elderly client's home that was probably going to be a simple fuse replacement, Roger Brown had exactly one hour. It was an hour he would never forget: his first solo in-the-field investigation. Having gotten the name of the cleaners who serviced 222 Craving Lane from Alvin Smallinsky, Roger had arranged to meet the woman who owned the business. The cleaning crew was high on Roger's suspect list for having left Merry the mysterious "I know it's you" notes. They had plenty of opportunity, now it was time to determine if they also had motive.

Roger rapped on the door with authority. He hoped whoever answered didn't catch on to the fact that he had none.

A young girl, fourteen or so, appeared wearing a t-shirt, jean shorts and flip flops, the kind with a plastic flower between the big toe and the others. She was eating an orange popsicle, the colour staining her lips and left cheek.

"Hello," Roger said, momentarily taken aback by the appearance of a child. "Is your mother at home? I'm looking for Luba Novo... Nokark...Norashka..." He started and fumbled badly with the long name.

"Navarykasha," the girl said smoothly, making it sound like music.

"I'm sorry, yes, that's it," Roger said, feeling like a fool. So much for hitting it out of the park on his first assignment. Well, self-assigned assignment.

"Hold on a sec."

The girl disappeared. Roger looked down at the inside of his hand where he'd penned the name, knowing he'd never remember it, and repeated it several times, never twice the same.

"Hello?" Luba Navarykasha was in her early thirties, with dark hair and eyes, and a smile too big for her mouth.

"Hello, yes, thank you for…" Oh geez, what was he thanking her for? "Thank you for seeing me, Mrs…Miss…Ms. Navarushacash… uh…"

She smiled again. "You call me Luba."

It was not just the name that clued Roger in to guessing the woman was Ukrainian, but her accent. It was an accent which only recently had become much more recognizable to the people of Livingsky. Even though Saskatchewan had historically been home to many Ukrainians thanks to the great European migrations of the late 19th and early 20th centuries and then again after World War I, in the ensuing years the population had become overwhelmingly Canadian-born, inter-married, and often accent-less. But another war, more than one hundred years later, once again brought Ukrainian families to Livingsky, this time by plane instead of boat, looking for respite from terror and repression and, in some cases, a new beginning.

"Hello, Luba. My name is Roger Brown. I'm a detective with LSI, Livingsky Sharpe Investigations."

"I don't know what that is."

Roger decided not to elaborate at the moment. Luba Navarykasha's familiarity with LSI was a key aspect of his investigative plan. "I'm looking into activities which occurred earlier this year at 222 Craving Lane."

Still looking confused, Luba said, "Yes, I know this place."

"You own the cleaning company that cleans the building at 222 Craving Lane, is that correct?"

"No company," she replied, "just me and some women do this work."

"I see." Roger glanced down at this phone where he'd pulled up an image on the screen of a photo he'd taken of his case notes. He repeated the date range between which the two notes had been delivered. "Did you…and these women clean 222 Craving Lane during this time period?"

"Uh-huh, yes. We clean on Monday and Friday night. Sometimes on Saturday if there is extra cleaning to do. Mr. Smallinsky tells us what to do."

"Ms....Luba, are you certain you are not familiar with LSI?"

"I don't think so, no."

Ah-ha. Did he just catch the woman in a lie? "Livingsky Sharpe Investigations is one of the offices you clean in the Craving Lane building."

Luba nodded. "Okay. That could be so. We just clean. We don't ask anything about who works there."

Humph. Fair enough. "Luba, have you ever met or do you know someone named Merry Bell?"

"Maribel? This is a woman's name?"

"Yes."

"First name or last name?"

"Both. Her first name is Merry, like Merry Christmas. Her last name is Bell, like...Jingle Bell." *Sheesh, Roger, do better.*

The woman thought for several seconds. "I don't know this name. Oh wait, wait, Sharpe, yes, I do know this name. I remember. You are right, this is on one of the doors in that building. I'm thinking I saw it there for sure. But Merry Bell I don't know. I don't see that name in the building."

Roger nodded. Having visited his wife's office which was next door to Merry's, he knew the sign on the door read: Livingsky Sharpe Investigations. Beneath it another sign, a white flash card handwritten in jiffy marker, read: Please come in. That was probably what Luba Navarykasha was recalling. Now what? Fidgeting under the expectant gaze of the woman, Roger began to doubt himself. Investigating was harder than he expected. But what did he expect? That Luba would curdle under the pressure of his expert inquisition techniques and admit to sending the notes? How was he supposed to know if she was telling the truth or lying through her teeth? How was he to know whether she knew more than she was letting on? And while he was trying to figure all of that out he was standing in front of her like a fool having no idea what to do next.

Merry Bell and every detective he'd ever seen on TV or in a movie made it look so much easier. As did Stella, who hosted *The Darkside of Livingsky* podcast with unquestionable confidence. Was that the problem? Was he an idiot for thinking Roger the electrician could ever be as smart and intuitive and crafty as Stella? Being a crossdresser presented a great many challenges to living life, but one of the things he was sure of was that Roger was Stella and Stella was Roger, and at no time did he wish for either of them to be gone. It was true that at times when he was Roger he pined to be Stella. But that wasn't because he didn't like Roger or thought Roger was an imposter hiding who he really was. It was because Stella gave him something Roger did not. Stella gave him peace. He needed Stella to live. But he also needed Roger. He liked who he was as Roger as much as he liked who he was as Stella. The problem was wanting both.

Stella easily discussed true crime with her listeners, assertively debating guilt and innocence, motives and criminal proclivities, and enthusiastically indulged in the drama of it all. Roger the electrician was simply less experienced at it, so he needed to give himself a break. What did stand to reason, it began to dawn on Roger as he stood on the woman's stoop, was that if Roger was Stella and Stella was Roger, the skillsets and what they knew as one should be available to the other.

Focusing on the logic of his case notes without having to refer to them, Roger cleared his throat and asked, "Is it true that your cleaning crew arrives at 222 Craving Lane in the middle of the night when no one else is around?"

"No," she replied matter-of-factly. "This is not true."

"Oh?"

"Yes, we come to the building after most of the peoples are gone, but is not middle of night. This building closes at 5:00 p.m., yes? So we come after that. Sometimes at six, sometimes at seven, no later."

Roger smiled. If the notes had been slipped under Merry's door in the middle of the night, she wouldn't have found them until morning. But Merry had found both notes when she returned to her office after hours. As such, they had to have been placed there sometime between when Merry left her office during the day and returned there later that same night, say around six or seven? He had Luba and her crew on opportunity. Motive was still unclear.

"Luba, earlier this year Merry Bell, on two separate occasions, discovered a mysterious, unsigned note slipped under the office door of Livingsky Sharpe Investigations. Would you happen to know anything about that?" If nothing else, Stella was a direct bitch.

To Roger's great surprise, the woman nodded. "The note on the floor? Yes, I know this note. I see one, maybe there was another, I don't know this."

"You saw a note slipped under Merry Be...the door belonging to Livingsky Sharpe Investigations?"

"I see note on floor. Maybe it came from under the door, I don't know this."

"Did you put it there?" Roger quivered in anticipation at the possibility that he had just solved his first...what was this? Not a crime really. Was this actually a case? Maybe. Sort of.

"No. Not me. Someone else does this. I don't know who. But I see the note when I come into the office to clean. I pick it up so I can clean the floor, then put it back where I find it. I move things when I clean, but I always put back."

"I see." Roger's mind was whirring. If Luba was telling the truth, that meant the note was slipped under the door before the cleaner's arrived. "Luba, you told me you work with some other women, is that correct?"

"Yes. I have a helper for this building. Lesya."

That was worth another *Ah-ha*. "Might Lesya have written this note?"

Luba shrugged. "I think no, but maybe. I ask her. Was note written in Ukrainian?"

Roger studied Luba's open, earnest face. She was either an expert at obfuscation and trying to outsmart him or had just revealed that indeed she not only didn't write the note herself but hadn't looked at it when she moved it to clean the office floor.

"The note was written in English."

Luba laughed lightly. "Then not Lesya who writes this note. She only knows Ukrainian for now. She tries for talking English but it's hard for her."

Roger sighed, heavily. He'd hit a brick wall. Stella would likely agree.

Thanking Luba, Roger returned to his vehicle to stew. Opening his casebook where he'd faithfully recorded every detail of his investigation to date, he turned to the page listing categories of prime suspects. He crossed out Cleaning Company. He'd already crossed out Craving Lane Tenants. There were only two categories of suspects left. The first was Former Friend/Acquaintances. He had been giving this category a lot of thought. So far he hadn't come up with a good idea on how to get started without asking Merry outright for a list of people she knew before moving away from Livingsky. The second category held greater promise. In truth, both Roger and Stella considered this the most likely category of all: Family.

The chance that it was a member of Merry's family who was trying to make a connection through these notes made the most sense. Granted, it wasn't the most conventional way for an estranged family member to initiate communication, but nothing about how Merry came to be Merry was conventional and the likelihood that family ties had been strained in the process was high. Not only did Roger think it probable a family member was responsible for the notes, he truly hoped it was so. He was convinced Merry was lonely since returning to her hometown. She needed to be with people who loved her, people who could help Livingsky feel like home again. Who better to do that than family? Roger was resolute. He would use his burgeoning detective skills to find Merry's family and reunite them.

What could possibly go wrong?

CHAPTER 15

Vigil for Dustin Thomson had been widely promoted on social media, TV, radio and pretty much every other news outlet available. Even so, Merry was not prepared for the vast numbers of people streaming into Riverside Park. The Saskatchewan Roughriders were immensely popular in the city, but this level of congregation went far beyond football fans. The people of Livingsky had come to pay tribute to a fallen son and collectively grieve the loss of a local hero. Merry noted that although large, most of the crowd appeared generally polite and respectful. But there were others here too. Making her way deeper into the park, she came across an area that more resembled a fairground than vigil site. There were booths selling food, drink, and all manner of Roughrider merchandise. Further in, closer to an enormous bandstand at the end of the park nearest the Truemont Hotel, were stalls manned by organizations advocating mental health awareness and hawking self-help books. One even went so far as to invite anyone who was currently experiencing mental distress to visit with an onsite counsellor in one of three portable compartments set up for the purpose. How had this happened? When and how did the police theory that Dustin had committed suicide become so commonly known and accepted that it promoted this level of exploitative commerce?

"Merry!"

Whoever had called Merry's name was temporarily obstructed by a passing trio of young men whose torsos and faces were painted entirely in Roughrider green. On their backs, in blazing white, was

Dustin Thomson's jersey number.

"Merry, we thought we'd see you here." It was Roger Brown. Designs by Brenda was close by.

"Oh, hello. What are you two doing here?"

Roger held up his phone. "I'm taking some video for *The Darkside of Livingsky*."

"Video? But it's a podcast."

"True," he responded with his trademark genial smile, "but my listeners will eat up the audio. I'll play them portions of tonight's program and then we'll discuss. To have something like this happen right here in Livingsky, especially to a celebrity, is a big deal for the true crime community."

"Take a look around," Merry commented dryly, indicating the nearby booths, "apparently the cat is out of the bag that the police don't think it was a crime. Canada decriminalized suicide in 1972."

Roger nodded. "True. But until it's proven to be one or the other, we'll be talking about it." He gestured to the ever-growing crowd. "Just like everyone else in Livingsky. Can you believe how many people are here?"

"Did you say there's going to be a program?"

Roger checked his watch. "Should be soon. It's nine o'clock now. Someone said they'll wait until it gets dark so they can use the big screen on the bandstand."

"Isn't all of this just the saddest thing?" Brenda pulled up looking smashing in a Miu Miu track suit with black racing strips against hazard yellow.

Merry compared the look with her own. Brenda's was bumblebee chic, hers more army ant casual. She'd worn a pair of light cotton pants with a camouflage print and a khaki t-shirt that fit just right. She'd debated shorts because it was one of those summer nights when the temperature resisted lowering in sync with the sun, but she wondered if that would be disrespectful given the event's purpose. Looking around, she needn't have worried. At the least Brenda would have to give her points for hair and makeup, both spot-on tonight. "The saddest," she agreed even though no one nearby seemed particularly unhappy.

"Such a good-looking man with everything to live for. Why would he kill himself? And," Brenda gave Merry a pointed look, "I suppose this means you don't have a case anymore?"

Merry bit the inside of her lip which she often found herself doing in Brenda's presence. "Like Roger said, nothing's been proven yet." Brenda didn't need to know her fake client had just gone *poof* into thin air.

"Do you think it's true what they're saying, that he jumped off of Sweetgrass Bridge?"

Correctly sensing Merry was not inclined to speculate on the veracity of rumours, Roger interrupted with: "What I want to know is how did all of these people learn about what the police think in the first place? I play close to attention and I'm pretty sure the suicide thing hasn't been reported in the news yet."

As Roger asked the question, Merry saw the answer revealing itself over his shoulder. Twilight had descended, bathing the park and its visitors in pewter shadow and hues of purple and maroon. With the arrival of dusk a massive screen suspended high above the stage area had come to life, the image it displayed increasing in intensity with every passing second. Merry's mouth hung open.

Roger and Brenda followed Merry's astonished gaze to the screen and the words emblazoned there:

I see beginning
I see end
From Sweetgrass Bridge I see forever

Swift flow, eddies
Cool
Damp air moss lichen river
stone

Deepening, darkening

Unexpected
From Sweetgrass Bridge
I see never
I see end

by Dustin Thomson

The poem had been leaked.

Merry gagged. Suddenly all of the hoopla and on-site mental health professionals made sense. That damn poem pretty much painted a picture of a depressed Dustin Thomson leaping to his death off Sweetgrass Bridge. Another uncomfortable thought hit her: would Sergeant Veronica Greyeyes think she was responsible for the leak?

As darkness blossomed in the park and more people noticed the weighty words on the screen, a surprising thing began to happen, unexpected in what until now had been more of a rally atmosphere. The noise level of the crowd plummeted, first in one section of the park, then another and another, eventually spreading throughout the large outdoor area until there was nothing left but somber silence as people began to read and re-read what many would surely interpret as the last words of their beloved sports hero.

Merry surveyed the people nearest her, including the Browns, and could clearly see what was happening. In that moment Dustin Thomson became a legend. For decades to come he would be remembered as the celebrated quarterback raised on Saskatchewan soil gone too soon, one whose tragic story would be recounted for generations.

What came next was as poignant for its sounds as the actions themselves. Gasps. Sobs. Cries. Grief. The people gathered in Riverside Park that night were, beyond anything else, desperately sad. Grown men, sport enthusiasts who were more apt to shout obscenities in response to perceived bad plays, were shedding tears upon heaving chests. Families and friends hugged one another. Roger and Brenda stood arm in arm, Brenda's head resting on Roger's strong shoulder. Merry too stood there, feeling sad. And very alone.

Long minutes later a lone spotlight appeared centre stage where a lectern and microphone had been erected. Stepping into the light, wearing her trademark smart business suit and heels, was Livingsky's mayor, Carol Durabont. Taking his place two feet behind her just outside the circle of light was her husband, Peter Wells. Merry felt a vice tighten around her heart. *Goddamnit.* Months had passed since she'd last seen the mayor's spouse with his blond hair, ice-blue eyes and irresistible dimples. *Irresistible dimples! Jeez, I'm beginning to sound like a Harlequin romance novel.* She liked a Harlequin romance just fine, but that didn't mean she had to act like she was living in one.

The first thing Merry Bell did upon returning to her hometown of Livingsky, Saskatchewan, even before finding a place to live, was open the offices of Livingsky Sharpe Investigations. If she was going to survive, she needed money, and investigating was the only thing she knew how to do. It was during her first case that she'd met Peter Wells and together they'd entered into a consensual and playful game of flirting. She did not know he was married or to whom. Nor did she know he was inextricably linked to shady goings-on in the mayor's office which had direct implications on her case. When all was said and done and Merry's case resolved, the guilt of Peter Wells and that of his wife remained shrouded in uncertainty and the possibility that they were anything but a squeaky-clean young couple dedicated to the city, their family and to each other was never revealed to the public. After a short self-imposed time-out taking a "well-earned vacation" the couple was back in the mayor's mansion. In their last chaotic moments together that only the two of them knew about, Peter had vowed to Merry they would never see one another again. That, of course, was impossible.

"Citizens of Livingsky," Carol Durabont began in her confident leader's voice, "I want to begin by saying thank you. Thank you for your presence here tonight, for showing your support and sharing your grief with the family and friends of Dustin Thomson, a young man, a Saskatchewan man, an Indigenous man, an accomplished man, but mostly a beloved man who will not be forgotten."

Wild applause erupted in the crowd like an explosion, soaring overhead and spreading across the city, reaching into every nook and cranny, to its very outskirts and beyond, echoes of which ricocheted off the forlorn structure of Sweetgrass Bridge and the deep, dark river below.

Merry studied the area closest to the stage where she expected to see the family and friends Durabont was referring to. She recognized Dustin's roommate, Calvin, and his sister Miranda Poile who must have been not far behind Merry on her drive back to Livingsky from Little Turtle Lake. One very important person was missing: Ruth-Anne Delorme. Merry gritted her teeth at the thought of her faux client.

When the noise finally died down, Mayor Durabont continued with her address, beginning with a recitation of Dustin Thomson's many achievements both on and off the football field.

Merry's gaze gravitated to the compelling shadow behind the mayor, separate yet inseparable. For an instant Peter's eyes met hers and they both flinched. Merry forced herself to look away. That's when she saw the couple standing off to one side of the main stage area.

"Excuse me," Merry said to Roger and Brenda. "There's someone I need to talk to."

"See you at work tomorrow?" Brenda chirped. "If you don't have a case anymore maybe we could do lunch or a drink after work?"

Bloody Sauvignon blanc time. "We'll see," Merry mumbled as she moved off.

Calvin Wochiewski was not who she'd set off to find in the crowd, but she'd literally run into him and it seemed rude not to stop. The young man was a mess. His hair was pulled back from his face into a stringy pigtail about the size of actual baby pig's tail, making his tear-puffed face all the more obvious. His clothes were badly wrinkled and he'd have done well to have a shower.

"Everybody loved him," were his first words to Merry.

Taken aback by the unveiled emotion on display by Thomson's

roommate, Merry did her best to offer words of comfort. "I know this must be very hard for you. People showed up tonight not only to show their love for Dustin but to support his friends and family. I hope you can find some comfort in that."

Calvin gave her a look that was hard to read. Had she said something wrong? Solace-giving wasn't exactly her strong suit. Glancing over his shoulder she saw that the couple she was intending to talk to seemed to be sticking to their spot. They were listening intently to Robert Calder, the Roughriders' coach, who'd replaced Mayor Durabont on stage. She'd been wanting to circle back to Calvin anyway so maybe she had time to kill two birds with one stone. "Calvin, do you mind if I ask you a question?"

"Sure." He said the single word in a way that sounded like he wondered what else could possibly go wrong.

"Did you ever meet a cousin of Dustin's named Ruth-Anne Delorme?" It was a longshot but worth a try. The better question would have been whether he could identify the woman pretending to be Ruth-Anne. Merry wondered whether she should make it an LSI policy that all new clients must be photographed. What she wouldn't give for a face pic of Delorme. She kicked herself for not taking a screen shot when she had her on FaceTime.

He thought for a moment but shook his head. "Nope, never heard of her."

"You said Dustin was too busy for a girlfriend, but do you think it's possible he had one anyway? Maybe an on/off kind of thing? Someone he saw when you weren't around?" People who worked nights and slept during the day missed things.

"Possible? I suppose. We were best friends, but Dustin didn't always tell me everything going on with him."

Not exactly a satisfactory answer, but the loudspeakers were beginning to play a particularly mournful tune and Merry knew she had to get as much out of the young man before he broke down in tears again. "One more question?" She didn't wait for a response. "Dustin's truck, the one you allowed me to search…"

"Did you find something?" Calvin asked, more alert.

"No, not really. I was just wondering why it's in the apartment building's parking lot?"

The man took a step back, as if he needed room to digest the unexpected question. "What do you mean? Where else would it be?"

"You said you last saw Dustin on Friday afternoon before you went to work. The next morning when you got home from work you said he'd already gone out and never came back, at least not before you went back to work again that night. Do I have that right?"

"Yeah, that's right."

"Was his truck in the parking lot when you left for work on Friday night?"

"Uh, yeah because he was still at home."

"And when you got back from work on Saturday morning—the day he disappeared—was the truck in the parking lot?"

"It was gone because he was gone out like I told you. Is this important for some reason?"

"It might be. Calvin, I want you to really think about this next question before you answer. When you got home from work on Sunday morning, was the truck in the parking lot?"

The man's reddened eyes widened. "Yeah. Yeah it was. Right where you found it."

"So if Dustin went to Sweetgrass Bridge with the intention to commit suicide like the police think, wouldn't he have driven there with his own truck? If that's what happened, how did the truck get back in the parking lot outside his apartment building?"

"Holy shit, man." Tears began to form. "I dunno. Do you?"

"I don't."

"Fuuuuuuuck."

—

Detective Sergeant Veronica Greyeyes did not look the same. Merry spent a moment studying the woman before she knew she was being studied which, knowing the cop's sharp instincts, wouldn't be long. Having only encountered Greyeyes in professional circumstances, it was strange to see her in the park, standing there like a regular member of the community, leaning into the side of a man Merry guessed was her husband, her eyes red and swollen as she joined in the communal grieving over a man whose loss seemed to affect everyone. The tears were the biggest surprise of all. Veronica Greyeyes did not strike Merry as the kind of person who cried easily and certainly not in public.

"Sergeant Greyeyes," Merry called out when she was near enough to know the other woman could hear her.

Greyeyes immediately straightened to attention and unconsciously moved a short distance away from the man. Her dark eyes found Merry and her hand instinctively moved to where a gun sometimes rested at her belt line. "Ms. Bell."

For a brief second the women stared at each other. It was not lost on Merry that if it wasn't for the efforts of Veronica Greyeyes—in part—she might currently be incarcerated in a British Columbia prison. For that she was grateful to the woman. She also liked Greyeyes and suspected the feeling was mutual. Still, there was something that held them back from fully trusting one another. Maybe it was just the inescapable cop-P.I. thing, an impenetrable barrier that would never go away.

In an effort to move beyond the initial awkwardness, Merry held out her hand to the tall, handsome man standing next to Detective Greyeyes. "Hi. I'm Merry Bell."

The man extended his hand along with a tentative smile. He was probably used to having to maintain a healthy dose of suspicion when it came to meeting people who knew his wife. As far as he knew, she could be a colleague from work or a crook hellbent on revenge for a past arrest. "Bobby Cook," he stated firmly. "I'm Veronica's husband."

"Nice to meet you, I'm…" *Uh, hmm, what to say?*

"Ms. Bell is a local detective," Veronica saved the day. "We worked the same case a few months ago."

The man's dark features relaxed a little. Colleague not crook. And maybe, Merry thought, that's not too far off, whether Greyeyes liked it or not.

Merry glanced up at the screen where Dustin Thomson's poem was emblazoned for all to see. "I want you to know I had nothing to do with that."

Greyeyes held up a hand. "I know. Someone sent a copy of the poem to the media. The intention may have been good, but whoever did it doesn't realize how something like this can jeopardize an ongoing investigation."

"Who would do something like that?"

"Well, if it isn't Sweet Lips!"

Oh for godsakes! Coming up behind Greyeyes and her husband was Gerald Drover in all his gangly glory.

"What did I tell you about calling me inappropriate names?" Merry shot back with a furrowed brow which did little to hide the blush of cheek that irritatingly always appeared whenever she saw the ridiculous man with the impossibly beautiful eyes.

Drover's gap-toothed smile somehow managed to signal his acceptance of the admonishment while clearly communicating his belief that Merry wasn't entirely sold on it.

Out of the corner of her eye Merry saw Greyeyes silently mouth the words: Sweet Lips?

"I think you know Detective Sergeant Veronica Greyeyes?" She knew he did. Greyeyes had arrested Drover on suspicion of arson. Merry had proven him innocent.

In lieu of a handshake the two exchanged curt nods.

"And this is her husband Bobby."

Knowing it would irritate the cop, Drover forced the man into a hearty man-hug followed by a clap on the back. "I'm very pleased to meet you, Bobby," he proclaimed with extra enthusiasm. "What do you do for a living? Are you a cop as well?"

"Uh, no," Bobby replied, newly aroused suspicion clouding his face. Colleague or crook? He looked at his wife for some kind of direction, but finding none he said: "I'm a teacher."

"Good for you. I admire teachers. Tough work. Almost as tough as your wife's."

"Daaaaaaaaad, let's goooooooo."

The whine had come from behind Bobby Cook. Its source proved to be a big surprise for both Merry and Drover.

CHAPTER 16

Standing behind Bobby Cook was his daughter, Aly, the same sullen sixteen-year-old Drover had introduced to Merry at the JOY Centre, the same girl who'd disturbingly hinted at a more intimate relationship with Dustin Thomson than was good for either of them.

"I didn't know you had a daughter," Merry directed the comment at Greyeyes.

"She's not my mom," Aly made clear.

Veronica exchanged a tight smile with the girl and said, "Aly is Bobby's daughter. Whether she likes it or not, I've been her mother factotum since she was eleven."

The girl had the sense to smile at the odd terminology which was obviously an inside joke between the two of them.

"Can we go or what?"

Merry tried to catch the girl's eye, but apparently she was not into having her parents know that she knew Merry or Gerald. Were the parents even aware that their daughter was a regular at the youth centre? Merry looked at Drover. He was a volunteer at JOY Centre and had known Aly Cook for longer. On this one thing, she would follow his lead.

"We should probably head home," Greyeyes said to her husband, ignoring Aly's dramatic eye roll that wordlessly moaned "finally!"

"It was a real pleasure meeting you, Mr. Greyeyes," Drover proclaimed with another clap across the man's back.

"It's Cook, Bobby Cook."

"Gotya. Well, Bobby, I'm sure we'll meet again." Drover winked at Greyeyes for no discernable reason other than to get under her skin.

Greyeyes, looking as miserable as Aly, moved off with husband and kid in tow, but not before gifting Merry a far from pleasant glare.

"What a super cute couple," Drover said in an extra bubbly voice knowing they were not quite out of hearing distance.

"Okay, okay, you can knock it off. You're not that funny."

"Then why are you smiling?"

Damn it. She was.

"Is that your type? Funny guys. Maybe I got a chance after all."

Finding it difficult to wipe the grin off her face, she responded with: "You've got zero chance." Was that true? She wasn't sure. She'd gone from feeling lonely in a crowd of hundreds to fighting off a belly laugh. All because of Drover? Really?

Gerald Drover was unlike any guy she'd ever had a crush on both pre- and post- transition. Then again, this pelican in cowboy boots was unlike pretty much anyone else she'd ever met, period. He was a clown on stilts with heartthrob eyes and lips. The dissonance was highly disturbing and endlessly confusing. He didn't make her swoon à la Regency-era debutantes the way Peter Wells did, but a chance glance in his eyes did elicit a blush in her cheeks and an uncertain flush in other areas. Then again, so did the flu.

The one thing Merry could not deny was that she was experiencing loneliness. She'd known loneliness before, especially as a child and teenager, pretty much for all of the years leading up to her leaving Livingsky, leading up to her transition. Before she'd become Merry Bell the loneliness came from the undeniable knowledge that she was not who she was supposed to be. Because she wasn't herself, didn't know herself, how could she expect anyone else to know her, care for her. Falling in love was impossible. Except once. Young love, at least it felt like love, felt so good. But it didn't…couldn't last.

The loneliness Merry felt now was different. Back then it was self-imposed. It was safety. It was comfort. This loneliness had arrived unbidden, like an unexpected, unwelcome guest. Both were thudding, dull aches born of wanting something that was missing. But instead of desperately desired body parts, the something missing, Merry was coming to realize, was the need for people, people who knew her, cared for her, gave a shit whether she lived or died.

Was Gerald Drover meant to be one of those people? Was that what the blushing and flushing was all about? Or could he be more than that? She needed people, that much was clear. But was that a good enough reason to lead him on, if that's what she was doing? Would a sexual relationship ruin the possibility of a friendship? Which was more important? The fact that, at least for now, he was also her landlord, added another layer of complexity to the whole matter.

"You show up in the most unexpected places," Merry noted, thinking it best to push on in another direction. "First the youth centre and now at Dustin Thomson's vigil. Are you here to get a better look at the cranes working on Riverside Plaza?" The massive construction project, one of Mayor Carol Durabont's babies, had come to a complete stop in the first place because its continuation was dependent on Gerald Drover agreeing to sell a building he did not want to sell. Had something changed? "Did someone finally get to you?" Merry had not planned on bringing this up, but it was better than figuring out the mess that was their relationship status.

Drover shrugged. "Nobody gets to Gerald Drover unless he wants to be gotten. You should remember that, Honeycomb."

Merry rolled her eyes. "Do you think it's strange that Aly acted like she didn't know us?"

"Who knows with teenagers? They do and say and don't say the stupidest shit. I wouldn't think too much about it if I were you."

"Is it possible her parents don't know she goes to the JOY Centre?"

"Uh uh. She started showing up before she was sixteen. Kids under sixteen have to fill out a permission form signed by a parent or legal guardian."

"She could have faked that."

"Doubt it. We might not look like much, but the JOY team is on top of stuff like that. Have to be when you're dealing with kids.

Greyeyes and her hubby know she goes there. What they might not know is that I'm involved or that you met Aly there."

"So Aly was taking a risk that if she didn't say anything, neither would we."

"Could be. Like I says, kids are unpredictable and their brains don't always work right."

"You're here for the vigil then? I wouldn't have pegged you as a football fan."

"You see," he said with a twinkle in his eye, "there's so much you don't know about me. How about we go get a drink and I can tell you all about me."

"Pass."

"Your loss. Why are you so interested in what I'm doing here?"

"I'm interested in why anyone who might be tied to Dustin's disappearance is here."

"So you're still on the case?"

Not quite sure herself, she gave the man a half nod.

"And you think I'm involved some how?" he asked, incredulous. "C'mon, Cinnamon Stick, at some point you gotta stop suspecting I'm involved in every bad thing that happens in Livingsky."

"You're not a suspect," she allowed, "but you introduced me to Aly, so you're involved." It was a stretch but it made sense...kind of.

"I think you're just looking for an excuse to hang out with me," he responded with his trademark lascivious smile.

Merry turned to walk away. "I gotta go."

"Okay okay okay," Drover did a quick circle around to get in front of Merry. "I'm here because I know Dustin from the JOY Centre. Mervin Jarvis and Marielle Oleksyn donated all the money to build the place, but without Dustin's annual fundraising efforts we probably couldn't keep the doors open or at least we wouldn't be able to offer the programing we do. He didn't just throw money at us either, he spent time there and at least a couple times a year he'd bring in some of his teammates to help out and meet the kids. Those were fun days. Even the kids who didn't give a lick about football got excited. The board offered to name the gym after him but he turned us down. Pretty humble guy. He doesn't…didn't want a lot of attention on himself."

Merry sighed. Praise kept pouring down on Thomson. Was this really the kind of guy who might have had an inappropriate relationship with a teenage girl? She really hoped not, but her findings as an investigator didn't always jive with what she hoped was the truth.

With a questioning look, Drover asked, "Do you believe he killed himself?"

Merry hesitated, then said, "I'm undecided."

"I know a few of the Roughies who are here tonight from when they visited JOY; I could introduce you if that would help."

"Thank you. That's nice of you."

"Told you." Gerald pointed at his chest, a narrow but sturdy tube sheathed in a heavy metal t-shirt. "Nice guy in here."

Gerald Drover was a scoundrel, often inappropriate and irritating, but yes, if truth were told, Merry had to agree there was a nice guy in the mix too.

"I appreciate the offer but I already tried talking to the players at Love Stadium. They weren't exactly forthcoming."

"I get that. Sports guys are all the same. One for all and all for one kind of stuff. They protect each other. But if you get them out of their element, one on one, they can be different."

Recalling her experience with Trent Brown outside the stadium, Merry had to agree with Drover's evaluation.

"See over there?" Drover ticked his head in the direction of a beer tent that was becoming increasingly popular as the evening wore on. "That big guy with the handlebar moustache? That's Dylan Cloutier. He's a Roughie."

"I met him," Merry said.

"Looks like he's had a few."

"Oh, I see. By 'out of their element,' you mean drunk." Merry grinned. "Gerald, you're a genius."

"And a nice guy, don't forget that part."

She gave him a look that intimated the matter was still up for debate. "I'd love to meet Mr. Cloutier again."

Dylan Cloutier was built like a meatloaf and bald as a bowling ball, which he made up for with a meticulously groomed, luxurious handlebar moustache whose tips extended well beyond the circumference of his wide face. As Gerald Drover expected, he and his fellow Saskatchewan Roughriders, likely unprepared and uncomfortable with the sky-high emotions the vigil for their lost teammate had elicited in the crowd, had taken to masking their own inner feelings with alcohol and perhaps a bit more. The men weren't falling down drunk or acting at all rowdy, but they were definitely feeling no pain, emotional or otherwise.

After being re-introduced by Drover, Cloutier readily agreed to speak with Merry off to one side of the tent where it was a little quieter.

"Thanks for being here for Dusty," the man blew the words in her face along with a significant spray of yeasty hops. He also wore a strong Tom Ford scent that Merry recognized and liked.

"I know it must be a difficult night for all of you. How nice to see so many people here. It almost feels like the whole city showed up. It must feel good to be part of a team everyone loves."

"Not everyone," he said jokingly, "there are a few fans out there who think we can do better on the field than we are this year, but we do our best. Especially Dusty. He never let us down, even on the toughest days. We'll really miss him."

As far as she knew, only his teammates referred to Dustin as Dusty. "Were you two close?"

"Sure," he said, his eyes a little less glossy.

"A lot of people here tonight seem to be having a hard time believing Dustin would commit suicide." She hadn't actually talked to "A lot of people here tonight" but he didn't need to know that. "What do you think?"

The glow faded from the footballer's face and Merry thought she detected a definite droop in his moustache. "It doesn't make sense, does it?"

Merry's head moved up and down but she said nothing.

"I don't know. When I was growing up I knew this kid who seemed like he had everything going for him and then one day he found his dad's gun and shot himself dead. I just couldn't get my head around it. Nobody could. You never know what's going on with people, I suppose."

"Do you think Dustin had something going on with him?"

"I don't know. He mostly kept to himself, y'know? Might be the quarterback thing, thinking he can't get too close with us, personally, I mean. Some of the guys thought it was because he was gay or maybe he had a secret girlfriend he didn't want anyone to know about."

Again with the secret girlfriend. "Why did they think that?"

He tried for a rascally laugh. "Most of the guys are young, good-looking, built, and single. We go out and there's always girls around. Some of the guys really get into that. Not Dusty. He didn't come out with us too often, but when he did he was pretty quiet, went home early." Cloutier swigged his beer. "Can I get you one of these?"

"Thanks, I'm good."

"Me, I don't think it was the gay thing. I mean it's okay if he was, but I'm pretty sure it was about a woman."

"Someone in his past?" Was the football player talking about the same woman Dustin's sister told her about earlier in the day?

"I don't think she was in his past. I think she was someone he wanted to keep quiet about."

"Why would he want to do that?"

"Why do you think?"

Merry shifted her shoulders to indicate she had no idea.

What Dylan Cloutier said next made the hair on her arms stand straight up.

CHAPTER 17

Doreen was waiting patiently for Merry beneath the railroad bridge that separated downtown Livingsky from Alphabet City where Redberry Road East (the right side of the tracks) meets Redberry Road West (the wrong side of the tracks). Redberry Road, one of the longest streets in the city, ran alongside the South Saskatchewan River as it sliced through Livingsky, east to west. The first several blocks of Redberry East belonged to the proposed Riverside Plaza site and the Truemont Hotel, the properties fronted by a long, narrow expanse of public park which was the site of Dustin Thomson's vigil. The last couple of blocks were poorly lit and Merry found herself quickening her step. The wrong side of the tracks was labelled that for a reason and she wasn't in the mood to tangle with hooligans.

She spotted the headlights sooner than she normally would have only because she was being extra vigilant. They were creeping up behind her much slower than the posted speed limit. By the time she'd left the vigil the speeches by various politicians, friends, and representatives of the Roughrider club were done and the large assembly was beginning to thin out, so it didn't seem likely the vehicle's driver would be someone searching for a parking place. It was getting late, so it was possible they were someone who fit the other demographic of people who visited the park after dark; the ones looking for drugs, companionship or both.

For the second time in as many days, Merry withdrew her car keys in preparation for a quick getaway.

Glancing over her shoulder she could see the car was getting closer.

Shit. This better not be Robby McAllister playing Sir Galahad again.

Three quarters of a block to go.

The sounds of rubber on pavement and purring engine were getting louder.

Merry's heart-beat quickened. Unless she broke into a full run the car was going to overtake her before she reached Doreen. If she ran and it turned out to be nothing she'd feel a fool. If she didn't run and it turned out to be something, well, that might not turn out too well for her. The vigil had been a sea of people, where were they now? There was safety in numbers. Was she the only one who'd settled for a crap parking spot under the railway bridge?

She looked over her shoulder again. Too late. The car had picked up speed and was almost alongside her.

Shit shit shit.

Looking straight ahead, keys gripped in her palm with the sharp ends pointing out between white-knuckled fingers, Merry stayed the course but did not increase her pace.

The car was right there. Next to her. Donning her best don't-fuck-with-me look she turned to face the vehicle.

It passed by.

"Thank you, thank you, thank you," Merry whispered under her breath to no one in particular.

Her gratitude was premature.

The bright red of brake lights pierced the night like bloodspots.

Stopping in her tracks, Merry assessed her options. The car had stopped almost directly next to Doreen, so that was out. If she turned and ran the opposite direction it would take the car a while to make a U-turn to follow. Staying put and finding out what the hell this was about was appealing to her naturally curious detective's nature but probably not the wisest move. The vehicle was a black Range Rover. Nice. Expensive. Unless they'd stolen the vehicle these weren't naughty kids on a joyride deciding to play scare-games or low-end thugs looking for trouble. High-end thugs or gangsters could afford this car, but why would they be interested in her? Had she inadvertently pissed someone off without knowing it? Did this have something to do with her investigation into Thomson's death? If it did, that was another strong argument for staying put versus making a run for it.

In the end, the decision was easy.

"Ms. Bell." The two words, spoken in a firm, confident voice originated from inside the car, the dark hole behind the back seat window which had silently slid down. It was a voice Merry recognized because she'd just heard it in Riverside Park.

Mayor Carol Durabont had come for her.

Merry first met Carol Durabont at the annual Mayor's gala not long after she arrived in Livingsky. She'd thought the invitation to the event was due to her tenancy at 222 Craving Lane, but the truth turned out to be something much more complex. Carol Durabont was nearing the end of her first four-year term as mayor of Livingsky. She'd handily beat out a three-term incumbent on the strength of her campaign slogan: "A New City for a New Millennium," promulgating the idea that outdated practices by city administrators going back to the turn of the century had kept Livingsky from living up to its full potential. She promised a growing base of change-minded young voters that she would "slash and burn" Livingsky's reputation as a sleepy prairie town and pledged growth and renaissance through increased immigration, more tourism, and an aggressive revitalization of downtown. At forty-three she was the city's youngest mayor and the first woman to hold the post and over the past three-plus years had proven she wasn't afraid to make tough decisions.

At the gala Durabont and her ever-present lieutenant Mackenzie Blister expressed special interest in Merry, and particularly her talents as a private detective. What Merry did not know was that the interest was more about their (accurate) belief that she'd been poking around in their business, business that could not withstand a great deal of poking. What Merry also did not know at the time was that the man with whom she'd recently been engaging in mostly harmless flirtation was the mayor's husband. When all was said and done, and Merry's investigation complete, Blister took the fall for all the dubious dealings, most of which Merry suspected had been at the behest of Durabont. Her husband Peter retreated within the shell of whatever their marriage really was, and Durabont herself came out smelling like a rose.

"Ms. Bell, may I have a word?" the voice within the gleaming black Range Rover asked.

Merry stepped closer to the spotless vehicle and idly wondered how Durabont managed to keep it so clean. She probably had minions for that, she guessed, like the nameless faceless, silent figure who sat behind the steering wheel. Near enough to see inside, Merry beheld the mayor's face for the first time. The woman hadn't even bothered to lean forward in her seat.

"Were you following me?"

She tittered. "Of course not. We were on the way home from the vigil and I spotted you."

Peering deeper into the car Merry noted that Peter was not with his wife. He'd been at the vigil too, so why wouldn't they go home in the same vehicle? It probably meant nothing, but Merry took a little joy in the fact.

"I've been wanting to speak with you, so I asked my driver to stop. It was a last-minute thing. I hope we didn't alarm you."

Sheesh. It's nighttime. Creepy car. Stranger danger. Why would I be alarmed? "Not at all. I was enjoying my walk. Beautiful evening out."

Durabont pursed her lips, either stifling a smile or unwise retort.

The Range Rover's heavy door swung open. "Why don't you come in and we can have a chat?"

Oh yeah, stepping into a stranger's vehicle late at night always turned out really good. "It's so nice out," Merry replied, "why don't we walk and talk?"

After several seconds of silence, Carol Durabont's leg slipped out of the vehicle, soon followed by the rest of her. Even in this circumstance Durabont exuded grace, style and an undeniable sexiness. She wore an expertly tailored, cinnamon-coloured business suit that showed just the right amount of shapeliness and said: I'm a fit, attractive, young woman but also a serious professional with work to do. Merry was surprised to find the mayor a little taller than she was, then noticed the heels compared to her own flats.

Giving Merry a curt nod, Durabont stuck her head into the vehicle and had a short discussion with the driver before closing the door.

"Which way?" Durabont asked, looking not particularly pleased to have not gotten her own way.

Merry watched as the large black SUV moved away and slid into a nearby parking spot. She motioned to the sidewalk which continued beneath the bridge alongside Redberry Road West and into Alphabet City.

"Is it safe this time of night?"

Durabont had disarmed Merry with her late-night pursuit and mysterious request for an audience, so Merry felt it only fair she do the same in return. "I'm sure your driver will keep a close eye on us." She turned and started walking down the sidewalk without looking back to see if the mayor was following, sure she would be.

"You're right," Durabont commented after a short silence of not-quite-companionable walking, "it is a beautiful night."

Merry mumbled agreement. She wanted to like Carol Durabont. The woman was impressive. As the youngest and first female mayor of Livingsky she was certainly a trailblazer and role model for young girls interested in politics. When they first met at the Mayor's Gala, before the mess they found themselves mired in and probably blamed each other for, they'd had a moment, a wordless communion. They were two women who were strong, powerful and confident, both taller than most other women and some of the men around them, and because it was a gala, both dressed well. They revelled in being who they were and their shared experience. In another world they'd have bonded, maybe become friends, but that was not to be.

"You said you wanted to speak with me?" Merry pushed the conversation, ready to know where this was going.

"Are you sleeping with my husband, Ms. Bell?"

Merry jerked to a full stop. That was not at all what she was expecting to come out of the mayor's mouth.

Durabont stopped as well, turning on the spot to look directly at Merry but saying nothing more, her face revealing little other than what might be seen as idle curiosity.

"Why would you ask me that?" Merry couldn't believe Peter would tell his wife anything about their interactions or what he may or may not have been feeling at the time. They'd only been in each other's company a handful of times. A couple of those times involved innocent flirtation, another involved men with bats, and their last a fleet of Livingsky police officers. Perhaps she'd become aware of it another way. It would not be entirely surprising to learn that Durabont and/or Mac Blister had had her under surveillance.

"You do know my husband, don't you, Merry? I believe we agreed to call each other by our first names the last time we met?"

Merry didn't recall such an agreement, but she certainly wasn't planning on addressing the woman as Her Worship or whatever you were supposed to call a sitting mayor. "We have met, yes."

"How would you categorize those meetings? Were they social? Professional?"

Let's see, Merry thought to herself, one was a meet-cute and another was a violent confrontation with hoodlums. Probably not the best answer. "I'm sorry, you have me at a disadvantage here. Has Peter said something to you about our rela…how we know one another?"

"Have you been married, Merry? Or in a long-term relationship?"

At almost thirty, Merry found herself uneasy admitting the truth. "No."

"Oh. Well, if you had, you'd know that a woman knows things about her partner, especially if that partner is a man, no words necessary. I saw something change in Peter after he met you."

Ah ha! Ever since her first case uncovered unscrupulous goings-on involving the embattled Riverside Plaza development spearheaded by Durabont, Merry had wondered if the resolution which involved Mac Blister being unceremoniously dumped by the administration had in part been a result of Peter giving his wife an ultimatum based on what Merry's investigation had revealed. Now she knew. Mayor Carol Durabont had no reason to even suspect Merry had been in the know unless Peter had told her so.

"Why would you think those changes in your husband had anything to do with me?"

Durabont's pretty face froze into a much-less pretty mask. After a quick gathering of her wits the expert politician did what politicians do best, she skirted the question by switching directions. "You don't trust me very much, do you, Merry?"

"I don't know you."

"I'm the mayor of this city. I would certainly hope that counts for something."

"As you know, I haven't lived here very long."

"I suppose that's a good point. Maybe given time, you'll come to change your mind."

"I noticed the cranes are back at work on Riverside Plaza."

"Yes, they are." The mayor smiled, obviously very pleased with the matter. "Things have a way of working out in the end, if you're willing to work with the right people."

Merry wondered what the other woman meant by that. Was it a dig at her departed Chief of Staff, Mac Blister, was she slyly suggesting she and Merry could reach détente as long as they were each willing to look the other way, or had the savvy politician found new devious ways to get what she wanted by partnering with a fresh slate of collaborators? In the end, it didn't matter. Durabont was an elected official and it was ultimately up to the citizens of Livingsky to determine whether or not she was doing a good job, hopefully without bulldozing whoever stood in her way. Merry planned to stay out of that bulldozer's way, at least for as long as she remained in Livingsky.

"I think we're done here. Thank you for the talk." With that the mayor turned heel and casually strode to the waiting Range Rover as if she'd just finished a friendly visit with a girlfriend.

"I never answered your question," Merry called after her.

Durabont stopped, swivelling about to look at Merry over the expanse that now separated them.

"The answer is no. I am not sleeping with your husband."

Even in the dim lighting Merry could see the woman's nostrils flare then relax. What she couldn't know was whether it meant the woman believed her or never would.

"I suppose," Durabont began as she slowly turned away, "we'll just have to learn to trust one another."

CHAPTER 18

Looking in the mirror was never easy for Merry. Starting from when she was a child, she struggled to understand the reflection she found there and why it insistently displayed a body that wasn't hers. As a teenager she watched in revulsion as puberty revealed horrors instead of the hoped for boobs and hips. Then as a transitioning woman she strained to reconcile the evolving image with decades of want and expectation. Often unable to, she made up for imagined deficiencies with clownish makeup and tight clothing. This morning's less than alluring visage had nothing to do with identity however, and everything to do with ruthless insomnia that plagued her for hours as she attempted to process everything she'd learned the previous evening at Dustin Thomson's vigil. Thanks to Brenda Brown, Merry had recently learned the basics of making up her face in a way that was less gawdy and more natural than her previous go-to; highlighting her best features which, Brenda graciously assured her, she had plenty of. Unfortunately, none of Brenda's tips seemed to be working this Wednesday morning, no amount of concealer or colour correction cosmetics could hide the dark circles and worry lines.

Despite its small size and the mostly useless antechamber that took up a third of the square footage, Merry had grown fond of her office at 222 Craving Lane. It was comfortable without being too homey, it was professional but not austere, and the view outside its sole window was disarmingly appealing: a vividly colourful wall of graffiti compliments of the building next door. The official home of

LSI would forever hold a special place in Merry's heart for being her first place of business as a solo private detective. Today that private detective was very tired and very conflicted.

Settled behind her desk, Merry opened the Word document where she'd been recording notes on her current case (if she could still call it a case when her client had disappeared). She began typing in the pertinent details of Thomson's vigil only stopping when she got to the bit that happened at the end, her conversation with Dustin's teammate Dylan Cloutier. When she'd pushed him about the possibility of Dustin having a secret lover, he admitted that one night after having his lips loosened by an extra shot or two of Patrón, Dusty (as he liked to call him), who typically withheld details about his private life, confided in him. Cloutier didn't think the disclosure amounted to much, but Merry certainly did. Dustin drunkenly confessed to an on-again-off-again, sometimes tortuous affair with a woman whose name he wouldn't divulge. He was in love, he'd claimed, but the woman refused to commit.

Cloutier goaded his friend to tell him more. All Thomson would say—and this was where Merry's mind detonated—was that the girl was perfect for him because they shared similar backgrounds, having both been brought up on the reserve and that her job, like his, was in the public eye and kept her very busy. Cloutier couldn't quite remember which it was but felt confident Thomson had suggested the mystery woman was either a fireman or a cop.

Merry typed the words then stared at them. Fireman. Cop. Cop. COP.

How many Indigenous, female, age-appropriate cops could there be in Livingsky?

Was Detective Sergeant Veronica Greyeyes Dustin Thomson's lover? Could it be? Is that why she was at the vigil? Crying. Was she upset because a man she loved had just died? Or was it something more complicated, more sinister? Had Dustin threatened to tell Veronica's husband about their affair? Did she respond by pushing him off Sweetgrass Bridge? Or had Thomson, endlessly spurned by Greyeyes and heartbroken, leapt to his death in the throes of a hopeless depression?

After palming her forehead with a couple of thuds meant to dislodge the insidious theories that had kept her tossing and turning in her Junk House bed the previous night, Merry opened a browser on her computer. She knew the only way to excise the burning questions in her head was to start finding answers. In short order she located the LPS website. There were suitably benign biographies for the head of the service, Police Chief Jay Cuthbert, and two deputy chiefs, Deputy Chief Ron Day (Operations) and Deputy Chief Natalie Bilinski, but no mention of other LPS members. Several minutes later, after digging in places most members of the public didn't know about, Merry was reviewing a list of the names and ranks for the 473 regular members, 61 special constables and 127 civilians who currently worked for LPS. She repeated the process with the Livingsky Fire Service. Cross-referencing potential candidates to google searches, database dumps and social media accounts, there were only three, including Veronica Greyeyes, who fit the bill of an Indigenous, female, age-appropriate, sworn (non-civilian) members. Merry grumbled as she thought about what that said about the recruiting and promoting of women and Indigenous people within the LPS and LFS.

Pushing back from the desk and getting up, Merry turned, crossed her arms and leaned against the window frame, trying to organize her thoughts by focusing on the neighbouring building's mesmerizing graffiti wall. It was a marvel how the artist—or had there been more than one?— managed to cover the entire side of a three-storey building. Had they snuck in scaffolding under the cover of night, or was this actually a piece of public art commissioned by the building's owner?

Graffiti used to be an exclusively derogatory term, referring to scrawls on public property or train cars usually done without permission, sometimes political, sometimes threatening, sometimes just for the fun of it. Over the decades certain graffiti artists and their fans reclaimed the word as a bona fide style of artistic expression. Is that what she was looking at? Did her little office on Craving

Lane offer her a front row seat to an exclusive art show? Well, exclusive for her and all the other tenants of the building and whoever happened to be traipsing down this particular back alley. Was this work of graffiti art at risk for being defaced…by graffiti? Merry's eyes roamed the slashes and jabs of bright colours and stylized symbols that might as well be hieroglyphics. Was it all meant to be there or was some of it graffiti (the bad kind) on graffiti (the good kind)? Moving her attention to the back alley itself she began to search the space for something specific. And there they were. Perched at each end of the alley was a camera, high enough so as not to be reachable by anyone without a ladder, but visible enough to act as a deterrent for anyone thinking of defiling the wall. Merry turned, slammed down the lid of her laptop and dashed out of her office.

At the front entrance of 222 Craving Lane Merry spotted what she hoped would be there. From there she made her way directly to the offices of Smallinsky & Co. which, other than the common areas, took up the entire main floor of the building. It was a lot of square footage especially since there was no "& Co.", only Smallinsky. Then again, Alvin Smallinsky owned 222 Craving Lane so he could take up as much space as he wanted. Merry knocked on the door. Hoping it was one of those knock and walk in kind of offices, she did just that, finding herself in a large reception area nearly as lavishly appointed as the much larger accounting firm of Sage, Cope, Jaspar & Novakoski. Unlike Sage, Cope, Jaspar & Novakoski, instead of a strangely compelling and freakily prescient AI receptionist presiding over the space, a sign requested she push a buzzer, but only if she had an appointment. Merry pushed the buzzer.

—

Alvin Smallinsky was a physically unremarkable man who looked like a young Warren Buffet and carried himself with the swag of Elon Musk. To some people he was easy to overlook, but they did so at their own risk.

"Merry, did we have an appointment this morning?" Smallinsky asked, stepping into the reception area from behind a set of double doors each emblazoned with a bronze plate inscribed with: The Offices of 222 Craving Lane CEO Alvin Smallinsky, CPA, 2007 Small Businessman of the Year Nominee.

"I'm sorry, I don't have an appointment. I hope I'm not interrupting anything."

"Of course you are," he huffed, not entirely unkindly, "which is why I recommend people make appointments. Is this something important? As you know, I am always available to speak with a tenant on serious matters."

As was his habit whenever he came into contact with one of his renters, Smallinsky made a speedy, not entirely concealed assessment of the general dress and comportment of his newest third floor tenant. In the short time he'd known Merry Bell, he found her to be an enigma. On the one hand, had he been aware of her appearance before offering her a rental contract, he might have thought twice about doing so. He personally believed that requesting photographs of potential renters was an excellent idea, but his attorney advised him otherwise. The hesitance would have had nothing to do with gender, age, race or anything like that, but rather solely with professional appearance.

After allocating significant funds to re-purpose what was once a decrepit, decades-old private residence into a sought-after professional services hub, Smallinsky's highest hopes for 222 Craving Lane was that each office space would be inhabited by the cream of the crop of Livingsky's professionals, movers and shakers like him. Brenda Brown of Designs by Brenda was a fine example. She never failed to comport herself in a professional manner and looked every inch the successful businessperson, regardless of how successful Designs by Brenda really was. Regrettably, due to economic pressures, irritatingly high vacancy rates, and a robust inventory of premium office spaces, Alvin was forced to adjust his expectations.

The first time he laid eyes on the private investigator, his hopes of a sharply clad, female James Bond type were quickly dashed. Instead, the woman looked like she was dressed to man the kissing booth at a fairground. *Do they still have those?* This was definitely not the Smallinsky/Craving Lane standard he was after. On the other hand, on a subsequent day, Merry Bell showed up looking like an entirely different woman. The clothes weren't expensive, surely, and perhaps not even new, but they fit rather well and made her look... respectable, as did the toned-down makeup and hairstyle. A few days later, she looked different again, this time an unusual blend of roadshow carnie and TV lawyer. He began to wonder if these wide variations of looks were all part of her role as a P.I. Were these disguises? Smallinsky wasn't sure, but he knew enough given the current environment of #MeToo and whatnot, that he most definitely couldn't ask. And here she was today, looking as if she'd slept in her car. And without an appointment to boot.

"Well, yes, this is rather serious," Merry told him. "I'm on a case and I need your help."

Smallinsky brightened. This was more like it. He could almost forgive the no-appointment thing (if not the messy hair). "Of course, Merry, I'd be happy to assist you on your case. Is this a forensics accounting type of situation we're talking about?" One of his favourite movies was *The Accountant* starring Ben Affleck. Could this be the start of something like that?

"Not exactly. A client who hired me has suddenly gone missing..."

"Oh dear, do you suspect foul play?" What sort of dark, potentially dangerous escapade was he about to be pulled into? How thrilling.

"Uh, no, nothing like that, at least I don't think so. You see I have reason to suspect that she was not who she claimed to be. If I had a photograph of her it would make it much easier for me to identify her."

"Mm-hmm, mm-hmm, I see. You think I might be able to photograph her? I do consider myself a bit of a photographer, amateur of course, but I did hold the position of interim president with the Livingsky Camera Club for several weeks."

"I'll keep that in mind, but that's not quite what I need at the moment. I've noticed that our...your building has a RING security system installed at the front entrance. I know those systems take video of anyone entering and leaving the building." She gave Smallinsky the date and time of Ruth-Anne Delorme's visit. "It would really help if I could see the footage and get a screen grab."

Coming to fully understand the breadth and depth of what Bell was asking of him, and how little she really wanted from him as a professional accountant or photographer, Smallinsky stepped back as he considered a reaction bordering on aghast. "I'm afraid, Ms. Bell, that I will not be able to meet your request. You are asking me to hand over proprietary information which contravenes the strict privacy policies we have in place here at 222 Craving Lane. As I'm sure you can appreciate, these policies protect you as well as your clients, not to mention my clients and the clients of all 222 Craving Lane tenants."

Merry did her best for the next few minutes to convince Smallinsky to change his mind but to no avail. The 222 Craving Lane privacy policies were sacrosanct. And when she was gone, Smallinsky thought to himself, he might even write them down somewhere.

—

Two hours later, while deep within the virtual bowels of her computer searching for the fake Ruth-Anne Delorme's real identity, Merry heard a musical "Yoo Hoo!" at the door.

Ah geez. Designs by Brenda.

"I hope you don't mind the intrusion, Merry," Brenda chirped. She was wearing a Mary-Kay-pink dress that fit her figure like Jell-O fits a mold and nude-coloured heels that were sensible yet sexy. Merry took note. "May I come in?" She was already in.

Merry did need a break. Her mind was clearer than it had been earlier in the day, but hours of online investigation took its toll especially when none of her tricks of the trade were producing results. "Sure, why not?"

Brenda grinned. She sat in the chair in front of Merry's desk and said, "So, I understand you and Alvin had a bit of a dust-up this morning?"

Dust-up? "I don't know if I'd call it that exactly."

"You know what I mean. Alvin can be a stick in the mud and a real stickler for rules, but he carries a great deal of weight on his shoulders as a successful businessman and the owner of this building. Can you imagine the tenant issues he has to deal with every day? Monty Churchill from the second floor came in wearing shorts the other day! Just because it was thirty degrees out he thought it would be okay. Alvin was fit to be tied."

"Tsk, tsk," was the best Merry could muster.

"I know you get it. Anyhoo, I thought I'd bring you this." She leaned forward and slipped a paper across the desk.

Merry studied the paper then looked up at the other woman in astonishment. "How did you get this?" It was exactly what she'd hoped to get from Smallinsky, a screen shot of faux Ruth-Anne Delorme entering 222 Craving Lane taken from the RING security video. "How did you even know I wanted it?" A worrisome thought crept into her mind: did Designs by Brenda have everyone's office bugged?

Brenda winked. "I've got my ways."

"Can you teach me?"

"Maybe. Some day."

"Brenda, thank you. This will really help me out and save me a lot of extra work. I owe you one."

Without hesitation she calmly replied, "Yes, you do."

Why didn't I see this coming?

"I also wanted to thank you…"

"Oh?" *Danger Will Robinson.*

"…and tell you how much Roger enjoyed working with you on that big case you had a while ago." Then she added as if it was an afterthought: "You haven't called on him again?"

Brenda was smiling sweetly but Merry knew the woman wanted an answer or a promise, nothing else would do. "Well, to be honest, Brenda, LSI is not as successful as Designs by Brenda. Things have been a little quiet. I'm just getting started and it's taking a little longer to get clients through the door than I'd hoped. So, I really haven't had anything for Roger to help me with." She hoped tossing a little bit of sugar in with the truth and white lie would make it easier for Brenda to swallow the mixture.

Nope. Brenda Brown was not so easily assuaged. "I'm sure things will pick up real soon," she said with a syrupy voice while pointedly gazing at the photograph of Ruth-Anne, then back at Merry.

"This? Oh well…" *Gee! Zus! This woman!*

"You must be working on something new? Isn't that exciting? A missing person case maybe? That's usually why a detective would need someone's photograph, isn't it? So they can show it around to people, see if anyone knows the person or has seen them around or whatever?"

"Mm-hmm."

"You know, this just came to me, but I think Roger would be really good at that sort of thing, don't you? He has this way about him, everyone likes him right away. He's always chatting people up, and they tell him things they don't tell their best friends." She snickered. "To be honest, it drives me a little batty sometimes."

Merry stared at Brenda for a count of five. Then, against what she knew might be her better judgement, she thought: *what the heck?* When Roger first suggested the P.I. intern thing, he'd made the argument that since Merry had been away from Livingsky for so long he'd be of great use to her because of the strong contacts he'd cultivated in the community through his interest in true crime and the podcast. "You're right," Merry said. "Tell you what. I do need to identify the woman in this picture. If Roger wants to show it to some people, he can go for it."

Brenda jumped to her feet, clapping her perfectly manicured hands together with delight. "What a wonderful idea! Merry, thank you! He'll be thrilled. I'm going to tell him all about it as soon as he calls. He usually calls or texts in between jobs, just to say hi, isn't that the cutest?"

Merry decided not to comment on the electrician's cuteness.

Brenda's evident delight in arranging (manipulating?) something she knew her husband would love was off-putting but also rather touching. She had to hand it to the Browns, by all appearances they were an undeniably devoted couple. Picking up the photo Brenda had brought her, she stood up and gently shepherded Brenda through the office door and anteroom into the hallway. "I'll just make a copy of this downstairs and bring it to you."

"No need," Brenda sung as she clip-clopped merrily on her way, "I already made one."

CHAPTER 19

Merry was bagged. She'd spent several hours showing the photograph of the woman who'd claimed to be Ruth-Anne Delorme around the youth centre, the Roughrider's club house, she'd even sent copies to Calvin Wochiewski, Robby McAllister and Dustin's sister Miranda, and still she struck out. It was as if her client—former client? fake client?—didn't exist. It was time to go home. She slid through a DQ drive-thru for a burger and fries then headed for the Junk House. The night air was hot and still and even with all of Doreen's windows rolled down she could barely work up a whiff of a breeze inside the car. It was after 8:00 p.m. but the sun was intent on blazing bright as noonday. At least she didn't have to worry about her food getting cold.

Turning the corner onto her street, Merry immediately slammed her foot on the brake pedal. Someone was trying to get into the Junk House compound. The former scrap metal yard was surrounded by chain link fence behind a row of unruly bushes that kept it pretty much hidden from view from anyone outside the fence. There was only one way in via a gate that Merry, by order of her landlord Gerald Drover, kept locked at all times. At the moment it appeared that two shifty characters were attempting to bypass that safety measure.

Alphabet City was the kind of place where the later in the day it became and the darker it got the less advisable it was for anyone who didn't belong there to roam. At first, this attribute of the neighbourhood convinced Merry this was not a place she wanted to live. Eventually its other charms, namely it being the only place—with running water and a solid roof—in all of Livingsky that she could afford, changed her mind. In time she came to understand that what kept people away from Alphabet City provided her a certain level of desirable security.

Until now.

Moving at a crawl, Merry willed Doreen's tires into silence as they slowly rolled over the crumbling surface of the half-paved road. She narrowed her eyes to get a better look at the pair fiddling with her gate. One was brandishing something she couldn't make out. Bolt-cutters? Some kind of weapon? As she got closer, she could see that one was a man, the other a woman. The item in the man's hand was too short for a baseball bat. A hammer maybe? Closer. Closer. Closer. It's a—it's a—it's a bottle of wine? And was the woman carrying a food platter?

Merry did a quick scan of the other side of the street and found the most unusual thing of all: a pearl grey BMW 3 Series. No BMW owner in their right mind came to Alphabet City at night. Except…

The Browns.

Several questions popped into Merry's head as Doreen inched toward the couple standing in front of the gate, looking like a pair of confused angels who'd somehow found themselves at the not-so-pearly gates of hell. *What the hell are they doing here? How did they find out where I live? How daft or naïve or both is Brenda Brown to bring her fancy wheels into this neighbourhood?*

Merry tooted her horn to get their attention. The two made like a pair of Mexican jumping beans. To be fair, Merry thought as she stifled a laugh, Doreen's horn was not known for its delicacy.

Stepping out of the car, Merry registered the relieved faces as the Browns recognized her and realized they were not about to be gang-banged.

"Oh Merry, thank god it's you!" Brenda exclaimed, running up to Merry and looking like she might hug her. "How on earth did you find us in this, this, this place?"

Merry stepped back. "Uh, I think the better question is how did you find me?"

Brenda's wide-eyed gaze moved from Merry to her husband then the padlocked gate then back to Merry. "You mean this isn't some kind of crazy mix-up? You actually live here?"

"Mm-hmm."

"Like right here? On this street? In this place? It looks like a minimum-security prison, not a home. And where is the house? The yard?"

Merry nodded at the gate. "Behind there."

"Oh Merry!" Brenda took a step closer and laid a trembling hand on her arm. "You poor, poor dear. You told me business was slow, but I had no idea how bad things really are. How stupid of me to have missed this." She looked at her husband as if communicating her plan telepathically, then said: "This is what we're going to do. You're going to pack up your things…you do have things, don't you?…of course you do… you're going to pack them up right now and you're going to come home with us. We'll figure this out together."

Likely having noticed the growing head of steam atop Merry's head, Roger spoke up. "Brenda, I'm sure Merry doesn't need our help. There are actually some very nice homes in this part of town. I re-wired a garage just a few blocks from here last month."

"How did you find…" Merry stopped there. Both Brenda and Roger had proved in the past that they "had their ways." It was useless to ask what those were, they were here now. She approached the gate and unlocked it. "Follow my car inside. There's plenty of space to park."

A couple of minutes later, Merry was reluctantly inviting the Brown's inside the Junk House, inwardly bemoaning the fact that her DQ would have to wait.

Once inside, Roger handed her a bottle of sparkling wine and Brenda offered up an impressive charcuterie platter under Saran wrap.

"It's unacceptable that you've been in Livingsky for, what has it been now, six months? And we still haven't been to your home or brought over a housewarming gift," Brenda declared.

Merry could easily hear the unspoken subtext: *Because we haven't been invited.*

"When you couldn't make it to the pool party," Roger added, "we thought we'd surprise you with this. I hope you don't mind."

"Let's open this now," Merry said, brandishing the wine bottle as she headed into the kitchen(ish) area to find glasses.

The Browns followed. In the absence of an invitation to take a seat they hovered around the small kitchen table with its cheery tablecloth that matched the drapery on the picture window that overlooked the yard's dramatic scrap metal landscape. Brenda busied herself uncovering the charcuterie platter and laying out the pretty napkins and miniature forks and spoons she'd thoughtfully brought with it.

"Our gift is the charcuterie *and* all the accoutrements, including the charcuterie board," Brenda announced. "I hope you don't already have one. The board is hand-carved by a local artisan. The charcuterie is from that cute new place on Connecticut run by a lovely young couple who moved here from Minneapolis after Trump was elected. He's a butcher and she's a cheesemaker. Isn't that just perfect?"

"Mm-hmm," Merry murmured again as she popped the cork, laid out glasses and filled them to the brim.

"Isn't that adorable, mismatched glasses are so on trend right now. They look vintage, where did you find them?"

Merry was about to ingest a significant portion of her drink when Brenda stopped her. "We have to have a toast."

Everyone dutifully raised their glasses.

"To your new home, new office, and most importantly: new beginnings."

Merry couldn't decide whether the look in the other woman's eyes as they clinked glasses was sincerity or artifice. "Thank you. You shouldn't have done all of this." *Really.*

"This place," Brenda started as both Roger and Merry winced, "is really…something, isn't it? Whatever made you think to settle in this, this—this part of town?"

"Oh, you know, nostalgia mostly," Merry lied and sipped.

"That explains it. Your family lived here when you were growing up then?"

"This cheese is amazing," Roger interrupted, offering Merry a small shaving of Manchego at the end of a delicate two-tined fork meant especially for the purpose. "I think it's from Spain."

Merry gratefully accepted the cheese and the interruption. He was right. The cheese was amazing.

"You know," Brenda began, stepping away from the table to take in the rest of the modest space, "I could really work some magic in here. We could replace the lighting with these funky LED units I saw last week at that new design store downtown run by a really sweet young girl who just graduated from Sheridan College. Maybe a pair of over-the-top chandeliers there and there, then some wallpaper on that wall to draw attention away from, well, other things. You should just see the spectacular designs coming out of Venezuela these days. There's one in particular I'm thinking of that would look amazing, and of course hand-dyed cork flooring, maybe some slate, we'd have to change up the window treatment…oh, Merry, we could completely renovate your living experience." Twirling on her heels to face Roger and Merry she breathlessly awaited their response to her ideas.

Merry could not imagine Designs by Brenda let loose in the Junk House. Fortunately she had an easy out. "Sounds great but my budget is zero dollars."

"Oh," Brenda pouted, "that's certainly not ideal."

"Well," Merry offered. "I could double it. Could you work with that?"

"Weeeeeelllll, if we…" Brenda stopped talking. Breathed in. Breathed out. Then looking at her husband she said, "I thought we agreed you would tell me when I'm being too much."

In unison Merry and Roger crowed: "You're being too much."

They all laughed. It was not lost on Merry how good it felt, just to have a careless, easy laugh with…whatever these two were to her.

"It's hotter inside than out, there's no AC and all I have is a fan, so what do you say we take this party out back?" Merry suggested.

Brenda looked doubtful. "You mean in the…the…is it a landfill?"

Merry grinned as she realized she actually felt a tad offended on behalf of Gerald Drover. "It's a scrap metal yard, not a junk yard," she corrected, hearing Gerald's words in her voice.

"Oh. I see. Is that…different?"

Roger made the decision. "Sounds good to me, let's go."

Merry led the little band of guests out the front (and only) door and around to the back of the Junk House. With dusk approaching and timers set by Merry engaged, the sitting area was a-twinkle with fairy lights and the yard's Stonehengian scrap metal monoliths shone with otherworldly glow thanks to strategically placed spotlights. Gentle floral scents from blooming caragana and honeysuckle bushes mingled in the summertime air as hummingbirds and honeybees arrived for a late-night snack.

"Merry," Brenda had stopped dead in her tracks, "this is lovely."

Merry shrugged and invited the Browns to sit. "Roger, would you mind refilling our glasses?"

Brenda wandered into an area just beyond the sitting area. Merry watched her lean forward to inspect something. What was it now? Unsightly weeds? A bit of garbage blown in from the scrap heaps? Was she going to suggest a full yard-makeover next?

"Merry, have you seen this?"

With Roger too slow on the uptake, Merry refilled her own glass and, suspecting she'd be needing it, took a healthy slug before going over to where Brenda stood entranced by something on the ground.

"Seen what? I've only just started getting things cleaned up back here so…"

"This."

Brenda was pointing at a patch of freshly tilled dirt that Merry swore she'd never seen before. In the middle of the bed was a collection of newly planted geraniums in full bloom, dazzling red.

"What the…?"

"There's a card, like the kind you see on bouquets," Brenda pointed out.

"What the…?" Apparently the only two words Merry could manage.

"Wait!" This came from Roger who'd now joined them at the flower plot.

The women, startled, jerked about to look at him.

"What is it?" Brenda asked her husband.

"Suppose it's another one of those notes?"

"What the…?" Merry again.

"One of what notes?" Brenda asked.

Merry began to regain her senses. "You're thinking it might be another note like the ones slipped under my office door a while ago?"

Roger's eyes had grown wide. "Could be, right?"

"Why would you think such a thing?" Brenda exclaimed. "It's been months since that happened. This is different. It's a note with flowers for goodness sake. From someone special, maybe?"

"Only one way to find out," Merry said as she reached down and swooped up the card. She pulled the note from its little envelope.

"What does it say?" the Browns asked in unison.

Merry read the short note to herself, then whispered, "Damn, he's done it again."

"Who did what? Is everything okay?" Brenda wanted to know.

"It's nothing. The note is from someone wishing me a happy birthday." What she didn't tell them was that the someone was Gerald Drover. It read: "Happy birthday, Sweet Lips. Hope you like the flowers. From your favourite slum landlord." *How does he even know it's my birthday?* Once again the cuckoo bird of a man and his disarming thoughtfulness was making her brain hurt.

"What?" Brenda screamed. "It's your birthday? Today? Why didn't you tell me? I would have brought a cake and streamers and noisemakers and…"

"That might be why," Roger said dryly with an eye roll that somehow came off as adoration for his wife.

"I don't like a lot of fuss on my birthday. But since you brought the bubbly, I suppose it wouldn't hurt to say cheers to my thirtieth."

"Thirty!" Another exclamation from Brenda. "Thirty is a milestone, a big one, it deserves more than Prosecco. We would have brought Veuve Clicquot."

"Well then," Roger raised his glass, "here's to fake champagne!"

They clinked glasses and drank. The cool, crisp liquid went down easily on the hot summer evening. Merry thought the fake stuff wasn't so bad.

"Oh my god, I just thought of something," Brenda blurted out after they'd settled in the sitting area. "We barged in here unannounced when you probably have plans with…friends? Family?"

"It's fine. No plans."

Seeing his wife about to respond and guessing she was going to ask something too personal, Roger announced: "I have a birthday present for you."

"What? How? You didn't even know it was my birthday until thirty seconds ago."

"It was going to be a housewarming gift," he admitted, "but now it's a birthday gift."

Feeling a little flushed and atypically warm-hearted after two glasses of sparkling wine, Merry sat back in her seat and said, "Lay it on me." Brenda's implication (whether it was innocent or not was up for debate) was obvious: why wasn't she celebrating her thirtieth birthday with friends and family? It wasn't something Merry wanted to dwell on so she welcomed the distraction of whatever the electrician/podcaster/wannabe detective thought would pass muster as a birthday gift.

Brenda squealed. Obviously she was in on the surprise.

"I found Ruth-Anne Delorme."

Merry jerked to attention, placing her wine glass on a side table. "What? You found her? Where? How? When? Tell me everything."

Roger smiled with deep satisfaction. "Well, first off, her name is not Ruth-Anne Delorme, which you already knew. It's Delores Tanner. Now before you get excited, I haven't learned too much about her yet. I need to do more digging. I'm just getting started."

"What do you know so far?"

"She's a 911 operator with the LPS."

At the mention of the police, Merry's mind began to stir with possibilities.

"From her social media accounts I'm guessing Delores makes questionable choices when it comes to men, and I'm pretty sure she's got a gambling problem. That's it so far. But I promise..."

"Honey, you did so good!" Brenda cried. "Didn't I say so, Merry? Didn't I tell you he'd be good at this kind of thing?"

"Yes," Merry agreed, half distracted by her thoughts, "you did say that." Pulling herself back into the moment she added, "Roger, thank you. This is very helpful." She meant it.

Roger accepted the gratitude from Merry with a nod and reached over to squeeze Brenda's arm in appreciation for her exuberant support of his investigative abilities. She mouthed the words "You're brilliant" at him.

Hours later, the charcuterie platter ravaged to a few smears of brie and tapenade, a rind of gruyere, a single olive and nary a whiff of bresaola, the bottle of bubbly and a box of white wine seconded from the fridge both empty, Merry was opening the Junk House gate to let the Browns out. After clearing the passage, the car stopped and the driver's side window rolled down. Leaning in, Merry waved at Brenda who'd drunk a wee bit more than an equal share and was half-collapsed in the passenger seat. Knowing he had to drive, Roger had wisely abstained after the Prosecco was gone.

"Thank you," she said to the couple. "This turned out to be a much better thirtieth birthday than I expected." The sentiment surprised Merry, almost as much as the fact that the words were directed at sworn frenemy, Designs by Brenda, and a podcasting electrician determined to self-anoint himself her assistant. Could it be? Might the Browns be something more than that?

In a gesture Merry thought seemed overly formal after spending a boozy night together, Roger held out his hand. On the first night she'd met Roger Brown, he'd also shaken her hand, using the opportunity to surreptitiously slip a piece of paper into her palm. Tonight, he repeated the performance.

CHAPTER 20

Detective Sergeant Veronica Greyeyes opened the door to the interview room and saw a familiar sight: Merry Bell. Bell had been a guest of the LPS on several occasions earlier in the year when she was both a suspect in the murder of the physician who'd performed her gender affirming surgery and a pesky investigator looking into an arson case over which Greyeyes had jurisdiction. Now here she was again. Neither woman looked pleased about it.

"We have to stop meeting like this," Merry quipped as Greyeyes took her seat and spread out a collection of files and a laptop, mostly for intimidation purposes.

"I'd prefer that as well," Greyeyes bluntly agreed.

"I'm glad you called me in today, although I have no idea why you did. Your message was rather vague."

Greyeyes reminded herself that Bell was smart, wily, and she'd best keep on her toes.

"There's something I want to talk to you about as well," Merry said.

"Oh?"

"So why *did* you call me in today?"

"Let's talk about your thing first."

Merry shrugged. "Fine by me." She pulled the photograph of Ruth-Anne Delorme from her purse and slid it across the table toward the cop. "Do you know this woman?"

Veronica frowned and felt her temper flare. They called this an interrogation room, but no matter who sat on the other side of the table, *she* was the one who did the interrogating, not the other way around. This was, however, a delicate situation. Different rules might be in order. She glanced at the photograph and swore under her breath. She knew she shouldn't have been surprised; Bell had proven her sleuthing abilities during the Redberry Road arson case. The big question now was: how much did the P.I. really know?

Taking the lack of response as obfuscation, Merry added: "You should. She works for you."

"Oh?"

"When I met her, she told me her name was Ruth-Anne Delorme, a cousin to Dustin Thomson. She became my client."

"I see."

"Her real name is Delores Tanner. She's a 911 operator who works, I'm guessing, a couple of floors below where we are right now."

"Is that right?"

"Cut the bullshit, Veronica. I want to meet with her today. Can you make that happen?" Then as an afterthought: "Please."

"That won't be possible today."

Merry made moves to get up. "Fine. I'll go find her myself. I'm sure the 911 operator's office or whatever it's called can't be that hard to find." At the door she stopped and looked back at the cop. "My thing is done. Yours? Forget about it."

"Wait."

Greyeyes categorized Bell's look as smug. She hated smug.

Merry returned to her seat and sat down, awaiting the other shoe.

"Talking to Delores won't be necessary."

"So, you do know her?"

The police officer managed a grudging half-nod.

"Seeing as she was pretending to be my client, I should probably be the one who decides whether or not I need to talk to her."

Fuck. This wasn't how this was supposed to go.

"Delores wasn't your client."

"Excuse me?"

"I was."

Merry looked as if a fully loaded semi had just sped by her at two hundred kilometers an hour, grazing the tip of her nose.

"This will probably come as a surprise to you," Greyeyes uttered, burying her eyes inside one of the files. "This isn't how I typically do things. I shouldn't have involved you in this but, well, here we are."

"Here we are?" Merry cawed, incredulous. "Where are we? You're going to have to do better than that, Detective Sergeant. What the hell is going on here?"

"I…as I've already informed you, I am not and have never been directly involved in the Dustin Thomson case. But, well, I found myself having some…concerns about the direction in which the case was heading. I thought if someone outside the department could look into a few things, privately, discretely, I could satisfy my-self that all was as it should be."

"That's a lot of words that don't make a lot of sense."

"You were at the vigil. You saw it for yourself. The police and now the entire city are convinced Dustin committed suicide. I had reason to believe—and don't bother asking me why—that the de-partment's conclusion might be inaccurate. Because of that I felt it was my responsibility, as both an officer of the law and a member of this community, to do whatever I could to ensure that the truth, whatever it is, be brought to light."

"I don't understand," Merry said. "Why didn't you just go to whoever is in charge of the investigation, or your boss, and tell them about your concerns?"

Greyeyes hesitated before speaking. Bell deserved more than she'd normally be willing to share. "Things aren't that simple. It doesn't always work that way around here."

Merry began to ask a question then stopped herself. "You're probably going to tell me not to bother asking about that either, right?"

Greyeyes said nothing but the look in her eyes provided the an-swer.

"So, let's see if I can start piecing this together. You hired De-lores, told her to pretend to be Dustin Thomson's cousin, then asked her to hire me? Delores was more than willing to play your crazy game because she needed money to pay off gambling debts."

Greyeyes fumed. *How the hell had she figured all of that out so quickly?*

"Well, well, well, Detective Greyeyes, I have to say I'm impressed. Surprised but impressed. I didn't take you for the kind of cop who would stoop to something quite so exploitative. And, I must say, you really need to nominate that girl for an Oscar."

Not for the first time since all of this began, Greyeyes regretted her decision to involve Merry Bell. Extricating herself from the mess she'd created, especially now that she knew what she did, wasn't going to be easy. "None of that matters now. Turns out my concerns were unfounded."

Merry registered surprise. "What? Are you saying you believe Dustin Thomson committed suicide?"

Veronica felt her cheeks burn and hoped the other woman didn't notice. "That's correct. I jumped the gun. I should have waited for the investigation to be concluded. I should have trusted the process. I made a mistake." She hoped the mea culpa would be enough to throw Bell off the scent of what was really happening. "You're off the hook, Bell. Your *client* is releasing you. The case is over. If you email me a final billing, I'll make sure it gets paid immediately." Greyeyes worried the content and haste of her wrap-up speech would sound exactly like what it was: a furious sweeping of the matter under the rug.

"You may have fooled me with the fake cousin trick, but I met Dustin's sister—his *real* sister—Miranda Poile. She is convinced, and she convinced me, that Dustin could not have committed suicide. She talked to him the day before he died. He was in high spirits and excited about some big news he wanted to share with her."

"What big news?" This was something Greyeyes didn't know. She was not fond of not knowing things.

"I don't know. My point is that suicide just doesn't track, Veronica. I think your first instinct was right. Something else is going on here."

"You're forgetting about the poem, it clearly…"

"That's a load of crap and you know it. You don't believe that poem is a suicide note any more than I do. You pretty much said so yourself when you first told me about it. And now that the poem has gone public, its actual relevance has been wildly blown out of proportion by mental health awareness proponents desperate to have a national celebrity as a convenient poster child. I don't blame them, but that doesn't make it right. You know that, Veronica, I know you do."

Fuck, fuck, fuck. As right as Merry was, she could not allow the woman to continue down this path. "I *don't* know that, not for certain." She knew she had to throw Bell some kind of bone. "If this wasn't a suicide, then maybe it was an accident…"

Bell didn't let her finish. "There was nothing at the bridge to indicate an accident. Ruth-Anne—or should I say *you* via Delores via fake Ruth-Anne—told me Dustin was always extra careful around water because he was a poor swimmer. That fact was something you obviously knew and passed on to Delores?"

Stop, Bell, stop.

"Which means if this was an accident, it was because he was clumsy or wasn't being careful, which is very unlikely for a high-performance athlete like Dustin. And I assume since there's been no mention of it by police there were no drugs or alcohol found in his system?"

Greyeyes slowly shook her head.

"Another theory is that he jumped in the river to save somebody, then drowned because he couldn't swim. Yet Robby McAllister—he was one of the lovebirds canoodling near Sweetgrass Bridge that night, but you probably know that—heard what he called a non-urgent yelp, maybe two, coming from the bridge. What he didn't hear was screaming or thrashing in the water."

"That doesn't mean there wasn't screaming or thrashing in the water."

"True," Merry allowed. "But if that's what happened, where is the person or persons he was trying to save?"

"Merry, you're making this more complicated than it is."

"No, I'm not. The problem is that the police, for some reason, are making this simpler than it is. The facts are still in doubt, Veronica. You know as well as I do that until the facts are actually proven, we need to keep investigating, turning over rocks, exploring every possible scenario, including murder."

Damn it. She needed this to stop. "Murder? Who said anything about murder?"

"That's why you sent Delores to hire me, isn't it? You had doubts. You knew something felt off. You're a good cop. You know murder is a possibility. There's more to this story than we know."

"Merry, you need to…" Pleading.

"For instance, more than one source talked about a mysterious person Dustin Thomson was having a relationship with, someone who broke his heart. Who is she? And why wasn't Dustin's vehicle at the bridge? How did he get there?"

"Veronica, suicide, accident, murder, whichever it is, there are too many questions without answers. You already paid me to investigate, so if it's about the money, don't worry about that, the retainer will cover more of my time. I think…"

"Stop right there!" The ferocity of Greyeyes' words ricocheted about the room like an out-of-control pickleball.

Merry pushed back her chair and regarded the other woman as if she were suddenly being confronted by a hostile stranger.

"It doesn't matter what you think!" The words came out lined with crushed gravel. "I was your client and now I'm telling you to stop your investigation. I'm also a high-ranking member of the Livingsky Police Service and I'm telling you to stop your investigation. Do I make myself clear?"

Merry was not easily cowed. "No. You don't. Actually, I don't understand you at all. What happened to change your mind so drastically? What don't I know?"

"There is a very real difference between an active police investigation and a private investigation," Veronica said with something very close to a sneer on her face. "One is carried out for the good of the people, the other is carried out for profit. Your profit. Which do you think is more important?"

Merry recoiled. "That's unfair."

"You're new to Livingsky. In a very short period of time you've developed a reputation for sticking your nose where it doesn't belong. That won't end well for you, Merry."

"Is that a threat?"

"It's an observation."

"The only reason I stuck my nose where I did in the first place was because of you. You hired me. You believed there was something to be gained by having both a private and police investigation. You started this, Veronica, not me."

"That's true. Now I'm ending it."

"Of course you are."

"What do you mean by that?" Greyeyes wished she could take back the question as soon as it came out of her mouth. She was close to getting what she wanted but now she'd poked the bear.

"You may as well admit it."

"Admit what?"

"You're the mysterious woman who was having the affair with Dustin Thomson."

Veronica Greyeyes felt her throat being strangled by invisible hands.

"That's why you're so desperate to call me off. You're afraid I was going to learn of your extramarital affair. Well, hon, it's too late. I know."

Greyeyes lips were twitching but no sound came out.

"It's why you secretly hired me, isn't it? You were Dustin's lover. When he disappeared, you were frantic with worry. You probably heard some of your colleagues postulating suicide. You couldn't say or do anything because, well, no one knew about the two of you. Certainly not your husband. Or your fellow officers. You knew Dustin well enough to know he wouldn't have committed suicide, so when the cops seemed to be leaning that way even before they knew he was dead, you had to do something without revealing yourself. Enter the fake cousin to hire me to look into finding out the truth. That about right?"

As Merry Bell spouted her horrifyingly accurate theories, Veronica was mostly worried about what else the P.I. had uncovered. The only way to find out was to stop wasting time on denial or speculation. "It's true," Greyeyes blurted.

Merry swallowed hard, then said: "What part?"

"All of it. It was over a long time ago but yes, Dustin Thomson and I had an affair. That's why I hired Delores to hire you. You're right about everything. But now things are getting too close to home. I didn't think the whole thing through. I can't risk Bobby finding out about me and Dustin. I want you to stop, Merry. I—we—need to trust the police. If their investigation concludes that Dustin killed himself, I will believe it. If it was some kind of accident, I'll believe that. But it wasn't murder, Merry, I just know it wasn't. You said earlier that you believed I was a good cop. My instincts tell me there's nothing nefarious going on here."

For a long moment the two women stared at each other, guessing what the other was thinking.

"Or," Merry began, a hard look on her face, "maybe your affair reignited. Or maybe Dustin wanted you back and you refused. Maybe he was so heartbroken he threatened to make the affair public, not because he was an ass, but because he was so in love with you and thought it was the only way to get you back. You invited him to the bridge that night, maybe to talk things out, maybe for a tryst. You picked him up. He might have suspected things weren't going to go his way romantically, but he'd never expect what you were really planning to do. His guard would have been down. When the time was right, you pushed Dustin Thomson off Sweetgrass Bridge."

It took a moment for the air to return to her lungs but when it did Veronica shot back at Merry with rage burning in her eyes. "Don't be ridiculous. I've never taken you to be a fool, but if you really believe any of what you just said, then you're the biggest one I know."

Merry said nothing. Her right cheek twitched as if she'd just been slapped.

"You got me, alright? It's true I hired you under false pretenses. It's true I had an affair with Dustin Thomson. I was wrong. I admit it. But that's it. The rest of what happened is a sad fairy tale without a happily-ever-after ending. Now do the right thing and leave it alone. Leave Dustin in peace."

"I'm doing the right thing," Merry asserted, her voice firm. "I'm doing my job. And it's not done yet."

Veronica stood. Merry followed suit. The two women faced off against one another like roosters at a cock fight.

"You don't have a job to do anymore. I told you once, I'm telling you again," Veronica growled, "this case is over. Now get the hell out of my police station."

Breaking the standoff, Merry stepped aside and moved toward the door.

"One more thing," Greyeyes warned. "If I hear of you having anything more to do with Dustin's death, I will come for you. And I assure you, you will not like it."

CHAPTER 21

Pulling up to the Brown's house Thursday evening, Merry was still shaken from her meeting with Veronica Greyeyes. Neither woman had pulled any punches. They'd put everything on the table and by the time they were done it was a splintered mess. She'd accused Greyeyes of having an affair and murdering a Saskatchewan Roughriders quarterback. Greyeyes in turn buckled her at the knees with admissions, threats, and intimidation. As horrible as the interaction was, as nasty as Greyeyes had been, Merry couldn't help feeling there was much more going on in that room than met the eye. It was true she and the LPS detective had had a bumpy relationship, adversarial at times, but beneath it all Merry had sensed respect, comradeship, and the beginnings of what could possibly become a friendship. Until today. In the past when they'd come to verbal blows, despite conflicting perspectives, their goals always aligned: truth, understanding and justice. Today was something entirely different. Today it seemed as if Greyeyes was a caged animal, at first playing nice in the hopes of being let out, then upon realizing that wasn't going to happen, moving into attack mode, claws and teeth bared.

When she came across troubling situations like this one in the past, Merry would find her way into the office of her old boss, Nathan Sharpe. He'd pull out the bottle of scotch he always kept in the bottom drawer of his desk and they'd talk. She didn't know how he managed it, but every time she'd leave feeling better and with a plan on how to proceed with whatever problem she had. But Nathan was 1,700 kilometers away. She had no one. Nathan assured her he would always be on the other end of the phone line whenever she needed him, but it was a privilege she didn't want to abuse. Besides, she was a big girl now, ready to reclaim her confidence as a P.I.. LSI was her baby and it was time she figured things out for herself.

The previous evening when the Browns were leaving the Junk House after a surprisingly enjoyable evening of charcuterie and wine, Roger Brown had clandestinely slipped her a note. Again. What was up with this guy and his penchant for secret-note-passing? He'd obviously read too many crime noir novels. They both knew it was a futile act anyway. Whatever the secret was, he'd eventually tell Brenda; he always did. Irksome, but admirable.

The message Roger had slipped her was both surprising and worrisome. And verbose. In it Roger explained how he'd taken it upon himself as an LSI intern—which he was not!—to open an investigation into discovering the source of the two mysterious notes Merry had received soon after moving to Livingsky from Vancouver. He'd made a discovery and wanted to share it with her. He asked her to meet him at his home tonight while Brenda was away attending a St. Peter's Abbey Hospital Foundation fundraising gala for which Designs by Brenda had been recruited to decorate the ballroom, pro bono.

Stepping out of Doreen, Merry did a quick check of herself in the reflection of the driver's side window. Makeup not bad. Hair a little on the too-fluffy side but still firmly in the 2020s as opposed to the 1980s. In deference to the heat, she wore a modest crop top, her midriff barely showing and the neckline near her former Adam's apple. *It's fine,* she told herself. She had bigger things to worry about tonight than how she looked.

Marching up the walk to the modern, glass-a-palooza house, Merry's irritation grew with every step. How dare Roger start an investigation into those notes? Yes, she'd told him about them, to chide him about his own penchant for sending secret notes. But she certainly hadn't asked him to do this. Maybe it was her fault for leading him on. From the very first day she met him he pretty

much begged her to let him become involved in LSI. As a favour
to Brenda she'd allowed him to tag along on a couple of stakeouts.
It was pre-Doreen and she couldn't very well use an Uber, so she
kind of needed him. More recently she'd agreed to let him take
a stab at identifying the woman who'd tried to pass herself off as
Ruth-Anne Delorme. To be fair, he had been helpful in all of those
situations. So, there it was: she *had* led him on. And now he was
taking initiative, no doubt to further prove to her what he was capable of. But Merry was not in the market for a sidekick or any
kind of intern, paid or unpaid. Like Nathan, she was a lone wolf. Of
course, Nathan did hire her...and a few other investigators...didn't
matter, whatever it was Roger had to show her tonight, she'd listen
then shut him down.

A sharp trio of raps and the front door opened.

Merry stepped back, her mouth forming a silent oval, stunned.
Stinging recognition slapped her on one side of the face, then the
other. Was this it? Was this the same feeling—the emotion—the
shock—that people who knew her pre-transition experienced when
they first met Merry Bell?

Roger Brown had not answered the door. The person standing
there was Stella, Roger Brown's crossdressing alter ego and host of
The Darkside of Livingsky.

"Come in, please." It was a softer, somehow sharper version, but
still Roger's voice.

Merry stepped inside the generous foyer.

Stella stepped back knowing Merry would need space to take in
the person he was presenting as tonight.

The first thing that came to Merry's mind was that, although
this person was also Roger, the Stella bits of it read Brenda Brenda
Brenda. From the casually chic, matchy-matchy outfit, feminine but
not caricature-ish, tailored to suit what was obviously a male body,
to the flawless makeup and tasteful wig, these were decisions made
in close consultation with Designs by Brenda. Roger the electrician
was someone who Merry thought of as an everyday kind of man, fit,
pleasant looking. He wore nice clothes but nothing flashy or reveal-

ing of what his body might look like. The same could not be said for Stella. They'd obviously used subtle padding at the hips, ass and breast areas, but all else was natural, the slim waist, shapely legs. The only telltale signs undermining the illusion were Roger's hands, forearms and thick neck.

"I'm staring. I'm sorry."

"Don't be. I understand. I'm sorry for springing this on you. I don't do this…reveal myself to people…so I'm a bit unsure about the right way to do it. Are you okay? Is this okay?"

"Yes, yes, of course, I just…I just, I'm surprised but absolutely okay with it. In fact, I'm honoured you feel comfortable enough to show me Stella."

Roger chuckled. "You might not remember, but a few months ago after I first told you about her, you invited me to come on our next stakeout as Stella…if I wanted. Well, here you go, watch what you wish for."

Merry did remember. Then she'd bought Doreen and promptly stopped asking Roger to drive her places. That was lousy of her. Her earlier irritation forgotten, she stepped forward and placed a hand on Stella's arm. "I'm sorry, I should have…"

"Stop being sorry for anything. Even when you made the offer I didn't know if I wanted to take you up on it, or if I was ready. I still don't. That's why I'm doing this here, at home, where I feel comfortable and safe and while we're alone." Reading the question in her eyes, Roger kept on. "Brenda's mom took the kids across town for another kid's birthday party. Seems like a weird time of day for a pre-school kid's birthday party, but to each their own."

"Got it."

"If you're okay with all of this, do you want to come downstairs to see my podcast booth?"

"Uh, sure."

"Yeah? No questions? Anything?"

"Nope."

"Brenda would kill me if she found out I didn't offer you a drink. Can I get you something, water, wine, beer?"

"Nope."

Several minutes later, after touring the podcast facility and Stella assuring Merry that nothing was being recorded, they settled in the main booth. The first moments were awkward. They'd sat together a number of times but never as Stella and Merry. In a way they were strangers about to have a conversation as friends. They began by discussing the Dustin Thomson case or what was left of it. Roger quickly agreed with Merry's intuition that there was more to the footballer's death than was currently apparent. He replayed her a segment of his most recent podcast where listeners discussed Thomson and their own thoughts about what really happened that night on Sweetgrass Bridge. Many of the speculations were outlandish, bordering on conspiracy theories, but overall they supported the idea that all was not as it seemed. Merry was surprised how few of the callers believed Dustin Thomson could have committed suicide.

Deciding it was time to break the mold they'd talked themselves into, Merry finally asked, "Stella, why did you invite me here tonight?"

"You read my note?"

"No. I chewed it up and swallowed it to avoid it falling into enemy hands." She smirked. "Of course I read it. What I don't understand is what it's all about, why you've done whatever it is you've done."

"Passing secret notes is too much?"

"Uh-huh."

"Listen, Merry, it's no secret I've wanted to find a way to work with you ever since we met. I want to be part of LSI, to stretch my involvement in the world of crime solving beyond talking about it on a podcast. Don't get me wrong, I love *The Darkside of Livingsky*, but I think I can do more. I know I can. And before you say it, let me assure you this is not about getting more subscribers. This is about me, about Stella and Roger, and what I'm capable of."

"You have been helpful in the past, that's true, but what you've done, looking into something I never asked you to look into, something that is personal to me, is out of line."

"But why? I know it's personal. That's why I did it. To help you. It can't have felt good to get those notes, to not know who sent them. If it was me, I'd want to know. I think you do too but maybe you're too…"

Merry held up a hand. "Stop. I never asked you to do this."

"No, you didn't. And it won't happen again. But won't you at least listen to what I've learned?"

She nodded, wondering if she'd regret it.

For the next several minutes Stella spelled out everything Roger had done to date to investigate the source of the notes. He concluded with: "As far as access and motive are concerned, I've ruled out pretty much everyone; everyone except someone from your past. It only makes sense, Merry. The person who sent those notes has to be someone you used to know, when you were somebody else."

"To be clear, I'm not somebody else. I've always been Merry."

"You're right. I should know better than that. What I meant to say is that it has to be someone who knew you when you looked like somebody else. Better?"

Merry shrugged.

"It has to be someone from your family."

Merry jerked up in her seat, a roiling mixture of anger and worry flaring up all at once like a neglected stubble fire on a windy day. *What has he done? Did he contact my family? Oh my god!* "What did you do, Roger? Do you understand how inappropriate this is? How thoughtless? How damaging? All because you wanted to prove to me that you could play detective!"

"Wait. What? Yes I wanted to prove myself to you but that's not the only reason I did this, Merry. I did this because I'm worried about you. I think you're lonely. I wanted to show you that you're not alone, that you have someone on your side, that you have a friend."

"What are you talking about? What friend?"

"Me, Merry, me. I'm your friend."

Fighting back tears, Merry leapt up from her seat and lashed out:

"A friend wouldn't have gone behind my back to contact my family."

"That's why I didn't."

Merry sucked in air as if she'd been underwater and might drown if she didn't.

"Are you okay?" Stella asked for the second time that night.

Merry fell back into her seat. After a moment, she asked, "You didn't talk to my family?"

"No. That's why I asked you here tonight. To tell you what I've done and ask your permission to go further on this." Stella tried a small smile. "I'm guessing that's a no?"

Not quite ready to smile back, Merry croaked: "No."

It was Stella's turn to place a comforting hand on Merry's arm. "I meant what I said, Merry. I do worry that you're lonely. I don't know what happened with your family before you left Livingsky, but don't you think enough time has passed that you might be ready to reach out to them? You're going through so much with transitioning, opening a new business, starting your life over in a city that must seem new and strange to you after being away for so long. Family can be a really good thing to have at a time like this. If I'm right about the notes and who sent them, it sounds to me like they might be ready too."

Stella was right about some things, Merry conceded, but she was very wrong about one of them. She needn't go any further in identifying the person who'd slipped the notes under Merry's office door, because she'd already—unwittingly—done it. And now Merry knew who did it too.

"This has been, how to describe it, a challenging night?" Stella said as they said good-bye at the front door.

Merry nodded. "Yes, it has. But we got through it."

"Are we okay, you and me?"

For the first time that evening, Merry managed a small smile. "We are. It was a pleasure meeting Stella. I hope we meet again."

"Thank you for saying that. I hope so too."

"Goodnight." Merry turned to walk away.

"Merry, one more thing."

How can there be more? "Yes?"

"It's about what we discussed earlier. I think your instincts are right. Dustin Thomson didn't commit suicide. The way Sergeant Greyeyes responded to you today is proof of that. There's no way she'd be so ferocious with you if she was only protecting herself."

A shiver shot up Merry's spine. "What did you just say?"

"I think you're right about Dustin."

"No, about Greyeyes. The word you used…ferocious."

"Yeah. That's what it sounded like to me when you described how she acted in your meeting."

"Stella," Merry said, eyes burning bright, "you are freaking brilliant!"

Leaving Roger/Stella gaping in the doorway, Merry turned on her heel and headed determinedly toward her car. *Ferocious.* When is anyone, human or animal, the most ferocious? Veronica Greyeyes wasn't protecting herself; she was a mother protecting her child.

CHAPTER 22

"Thank you for meeting me here," Merry said to Gerald Drover at the front entrance of the JOY Centre.

"We don't let just anyone walk in here. Every adult needs an up-to-date Criminal Record and Vulnerable Sector Checks and an approved reason to be here. If you don't, you gotta be escorted by someone who has all that stuff. Like me. Aren't you glad you know me, Sweet Lips?"

"The jury is still out on that one," she responded, "but the flowers you planted in my yard helped."

"You liked those, huh?"

"I did. How did you know it was my birthday?"

"I have my ways."

Why do people keep saying that to me? "I really appreciate your telling me that Aly comes here on weekday afternoons during the summer months."

"Lot of kids do. They're bored as shit and looking for something to do. Better they come here than hang out on the streets. Nothing good happens out there. Why do you want to talk to her anyway?"

"Are you asking as a concerned JOY Centre volunteer or as a big snoop?"

"Can it be both?" he asked, giving Merry his widest gap-toothed smile.

"Can we go inside?"

"Can we go for dinner after you're done?"

—

Aly was in the common area, in the same spot where Merry first spoke with the young girl days earlier. Her head was buried in the glow of her phone, oblivious to anything or anyone around her, feet on the couch and a light camo jacket draped over her legs as if she were cold.

Merry took a spot at the opposite end of the same couch and cleared her throat to get the girl's attention.

Didn't work.

"Aly. Hi. Do you remember me?"

Aly looked up, only one eye visible behind strategically arranged bangs.

"We met here a few days ago and again the other night in the park for Dustin Thomson's vigil. You were with your mom and dad."

"She's not my mom."

"Got it." *Phew, poor Veronica has her hands full with this one.*

"What are you doing here?"

"I thought we could talk."

The girl shifted, pulling the jacket up to her chest leaving only one hand—the one with the phone—uncovered. "About what?"

"You were a little upset the last time I was here. I just wanted to see how you are."

"Whatever."

"You were right, Aly."

"Huh?"

"You told me you thought something bad happened to Dustin. You were right. Something bad did happen."

"Told you so."

"That must have been hard for you when you heard the news."

"Yeah. So?"

"Do you want to talk about it?"

She grunted, eyes fastened on the phone screen.

"You think I don't know what you're going through, and I don't, not exactly, but I went through some tough stuff when I was your age too."

Aly snorted. "So, you're one of those oldies who thinks we can get all best-friendsy and talk about shit just because you were a teenage girl once too. Whatever. I've heard it all before."

"Actually, I wasn't."

The phone moved down an inch, the eyes moved up.

"Wasn't what?"

"A teenage girl."

The phone slid under the jacket as Aly gave Merry a questioning look. "What do you mean?"

"I was never a teenage girl, at least not physically. When I was your age my body was the body of a teenage boy."

"Holy shit. You're transgender."

"Yes, I am."

"There's a kid at my school who's transgender." Aly shifted her feet to the floor, the jacket falling away.

Merry saw what she thought she'd see.

"They don't look like you do though. You can totally tell he's a boy."

"He's not a boy. He's a girl in a boy's body."

"Yeah, yeah, yeah, sorry, I know that. I just don't say stuff right all the time."

"I'm only telling you this because I know what it's like when your body is doing things you don't understand or don't expect."

Aly's face reddened and her hand instinctually dropped to the small mound at her belly.

Merry's eyes followed the movement, intentionally. She wasn't showing much but the signs had been there all along; the bulky clothing, the way she sat in strange, body-shielding positions. She was already a prickly teenager, but the poor girl was not only dealing with the raging hormones of puberty but those that flooded your body when you were pregnant.

"How long have you known about the pregnancy?"

"A while," she sniffed.

"Aly, I know this might be hard to discuss, but when I was here last time, you talked about Dustin in a certain way. It made me wonder if you were closer than a coach and student should be. Is that the way it was? Is Dustin Thomson the father of your baby?"

The young girl jumped up from her seat and scrambled to gather her things. "You don't care about me. You're just here playing Miss Fancy-pants private detective. You just want to know what I know. Well, that's private. That's between Dustin and me. You can fuck off, lady!"

"Hey, hey, hey, language." This came from Drover who'd been standing more than hearing distance away, until the last part.

Aly shot Gerald and Merry a sour look, flipped both of them the bird, and ran off.

"Whoa," Drover said, approaching the couch. "I don't know what the hell all that was about, but I'm guessing it didn't go well."

Merry remained sitting, her mind buzzing. "Actually, it did."

—

Arlene dropped three Gus & Gran specials of the day, Shepherd's Pie, on the table along with three pints of lager.

"You want anything else?" It was said more as a dare than a question.

"I think we're good, thanks," Merry told the cranky looking server.

With a wink for Gerald, Arlene sauntered off. He did not wink back. He was not in the mood. The perturbed look on his face, along the lines of *This is not how I saw my Friday night going*, was directed at the man sitting next to him on the same side of the cracked leather booth, Roger Brown.

Gus & Gran's, an Alphabet City mainstay since long before Merry left Livingsky, was a honkytonk kind of place that took up most of the main floor of the Coronet Hotel, known for cheap rooms and the occasional stabbing. The bar/restaurant was popular with the denizens of Alphabet City (which now included Merry), low level thugs, and university students looking for cheap beer. There was a pool table, dart boards, a long bar with swivel stools, a handful of stand-up deuces and a few booths usually reserved for canoodling or drug deals or both. The lighting was always dim regardless of the time of day and the air was thick with a foggy haze that reeked of nicotine and pot even though smoking indoors had been outlawed for years.

"Thanks for meeting us here on such short notice," Merry said to Roger, doing her best to ignore Drover's annoyance.

"I told you I wanted to help, so here I am. Besides," he said digging a fork into his pie, "Brenda has come up with this fun new tradition she calls Fasting Fridays. How she thinks eating nothing on the first day of a weekend is fun I don't know."

She probably makes up for it with extra-large glasses of Sauvignon blanc, Merry guessed but didn't say so out loud.

"Yeah, whatever, so what's *he* doing here?" Drover spoke up, already halfway through his pint.

"It's this case," Merry said, "or whatever it is, since I don't really have a client anymore. It's driving me crazy."

"Youse was looking a little shook up after your talk with Aly at the centre, but still, what's it gotta do with this guy?"

The two men had met before. The last time was also at Gus & Grans during a wrap-up meeting for LSI's very first case which had exonerated Drover of arson relating to a suspicious fire at one of his properties. Merry had let Roger handle the presentation of the bill which of course led to a bit of sparring—good-natured, Merry had thought—between the two.

"Roger has been very helpful to me, first on your case and again on this one."

Roger chewed and grinned at the same time, surprised but grateful for the compliments, especially given their most recent interaction.

"When I get like this, I find it helps to talk things out with someone," Merry explained, wishing for the thousandth time she still lived in Vancouver and Nathan Sharpe worked in the office next to hers.

"Yeah, so that's why I'm here," Drover groused, "but why is he here?"

"I asked Roger to join us because he's familiar with the case."

"So in this here scenario I'm nothing but a pretty face buying dinner?"

"You're buying dinner?" Roger asked.

"Not yours," Gerald growled with a baleful glare.

"Yup," Merry said brightly, "that sounds about right."

He shook his head, causing the top of his ginger mullet to quiver, and signaled Arlene to bring him another beer.

Merry moaned with pleasure as she took the first bite of the Shepherd's Pie. It was an unsolved mystery how a place like Gus & Grans that was waaaaay more bar than restaurant and got food to the table in a disturbingly short period of time after it was ordered always managed to deliver some of the most mouthwatering dishes in the city.

After Merry's meeting with Aly, she'd fully intended to blow off Gerald Drover and his invitation to dinner, but as the word "no" was forming on her tongue, she stopped herself. Once again it was a Friday night and her plans included spending time alone in her darkened office, probably getting tipsy on scotch as she attempted to purge her brain of the unthinkable suspicions that had begun to sprout there like noxious weeds. Although she hadn't appreciated it at the time, Roger voicing his concerns about her state of loneliness had sunk in over the past twenty-four hours. She wasn't sure she completely agreed with his assessment, but she had begun to wonder whether she should try something new, like saying "yes" to Drover's invitation.

"So, what's up?" Roger asked as he continued to enthusiastically enjoy his Fasting Friday dinner.

For the next several minutes Merry repeated the pertinent facts of the Dustin Thomson case, most of which both Roger and Drover were aware of, more as a sort of base from which she could launch into the disturbing thoughts that were wracking her brain. The first of those suspicions was the one that drove Merry back to the

JOY Centre: could it be that Detective Sergeant Veronica Greyeyes had learned of Aly's pregnancy and, suspecting…or knowing… her daughter was involved in Dustin's death, went into mother lion mode, doing everything she could, pulling every string, using every bit of professional collateral she had, to protect her child and keep the truth from being found out?

"How did you even come to suspect Aly was pregnant?" Roger asked.

"I didn't at first. She was always hiding her body with baggy clothes and coats even though it's summer. That in itself isn't all that unusual, especially for young girls, and especially if they're having body image problems which unfortunately happens all of the time at that age. Another possibility was that she was hiding an injury or bruises. But there was something about the way she moved and carried her body at the vigil that made me think otherwise. Then when you described Greyeyes as ferocious, the idea just stuck."

When Merry confronted Aly at the JOY Centre she confirmed the pregnancy. She'd previously claimed some kind of intimate relationship with Dustin Thomson, so putting two and two together wasn't hard. Neither was the thought that Dustin didn't take the news of the pregnancy very well. But could Aly somehow be responsible for his death at Sweetgrass Bridge? The girl had anger issues, but she was also a petite sixteen-year-old and he a muscled athlete, almost ten years her senior. Did any of this make sense? Was it possible?

Yes.

Or was another scenario more probable?

All of this time Merry was plagued by a nagging thought that refused to go away, a belief that something else was going on here, something she couldn't quite put her finger on because the finger was already pointing in too many directions.

"Merry," Roger began, "do you think Aly's mother might know about the pregnancy?"

Merry looked at Roger and slowly nodded. Therein lay the second worrisome suspicion.

Roger dropped his fork and gulped his beer to wash down a chunk of pie crust that had suddenly gone dry and lodged in his throat. "Wow. Do you think...?"

Another nod. At first she suspected Veronica because of her affair with Thomson. Suspicion then turned to Aly because of her pregnancy. But now it swung wildly back in the direction of Greyeyes. What if the reason she wanted to halt the investigation wasn't because she was protecting her daughter? "What if she was protecting herself after all?"

As Roger and Drover stared at her, stunned by the words, Merry buried her head in her hands, a wave of misery washing over her. Maybe this wasn't about a child's fury at a man refusing to own up to his paternity. Maybe this was about a grown woman's rage at a man she was having an affair with who'd impregnated her daughter. Maybe this whole damn thing was about one very simple thing: vengeance.

CHAPTER 23

Old habits die hard. So do new ones. Once again Merry was alone in her dimly lit office on Craving Lane on a Friday night staring out the window at a wall of graffiti nursing a glass of Oban. The evening at Gus & Gran's had come to end not long after Gerald Drover wedged himself into Merry and Roger's conversation about the Dustin Thomson case. From the very first day when fake Ruth-Anne Delorme contacted Merry, the case had hinged on figuring out what kind of case it really was. Was Dustin's disappearance due to an accident? Suicide? Or murder? Merry's gut kept insisting it was the latter. Yet hard as it was to come up with a reason for somebody to want to kill a popular Saskatchewan Roughriders' football player, and a likely candidate to have committed that murder, her gut still roiled with the possibility.

As she and Roger debated whether the culprit was Aly Cook or her mother, Sergeant Veronica Greyeyes, despair over the possibility of either being true spread through Merry like an invasive disease. A child of sixteen…a murderer? Horrific to consider. And Veronica Greyeyes? This was the woman whose actions helped clear Merry of a murder charge. This was a woman who, despite their sparring ways, she'd come to respect and even admire. It couldn't have been easy for an Indigenous woman to get where she was in the Livingsky Police Service in what had historically been a white male dominated career. Then again, did she really know Veronica Greyeyes? They weren't friends. Merry hadn't met the police detective's husband until the night of the vigil in the park, nor had she known Aly even existed until then. Yet her admitting to having an affair with Dustin Thomson had rocked Merry. But why should it? Their interactions to date had been solely professional, often bordering on acrimonious. There was no personal relationship. How was she to know whether Greyeyes was the type of woman to cheat on her husband, if that's indeed what happened, and if it did, who was Merry to judge her for it?

Veronica Greyeyes was probably exactly the type of person Merry Bell should pursue as a friend. As the new kid on the playground, was it up to her to find and make new friends? In her head she could hear Stella/Roger Brown answer the question: Yes! She needed to try harder, to meet people halfway. She'd done none of that. Instead, she holed up in her office or the Junk House and licked her wounds. Wounds collected over a lifetime of hardship and uncertainty and fear. Wounds which had scabbed over but never seemed ready to heal, at least not while she was in Vancouver. If she was being honest with herself, Merry knew there was more than one reason she'd come back to Livingsky. It wasn't only because she couldn't afford Vancouver prices anymore. It was because she needed to go back to where Merry Bell began, she needed to repair what had been broken, if that was even possible.

One of Merry's earliest doctors had been a philosophical fellow who likened the transition process to the four stages of a healing wound. The first and most urgent stage was to stop the bleeding before you died. Merry could relate. She'd known dark and desperate times, times when death presented itself as a viable even desirable option. The second stage was clotting, the formation of a protective scab, where although there might be inflammation and the wound itself might look red and raw and unhappy, this was the true beginning of healing. The third stage occurred once a wound was clean and stable; only then could the body and mind begin to rebuild. This, in Merry's current estimation, was where she was in the process. Returning to Livingsky had given her a clean start, a stable place to heal. She'd loved her life in Vancouver; it was a beautiful, vibrant city that offered seemingly endless opportunity, but it also pulled and pushed and came with its own stresses and tensions, its own sources of inflammation that threatened repeated infection over healing. The needs of the person who'd run away to Vancouver all those years ago were not the same as the needs of the person who eventually left it.

The final stage of healing a wound was maturation. Even after the scab is gone and the area looks closed and repaired, a wound is still healing. For how long? Nobody really knew. But when it did, Merry would have to figure out where the new, fully healed Merry Bell belonged.

In the meantime, she had other things to worry about. Could she afford to turn on a highly ranked officer of the Livingsky Police Service? In her first case she'd pissed off the city's mayor, and now this? Maybe the decision as to whether or not she stayed in Livingsky wasn't going to be hers to make. At this rate, the people who ran and looked after the city might very well kick her out.

In the end, it was Gerald Drover who saved Merry from having to betray Greyeyes.

"Can I talk now?" he'd asked once he'd finished his Shepherd's Pie and begun working on a third pint of lager.

"Gerald, I'm sorry, I know this has probably been a bore-fest to listen to," Merry said.

"Yeah," Roger agreed. "Now that you're done Medieval feasting over there, don't feel you have to stay."

Merry gave her wannabe assistant a puzzled look. Though his words were vaguely aggressive, his wide-open, friendly face read nothing but happy-go-lucky Roger the electrician. She'd seen it before, bits of Stella peeking out from behind Roger, this time having a little fun by provoking the guy who didn't want him there.

"I hate to be the one to put a stale cracker in your P.I. soup," Drover notified the duo with a smug tone. "But I'm gonna."

"What are you talking about?" Merry asked.

"Dustin Thomson is not the father of Aly's baby."

"What?" Merry and Roger responded in unison.

Merry pushed aside her plate and drink and leaned in closer.

"How do you know that?"

"Because it all went down at the JOY Centre, Sugar Bits."

"All of what?" Roger asked, not for a moment considering that *Sugar Bits* was meant for him.

"All of the stuff that leads up to making a baby. The dad is a punk named Jeremiah. He's been coming to JOY for a couple years now. Always hits on the new girls. Aly fell for it."

"How can you be sure he's the father?"

"Well, I guess I can't be one hundred percent sure, but I'm thinking it's a pretty good guess because I caught them doing the naked chicken dance behind the JOY building one night." Drover, looking extremely pleased with himself, signaled for another beer and a round of shots, likely more to irk Roger than because he was thirsty.

"Oh wow," Roger exclaimed, scratching his head.

Merry's chin sunk until it hit the tabletop. The implications of what she'd just learned were mind boggling. On the one hand she was glad to have been presented with reasonable doubt that Aly and her mother were guilty of murder, and that Dustin Thomson was a creep who took advantage of his position of power to prey on young girls. Merry realized that even though she'd never met him and knew nothing about football, she really wanted to believe—as pretty much everyone in Saskatchewan did—that Dustin Thomson was an all-around good guy, someone young people could look up to and emulate. On the other hand it meant she was back at square one. *Damn.*

"Maybe the police—and everyone else for that matter—is right," Roger said. "Maybe Dustin Thomson wrote that poem about seeing never from Sweetgrass Bridge and jumped off of it for reasons we may never know."

Merry could feel Shepherd's Pie creeping up her esophagus. Roger might be right, yet the sickening feeling that something was missing wasn't going away. But what was it?

"I gotta go."

"Uh, what's that you're saying, Sweet Lips?" Drover's mullet was leaning heavily to one side.

"I need time to think."

"I'll come with you," Roger offered, beginning to slide out of the booth.

"Alone." She smiled at Drover. "Thanks for dinner. I owe you one."

The men watched her weave through the crowd and disappear.

Arlene delivered the beer and three tequila shots. "Where's your friend?"

"She had to leave," Roger told her.

Arlene picked up the extra shot, downed it, winked at Drover, then ambled off to the next table.

Drover looked at Roger. Roger looked at Drover. This was definitely not how either of them saw their Friday night going.

—

In the quiet of her office, facing the hypnotic yet strangely calming graffiti wall outside the window, Merry played with the ever-changing pieces of the puzzle that was Dustin Thomson's death. Learning that Thomson was most likely not the father of Aly Cook's baby moved the teenager way down the list of suspects in his murder (if indeed that's what it was). Down, but not entirely off. Embarrassed that the father was some random bad boy, her drama-heightened teenage girl brain might have somehow convinced her to try to persuade Thomson to believe he was the father anyway (which would have been difficult if their intimate relationship was also a figment of her overactive puberty-controlled imagination), with the same tragic results. Far-fetched but not impossible, especially if Aly's anger issues were more severe than anyone knew.

Another of Merry's theories was that Veronica Greyeyes had attempted to halt the investigation because she knew of the pregnancy and believed her daughter might have done the unthinkable. That only worked if Aly told her parents the same lie she tried to pass off on Merry, that Thomson was the father. The fact that Veronica had been, or still was, romantically involved with Thomson took things to another level. If she believed her daughter's lie, she might have been enraged enough to woo Thomson to the bridge and killed him for the despicable act he'd committed.

But all of Merry's suspicions fell apart when she studied the timing. Although she didn't know the details of Greyeyes and Thomson's affair or how or even if it had ended, or what Veronica believed about Aly's pregnancy, what Merry did know to be true was that Veronica Greyeyes (through fake Ruth-Anne Delorme) hired her to look into Thomson's disappearance days before anyone knew of his death. Veronica would never have hired her if she knew of or was responsible for Dustin's death for one reason or another, nor if she suspected her daughter was. Which left Aly as a suspect, killing Dustin before revealing her pregnancy to her mother, causing Greyeyes to attempt to halt the investigation. But Aly's baby was not Thomson's, leaving her little reasonable motivation to kill him.

All of which led Merry back to having no motives and no suspects.

Swivelling her chair to face the computer, Merry reached for the Oban. As always, the luscious notes of apple and honey morphing into tart lemon and malt and eventually a tingling oaky spice reminded her of her old boss, Nathan Sharpe. It also reminded her of his wise words whenever she felt she'd reached a dead end with a case. The best thing to do when you're at a dead end, he advised, is to go back to the beginning: review every note, every interview, every piece of evidence no matter how insignificant or how much it reeked of red herring. That's exactly what she intended to do.

Ninety minutes later Merry swore and slammed down the lid of her laptop. Nothing, she'd found nothing.

Merry prided herself on making meticulous notes throughout the stages of a case. It was a good way to keep facts straight and separate from theories and suppositions. Sometimes just re-reading what she'd done to date helped her decide what the best next move was. Tonight, she'd hoped to find something forgotten or overlooked, something that would explain why she simply could not let this go. Dustin Thomson was more than a star quarterback; he was more than a celebrity whose face was recognizable to pretty much half the population of Saskatchewan and maybe even the country. He was someone's brother, someone's son, someone's best friend, someone who one sweet summer day found himself on Sweetgrass Bridge in the light of a luminous moon and never came home again. Dustin Thomson was worth whatever trouble she had to go through to find the truth about how that came to be.

Merry lifted the computer's lid, stared at the screen and positioned her fingers atop the keyboard. They didn't move. There was nowhere for them to go.

I've failed.

The gloom of those two ugly words threatened to overcome her.

"Nope! Uh uh!" she bellowed at the world. "I am Merry Bell. I am awesome. I don't fail." If her gut was telling her there was something more to all of this, then she believed it and would not rest until she found out what it was.

Throwing open a desk drawer, she pawed through hanging files until she found the one she was looking for. It was labelled *Dustin Thomson* and contained all the miscellany she'd collected throughout her investigation that weren't digital, receipts for gas, groceries, lotto, a parking ticket, random photographs, scribbles on scraps of papers and napkins.

"I'm going to find you," she whispered, knowing that sometimes answers could be found in the bits and pieces of life.

And she was right.

CHAPTER 24

When Merry pulled into the parking lot at nine-thirty Saturday morning, Greyeyes was already there drinking a Starbucks in her unmarked police vehicle. The office didn't open until ten, but Merry wanted to be there early. Obviously, Greyeyes had the same idea. She also happened to snag the best spot from which someone in a car could keep an eye on who went in and out of the business. Merry directed Doreen into a nearby space, grabbed her own coffee—a much cheaper Tim Hortons variety—and slipped into the passenger seat of Greyeyes' sedan.

The two women exchanged greetings, which although not frosty, weren't the calibre of two good friends meeting for a chinwag over morning java. Their last contact had been fiery and they were both still feeling the aftereffects of it.

"Thanks for coming," Merry offered, eyeing Veronica's coffee with jealousy, remembering the days when she could afford a grande, quad, nonfat, one-pump, no-whip mocha.

"There's nothing I'd rather do first thing in the morning of my day off," Greyeyes' response was drier than her cappuccino. "Now tell me again why I'm here."

"First, I want to apologize for the last time we talked. Things got a little heated. I'm a professional and I don't like how I conducted myself."

Leisurely sipping her drink, Greyeyes silently eyed up the other woman.

"As my client…" *who hired me via questionable means*, "…you requested that I conclude my investigation. I should have accepted that and done as you asked."

"Yes, you should have."

Merry's temper burbled but remained under control. She wasn't the only one at fault for the situation at the police station getting out of hand. Greyeyes had threatened her, for god's sake. But for right now she needed the cop, so no matter how good it might feel to point out the errors in Greyeyes' actions, she wouldn't do it. At least not now.

Greyeyes sucked in her cheeks, looked out the window for a beat, then back at Merry. "I could have handled the situation better as well."

Merry stifled a grin. Not exactly an apology but close enough. As a police detective, Greyeyes was probably unfamiliar with the concept anyway, especially when it came to dealing with civilians. Merry could appreciate that being a cop wasn't easy, so she was willing to give the woman a pass. A small one.

"Are we done with that then?" Greyeyes asked.

Obviously the cop was not one for prolonged sessions of talking about feelings. Merry was good with that.

"Yes. But there's one other thing I want to clear up."

Greyeyes' mouth tightened but she said nothing.

"I accused you of murdering Dustin Thomson." Then she added (because she had to get some self-satisfaction out of this): "Your former lover."

Greyeyes made the kind of noise in her throat that, were it made of words, Merry likely wouldn't have liked them.

"I was wrong to do that. I know it isn't true."

"Of course it isn't. I'm a Livingsky police officer. I uphold the law, not contravene it."

"Veronica, you know as well as I do that being a cop does not automatically make a person incapable of committing a crime, even a very serious one."

The detective responded by making the same noise in her throat.

"You weren't the only one I suspected."

"Okay, who are we talking about here?"

"Aly."

A few spits of Greyeyes' coffee erupted from the small hole in its lid as she suddenly shifted in her seat to face Merry. "What are you talking about, Bell? And," she said with an ominous tone, "I want you to be very careful about what you say next."

Merry *had* thought a lot about what she was going to say next. If Veronica and her husband Bobby didn't know their daughter was pregnant, they needed to.

—

Merry Bell did as Greyeyes requested. She was careful and meticulous in laying out the facts as she knew them and how they fed into her suspicions. Sitting inside the car, so close to one another, the conversation seemed more an intimate communion than a typical cop-detective interaction, and as Merry spoke Greyeyes' mind leapt back to the terrible scene that had played out in her home. It started out as a typical Wednesday evening, she'd just come upstairs from the basement after finishing a quick after-shift workout in their modest home gym, Bobby was fixing dinner in the kitchen, Aly was pretending to do homework at the island. That should have been her first hint that something was up. Rarely did Aly do anything at the kitchen island. Too much risk of being discovered doing whatever it was teenage girls did on their phone, which seemed to demand as much time and attention as a full-time job. After a quick shower she returned to the kitchen to find father and daughter in mid-confrontation, a very tense one. "What's going on here?" she'd asked innocently. From there things went downhill very fast.

The revelation that sixteen-year-old Aly was pregnant was not the last nor even most shocking one: the father of the child was Dustin Thomson.

At no other point in her life could Veronica Greyeyes remember feeling like her body might detonate, exploding right there in the kitchen of their lovely home, splashing guts and blood and brain matter all over the cupboards and floor. It was going to be a bitch to clean up. For what seemed like forever she was unable to speak. All she could do was stare at her daughter, at her husband, and then she began to wonder if maybe she wanted her body to explode. Only something that extreme could make the pain of what she was going through go away. An easy fix.

How could she possibly say anything? Was she supposed to tell her husband that the man who'd impregnated their teenage daughter had also been sleeping with his wife? Was she supposed to rail at the ghost of Dustin Thomson and berate him for having sex with her daughter? Did he even know Aly was her stepdaughter? Did he know she was only sixteen? And what about Aly? She was only a child. She'd been taken advantage of, abused, by someone she knew. And she and Bobby knew nothing about it. They'd been oblivious. She'd known of parents in the same situation, responding with disbelief, acting shocked, blaming everyone but themselves. But deep down inside she couldn't help but judge them and silently scold them for being poor parents. Now it was her. She was the poor parent.

Veronica felt a depth of pain and grief and guilt and anger like she'd never felt before, the warring emotions never meant to exist in one place at the same time, threatening to tear her apart. The battle within her raged on even now.

What happened on that interminably long, impossibly horrible night, the hours of talking, crying, pleading and regret, the "trying to figure it out," now seemed like a hazy dream. The night ended, somehow, with Aly exiled to her bedroom, she and Bobby to theirs. But it wasn't the end. It was followed by more hours of raw discussion and, at least in Veronica's case, telling lies. There were no easy answers to be found. By the next morning, Veronica knew only one thing for certain: Merry Bell's investigation into the possibility that Dustin Thomson was murdered had to be stopped.

Veronica knew she wasn't the one who'd driven Dustin Thomson to Sweetgrass Bridge that night. But someone had. Could it have been Aly? Maybe she suggested a late-night visit to the infamous

ANTHONY BIDULKA   233

spot for…a romantic rendezvous? Just the thought made Veronica want to throw up. Aly had recently earned her learner's permit so she would have convinced Dustin to let her drive. He'd have been expecting one thing, but Aly would have had something entirely different in mind. She would tell him about the baby. Did she expect him to start making plans for their future together? What happened then? It wasn't difficult to imagine that things did not go according to Aly's plan. Getting a sixteen-year-old pregnant could end Dustin's career. Did he refuse to own up to it? To believe it? To support her through it? Did he suggest an abortion? The situation would have escalated in a hurry. Aly for sure had anger issues, but was she truly capable of murder? Could a petite teenager push a quarterback off a bridge? What if his guard was down? Maybe…

"Veronica?"

Greyeyes heard her name being repeated and snapped out of it. Now was not the time to lose focus. She had to stay sharp. Merry Bell needed to tread lightly here. If she didn't, if she took them down a dangerous road, Greyeyes truly didn't know what she would do. *What am I capable of?*

"Aly is pregnant."

Greyeyes gagged. *How the hell had she found out?*

"I know this is none of my business, but I wanted to say something to you in case you and Bobby didn't know. Aly is only a child and she's going to need your help."

"You said you think she had something to do with this. Why?" Veronica demanded to know.

"I did. Past tense. I don't anymore."

Greyeyes gulped for air. *I still suspect her, God help me, why don't you?* With beseeching eyes, she asked, "Why not?"

"When I first met Aly at the JOY Centre she led me to believe she'd had a relationship with Dustin Thomson that was more than just friendship."

Fuck no! She knows. What am I going to do if…

"When I found out she was pregnant I naturally suspected Dustin might be the father."

He is the father.

"He's not the father."

What? "What?"

Merry gave Veronica a strange look. "Did you know about the pregnancy?"

Veronica hesitated. What should she say? If she denied knowing she could play dumb a little longer until she figured out how to deal with whatever situation Merry was leading them into. If she told the truth, well, things would devolve quickly, making their last explosive conversation seem like a tea party.

"We did. We learned about it quite recently," Veronica admitted. Taking a breath, she asked, "Why did you change your mind about Dustin being the father?"

"Apparently Ger…someone who volunteers at the centre caught Aly having sex with her boyfriend."

"She has a boyfriend?" Veronica blurted out before she could stop herself.

"Well, from what I understand, calling him a boyfriend might be a bit of a stretch."

Veronica shook her head. "She was having casual sex with someone she barely knew." *I'm such a bad parent.*

Merry nodded. "I think she made up the story about having a relationship with Dustin to, I don't know, maybe make herself feel better about the pregnancy. Or maybe it was wishful thinking, making a baby with a handsome celebrity who's in love with you sounds way better than getting knocked up by some asshole."

And easier for your parents to swallow when you tell them you're pregnant.

"Who knows what goes on in the heads of teenage girls," Merry kept on, "I know I was an ugly mess at that age. And with Dustin missing and unable to refute her story, the whole ruse worked even better. I'm sure he liked Aly, encouraged her to play sports, but I'm pretty confident he didn't have sex with a teenager."

In a strange way, Veronica felt relief. Yes, her teenage daughter was still pregnant, but at least it wasn't with a man she herself was once involved with, once...loved? At least it wasn't a case of an adult taking advantage of a minor. At least it was the result of actions that, whether she liked admitting it or not, were probably under Aly's control and performed with her consent.

"What the volunteer saw isn't irrefutable proof," Merry said, "but a DNA test will confirm it if Aly doesn't."

Grudgingly Veronica once again found herself admiring Bell's ingenuity and abilities as an investigator. After all, it resulted in her and her daughter being taken off the suspect list for the death of Dustin Thomson. Still, the detective had played fast and loose with the rules of engagement, so there was no need to let her off the hook completely. "Now that you've come to your senses and realized neither I nor my daughter are criminals," she said with a touch of accusation in her voice, "what's next?"

"Now," Merry replied with a smile, "you and I catch a murderer."

With the morning sun heating up the insides of the car, both Veronica and Merry rolled down their windows to let in some fresh air and let out some pent-up tension.

"With Dustin not being the father of Aly's baby, neither you nor Aly had a good motive to kill him," Merry explained her thinking. "At that point it would have been easy for me to conclude that everyone else, including your friends at the LPS, was right: that he either committed suicide or his death was some kind of accident, and we might never know for sure which one it was or why it happened."

"So why didn't you? At least I assume that's why you convinced me to meet you here this morning." Greyeyes indicated the strip mall in front of them. "I think it's time you told me why we're in this parking lot. Do one of the businesses here have something to do with the case?"

"Ah-hah!" Merry crowed, hoping to lighten the mood. "So, you do admit I still have a case?"

Greyeyes was not amused. "Keep talking or I'm leaving."

"It's because of you I couldn't bring myself to believe Dustin Thomson killed himself."

"Me? Now what are you talking about?"

"Believe it or not, I respect your opinion, Veronica. You so believed he couldn't have done that to himself that you jeopardized your career, your reputation, your relationship with your husband to hire me to find out the truth. That is something I had to pay attention to.

"Then I met his sister Miranda, and his teammates, his coach, and so many others, all of them saying the same thing. None of them could believe Dustin would kill himself. Even so, it still could have been an accident, but none of the evidence supported that. So I went back to the beginning. One of the first things I did after you hired me was search Dustin's apartment and his truck. I found something that day that meant nothing to me at the time, but I kept it anyway, just in case. Well, just in case happened."

"What was it? What did you find?"

"The glove compartment of Dustin's SUV was filled with the kind of junk we all have in there, stray papers, old parking tickets, candy wrappers, that sort of thing. When I went through everything I found a receipt from a stop he made at a 7-11 convenience store."

"What's so important about that? He bought gas? Chips? Some gum?"

"He did buy gas. He also bought a lottery ticket."

"So what? He's allowed to waste his money."

"Suppose it wasn't a waste?"

Veronica knit her brow. "Are you saying he won the lottery? How do you know?"

"I don't."

"You're losing me here."

"I found the receipt. But where's the ticket?"

Greyeyes let out a stream of exasperation. "Stuck in the pocket of a dirty pair of jeans, between the couch cushions, in the garbage, it could be anywhere."

"Could be, and maybe it is. But what if something else happened to it? Do you remember how Dustin's sister Miranda told me what a good mood he was in the day before he disappeared, how he was excited to share some big news with her?"

"You think he was going to tell her he won the lottery?"

"Why not? It's a long shot but people do win. Suppose one of those people was Dustin Thomson. He was beginning to make good money with the Riders, but not change-the-life-of-your-sister kind of money. This could have been big for him and his family."

Greyeyes scanned the building they were parked in front of and saw why Merry had brought them here. "The Saskatchewan Lotteries office, that's why we're here?"

"Bingo. Excuse the pun…is that a pun?"

"No."

Merry could sense she was losing the cop's interest. "What's that look on your face?"

"Merry, whereas I appreciate you digging up clues and coming up with theories no one else would have thought of in an effort to make sense of what happened to Dustin, even if by some chance you're right, I'm sorry to tell you that no one at Saskatchewan Lotteries is ever going to tell you who won a lottery, how much, or when. They only release that kind of information when they want to and with the knowledge of the winner."

"I already know that. I called. But I can be very persuasive when I want to be," Merry said with a grin.

"Really? They told you Dustin won the lottery?"

"No," she confessed. "But they did tell me something almost as important."

Greyeyes waited a beat then said, "You're going to make me ask?"

Merry sighed contentedly, savouring the sweet feeling of her knowing something the cop did not but obviously wanted to.

"What did they tell you, Bell?"

"A lottery ticket that sold in Livingsky on the same date as appears on Dustin's receipt won a significant prize and…" She stopped there for dramatic effect and because she knew it would get a reaction.

"Get out of my car," Greyeyes fumed.

"Okay, okay," Merry relented with a wink. "They told me the winning ticket had not yet been redeemed and…" Stop.

"I swear to god, Bell, if you don't…."

"…the last day the ticket can be redeemed is today."

Greyeyes thought things through for a few seconds then said, "So, if you're right and the winning ticket actually belongs to Dustin, no one will show up. It's behind a couch cushion or he put it somewhere no one knows about for safe keeping."

Merry nodded enthusiastically. "Or, if I'm right, the ticket belongs to Dustin, and someone who knew it's a winner killed him for it…"

"…the killer will show up today to get their payoff."

"Mm-hmm. They'd want to wait as long after Dustin's death as possible to try to avoid suspicion or unwanted attention, especially if it was common knowledge they were associated with Dustin."

"There's one other option."

"I know," Merry conceded. "The ticket belongs to someone else entirely and assuming they know what they've got, they show up today to claim their money in all innocence."

"Yup," Greyeyes said taking a sip of her coffee and eyeing up her car-mate. "How do you propose we tell the difference between the last two options?"

"We're two exceptionally smart and resourceful women," Merry answered with confidence. "We'll figure it out."

Three hours later they did exactly that.

CHAPTER 25

"You're listening to an extended episode of *The Darkside of Livingsky*. If you've just joined us, I'm your host, Stella, and tonight I am joined by a very special guest, Merry Bell, owner, operator and principal lead detective at Livingsky Sharpe Investigations, better known as LSI. For those of you who aren't familiar with LSI, you're obviously not getting into enough trouble!" Stella cackled.

Ensconced in her darkened office across town, safe from view by anyone other than Stella who was conducting the interview via Zoom, Merry rolled her eyes. Roger had been understandably surprised when she'd agreed to appear on the show to talk about Dustin Thomson and the apprehension of his murderer and was now going overboard expressing gratitude.

"LSI is the preeminent private investigation firm in Livingsky," Stella prattled on, "a satellite of nationally renowned Sharpe Investigations based out of Vancouver, our neighbour to the west.

"Merry has been regaling us with heart-pumping and heart-breaking details of the mystery and intrigue that led to the tragic discovery of famed Saskatchewan Roughriders' football player Dustin Thomson in the dark, churning waters below Sweetgrass Bridge earlier this summer and the subsequent identification of the person responsible for the heinous act that ended the young quarterback's life. If you've missed our conversation so far, shame on you. But lucky lucky you, all you have to do is find this podcast, *The Darkside of Livingsky*, wherever you get your favourite podcasts and download the entire recording. While you're there, don't forget to subscribe.

"Now, Merry, before we move on, I have a very important question for you."

"Okay, shoot."

"Do you think I've done quite enough self-promotion yet?" Stella winked at Merry.

Merry laughed. "I think you've covered that off quite nicely."

"Thank you. I think so too. Now what do you say we move on to what I think is the most important part of this case: Merry, how did you catch Dustin Thomson's murderer?"

"Well, first of all, Stella, I want to make it very clear, again, that a successful outcome in any murder investigation is rarely accomplished alone. LSI worked closely with the Livingsky Police Service as well as contributing associates, such as yourself." "Contributing associate" was Roger's newest bid to formalize his role with LSI with an actual title. Merry, feeling generous, decided to use it for the purposes of the podcast only. And it didn't hurt to throw in some kudos for the LPS, just in case Greyeyes was listening, although she highly doubted it.

It wasn't the first time Roger had asked Merry to join Stella on the podcast, but it was the first time she'd said yes. Insanity, according to a definition often attributed to Einstein, is doing the same thing over and over again and expecting a different result. Merry knew she needed to make a change if she expected LSI to survive, if she expected Merry Bell to survive. Several months in and her business was still struggling. She was barely making ends meet, having to take on crappy side jobs just to afford food, clothes, chocolate, adult beverages, rent on the office and the Junk House. And who knew makeup and other girl stuff was so fricking expensive? Advertising was the bedrock of most business plans. Law firms did it, even doctor's offices, so why shouldn't LSI? How were people supposed to hire her if they didn't know LSI existed and what services she offered? When Roger shared his subscriber numbers with her, it was a no-brainer that given her current advertising budget—zero dollars—a stint as an expert guest on *The Darkside of Livingsky* made a lot of sense.

"As you know, Merry, on this podcast we do a great deal of theorizing and speculating about criminal investigations. With this being a Saskatchewan-based podcast, the death of Dustin Thomson was of particular interest to our listeners. But it was more than that, much more. For many of us, he was a hero, someone we knew and cared about. Dustin's success was our success. His tragic ending was a tragedy for us too. So it was a shock when it was revealed that his death was not suicide, as was originally believed, nor an accident, but a murder. Then our shock turned into disbelief when the actual murderer was revealed. Can you walk us through those final hours, beginning with you and police detective Sergeant Veronica Greyeyes sitting in your car in a Livingsky strip mall parking lot. What happened next?" Stella asked breathlessly.

Merry knew this was the climax of the podcast, the most important part, but she hated it. There was nothing about what happened next that felt good. "We'd been waiting there, in the Sask. Lotteries parking lot, for several hours. I have to admit, I was beginning to doubt my theory about the lottery ticket and who might claim it."

"Did you consider calling it quits?"

"Not really. If it was going to happen it was going to happen on that day. The next day the lottery ticket would have expired. Detective Greyeyes and I agreed from the beginning we would stay until they locked the front door."

"Let me tell you, Stella would not have been nearly as patient. What happened then?"

"It's a busy mall. Vehicles came and went all day. None of the drivers entered the Sask. Lotteries office. Then, midafternoon, a white 2003 Dodge Ram pulled into the lot. It was a vehicle I'd seen before."

"Oh my god," Stella pumped up the auditory drama.

"I knew the owner of the truck. And within moments both Sergeant Greyeyes and I were able to positively identify the owner and driver as Calvin Wochiewski."

"Calvin Wochiewski was Dustin's roommate," Stella added.

"That's correct."

"Were you shocked to see him there? Or had you already suspected he was the murderer?"

"To be honest, I didn't suspect Calvin until I went back and reviewed every piece of evidence I'd collected. Nothing was too insignificant to be considered."

"That's when you found the lottery ticket receipt you mentioned earlier."

"Yes. Once I learned that a ticket purchased on that same date was a winner, I began to construct a possible scenario where a winning ticket purchased by Dustin might lead to his being killed. Even then I didn't know it was Calvin. And seeing him at the Lotteries office wasn't enough. As soon as he arrived, Detective Greyeyes and I immediately went to work to support our theory. I contacted one of the witnesses who'd been at Sweetgrass Bridge the night of Dustin's death. The first time I talked to the witness I had asked him if he'd seen Dustin's vehicle in the parking lot that night. What I should have asked him was if he saw *any* vehicle there."

Stella gasped loud enough that her listeners were sure to hear the reaction. "The witness saw Calvin's white truck at Sweetgrass Bridge?"

"Yes. They assumed another couple was inside doing exactly what they were doing there that night, so they didn't look too closely or think much of it at the time or even afterwards."

"That places Calvin Wochiewski at the scene of the crime."

"Not exactly. Unfortunately the witness didn't see Calvin, only his truck. Up until then he was never a person of interest in the police investigation, so beyond initial questioning they never dug any deeper. While I was talking with the witness, Sergeant Greyeyes contacted Calvin's place of work. She quickly learned he'd lied about being at work that night. That was all we needed to proceed with apprehending Mr. Wochiewski.

"I can't go into the exact details, but much later, after Calvin was already in custody, DNA evidence definitively placed him at Sweetgrass Bridge." Merry sighed then continued. "As you and your listeners know, Calvin Wochiewski eventually pled guilty to killing his roommate and friend, Dustin Thomson."

"What a sad outcome," Stella said, "for everyone. In the end it was all about greed, about money, the root of all evil, some people say."

"I believe it was about much more than that," Merry countered.

"What do you mean?"

"Dustin Thomson and Calvin Wochiewski were best friends, since childhood. Their friendship was real, until something unforeseen came along and broke it. Calvin was proud of Dustin's accomplishments as a football player. He was once a player too."

"I didn't know that."

"In high school. He knew he wasn't good enough to make it as a professional and that Dustin very obviously was. He accepted that. He supported Dustin's career and celebrated his success. But then came the lottery win."

Stella nodded sagely. "Calvin thought it was unfair, too much of a good thing for someone who already had so much."

"Again, I think it was more complicated than that. Since all of this happened, I've learned a lot more about their friendship."

"They met when Dustin moved to Livingsky from Little Turtle Lake, right?"

"Yes. Dustin's mother was ill and needed to be closer to her doctors. Dustin still spent the summers between school years with his kôhkom at Little Turtle Lake. The boys became so close that Calvin ended up spending a lot of time there too. He came to love the old woman like his own grandmother. She loved to gamble, so for years whenever they visited, they brought her a lottery ticket as a gift. She would joke that if she ever won, she'd buy each boy a fancy car. After she died, Dustin and Calvin decided to keep up the tradition and once a week they each bought a lottery ticket in her honour."

"That's beautiful," Stella remarked, "but somehow I suspect this is where the train left the track?"

Merry smiled sadly. Stella was correct. The sweet tradition turned horribly sour. This was where, as Stella predicted, the evilness of money reared its ugly head. "When Dustin's ticket actually

won, Calvin believed the promise of their kôhkom should be honoured. He felt the monies should be spend on buying two hot cars
and pay for a grand extended driving adventure across Canada and
the U.S. until all the money ran out. Dustin did not feel the same."

"Could he really have believed that was going to happen?"

"I'm not sure. It was the chance of a lifetime to live out a dream.
I spoke with Calvin before they took him away. He said he'd been
hopeful but wasn't surprised when Dustin shot down the idea. He
did, however, expect Dustin to give him some of the winnings so he
could have a better life, maybe buy the car, go on the cross-country
adventure himself. Instead, Dustin was all about giving the money to the reserve. He wanted to fund similar youth programs, like
those at JOY Centre, at Little Turtle Lake. Calvin felt Dustin was
oblivious to what was going on with him, that he was more interested in helping people he didn't know instead of his own best friend."

"The friendship was over."

"In his twisted thinking Calvin believed he was the only person
willing to use the money the way their grandmother wanted. He
knew he wouldn't get it unless he took it. Sweetgrass Bridge was a
special place for Dustin and Calvin. After kôhkom died, they would
often go there because there were trees and it was near water and
it reminded them of her and Little Turtle Lake. That night Calvin
convinced Dustin they should go there to raise a toast to thank her
for the windfall."

"Instead, he planned to push his friend off the bridge."

Merry made a sound that caught Stella's attention.

"Isn't that what happened?"

Merry's head moved in a robotic fashion, once up, once down.
"Probably. We may never know the real plan. Calvin might have
believed he could change Dustin's mind about how to spend the
money by taking him to the bridge they both associated with their
grandmother."

"But he still pushed him off the bridge?"

Merry hated that the answer was a simple "yes." Were friend-
ships that frail? That susceptible to cracking apart and erupting into

violence and murder? If that was true, why would anyone go out of their way to make a friend? Wasn't the safer, more rational choice to be alone, to trust no one?

"Our poor Saskatchewan Roughrider, he wouldn't have suspected a thing," Stella murmured.

"No," Merry glumly agreed. "And maybe that's a good thing."

Sensing the energy draining from the interview, Stella wisely decided it was time to change gears. "To all you listeners out there, I know you're chomping at the bit to get to the call-in portion of the podcast. I'm looking forward to discussing all these details in depth with you too. Private detective Merry Bell has been our guest tonight. She's been incredibly generous with her time and knowledge. Merry, I know you have another commitment and have to leave us," Stella announced, as pre-arranged with Merry, "so on behalf of myself and my listeners I want to thank you for joining us tonight on *The Darkside of Livingsky* and for this fascinating behind-the-scenes look at your investigation into the murder of local hero and legend, Dustin Thomson.

"Anyone out there needing a private investigator, you've just met one of the best. I've posted contact information for Livingsky Sharpe Investigations on the show notes page. Goodnight, Merry. I hope we have the chance to do this again."

Stella meant her last words and Merry knew it. She just wasn't sure she could make that promise. Instead, she upped the cheeriness in her voice, chirped "Thank you, Stella and goodnight, everyone" and hit the "Leave" button. Once the connection was broken and the screen was blank, she whispered: "Somebody, please hire me."

Hearing an unfamiliar rustle, her eyes darted to a corner of the room. She found a small mound of brown sugar curled up there, gently snoring. Somehow in all the kerfuffle of Dustin's roommate being arrested for his murder and no one stepping up to care for him, Marco the Lagotto Romagnolo had ended up going home with Merry. She met him when she first interviewed Calvin Wochiewski and had fallen in love—who wouldn't?—but she never expected the furry Italian to become her roommate. What was she thinking? Her life was a mess. She could barely take care of herself, never mind a young dog. On the bright side, Alvin Smallinsky turned out to be a closet dog lover and was immediately amenable to her bringing Marco to Craving Lane as needed, even offering to look after him should she need to leave her office unexpectedly on P.I. business.

Lowering herself on the floor next to Marco, Merry buried a hand in the dog's soft fur and sighed. She wanted nothing more than to take Marco home to the Junk House where they could enjoy the final golden rays of a summer night beneath the magical fairy lights of the scrap metal yard with a glass of wine, a chew toy, and a good book. But the night was far from over. There was one last thing that needed doing and she wasn't looking forward to it.

CHAPTER 26

The door to Designs by Brenda was half open. Merry, brandishing a fresh bottle of wine and two glasses, pushed it the rest of way. Seeing Brenda intently studying something on her desk, she announced her presence with: "Sauvignon blanc time?"

Startled, Brenda looked up. Seeing her office neighbour and the wine, she shoved what she was reading under a stack of fabric swatches and with an uncharacteristic lack of gracefulness jerked into a standing position. "Oh. Hello. Gosh. Merry. I'd love to but I'm already late. I told Roger I'd be home…well, right about now. Maybe another time?"

Merry couldn't help but frown. This was new. Designs by Brenda never turned down Sauvignon blanc time. That was Merry's gig.

"I was hoping we could talk. It won't take long."

Brenda scrambled to shove papers into a lovely off-white leather folder. "Now where's my coat?"

"It's twenty-five degrees outside," Merry commented as she assessed the woman for signs of a stroke.

"Of course, how silly. Well, thanks for the drink. See you tomorrow." Brenda hustled towards the door.

"I think it's important we talk, Brenda."

The woman stopped in her tracks. She slowly turned to face Merry, a defeated look on her face. "I know what this is about."

"You do?" This was unexpected but not entirely surprising. Merry had only just recently discovered what Brenda knew all along.

"Yes, and I'm sorry. We both are."

"Both?"

"Roger and me. He told me about what he did, starting an investigation into those notes slipped under your door without your knowledge."

Brenda was wrong. Roger's ill-advised investigation was not what Merry had on her mind.

Brenda nattered on: "He told me how he concluded your family was responsible for sending those notes and that he invited you to the house to ask your permission to contact them. That was very wrong of him. He shouldn't have done it. I blame myself. I should never have encouraged him to play detective with you. He shouldn't have done it," Brenda repeated, "but I hope you understand why he did."

The words Roger used to explain himself stuck with Merry like burnt rice at the bottom of a pan: *I did this because I'm worried about you. I think you're lonely. I wanted to show you that you're not alone, that you have someone on your side, that you have a friend.* "He said he did it because he thinks I'm lonely."

Brenda's moist eyes reached out for Merry. "He did it because he's lonely too. We both are."

Merry's brow creased. What was this woman talking about?

"Roger is a crossdresser. Has been since the day I met him, since before I met him. I am his wife. I am the wife of a crossdresser. Is there a name for that, for what I am? I don't even know. We're certainly not mainstream people. Are we part of the LGBTQ community? I don't know. Some other community? Is there a crossdresser and their spouses' community? If there is, we can't find it. At least not in Livingsky. We don't know where we fit. We have no one to relate to, no one to talk to, no one to help us get through the rough patches, because we certainly have them, no one to guide us how to do things we have no idea how to do—like tell our kids why their dad goes into the basement to host a murder podcast and wear a dress—no one to just be ourselves with. It's lonely, Merry, it's achingly lonely."

The room fell into deep and heavy silence, permeating the walls and ceiling, weighing on them like heavy rain. For a long time, the two women stared at each other. Brenda at first appeared shocked that the words had come out of her mouth, then doubtful that they had. Merry, her arms fallen lifelessly to her sides, weak-kneed, felt the wine bottle and glasses begin to slip from her grasp but recovered them just in time.

"Brenda," Merry began in a hushed tone, "I didn't know. I should have. I wasn't thinking. I'm so distracted dealing with my own crap, I didn't see yours. It's no excuse and I'm sorry."

"Thank you," Brenda whispered, still shell-shocked by what she'd just admitted out loud.

"I know what you're going through. I have felt loneliness all of my life, one kind of lonely before I began my transition, another kind after. Transgender people often wonder the same thing: where do we belong? Are we really part of the LGBTQ community? Just because the T is there in form doesn't mean it is in function, it doesn't even mean it should be. Maybe we're just who we are and that's all that matters. I don't know the answers, Brenda. I haven't met anyone who does. Strangely enough that makes me feel better."

"Humph," Brenda ticked her head to one side, "that does make me feel a little better. You know what else would make me feel better?"

Merry raised a questioning eyebrow.

"Sauvignon blanc time. Why are you just standing there? Open and pour."

Merry did as instructed, grateful for the extra time to consider her next move. This conversation had veered wildly off course. The wine had been meant to lower Brenda's defenses while Merry confronted her, not to soothe her in the aftermath of a personal meltdown.

The women and their wine settled on a loveseat Brenda had managed to find room for in the small office crowded with enough design knick-knacks and samples to fill a Wayfair warehouse.

"Brenda, I wonder if you and Roger should consider seeing a counsellor to talk about this. I did. It helped me immensely. I still have things to work out, but it helps, I promise."

"We do. And you're right, it does help. I really don't know where all of that came from," she waved her hand in the air to indicate her recent outburst. "I guess maybe I'm just tired. I've been so busy, clients clients clients, all the time wanting this and that and the other thing."

Merry wondered where all these clients clients clients came from as she'd yet to see a single one darken the door of Designs by Brenda in the months since she'd been at 222 Craving Lane. But no matter, Brenda seemed happy to move on, and so was she. It was time to take this china shop bull by the designer horns. "I'm glad you brought up the notes earlier. That's actually what I wanted to talk to you about tonight."

"I know, and again, I'm sorry, we both are. I'll tell Roger to back off."

"I don't want to talk about Roger. I want to talk about you."

"Me?"

"The notes, you remember what they said: *I know it's you*?"

"Mm-hmm." She sipped wine.

"Brenda." Merry stopped there, waiting for the woman to come clean on her own.

"What is it?" Brenda asked, the pitch of her voice higher than normal.

So much for coming clean. "Brenda, I know it's you."

Brenda laid down her wine glass and brought a delicate hand to her burning cheeks. "Wh-what are you saying?"

"I know it was you who sent those notes."

"No, it was not."

"You denied it the first time I accused you of sending them. I believed you. Not this time."

"Merry, I think you're just upset about what Roger did. It's made you paranoid about who could be doing this to you, sending such threatening notes…"

"It was you, Brenda, I know it. Do you want to know how I know it?"

The designer was motionless, like a child hoping that if she remained perfectly still no one would see her.

"When I confronted you about the notes months ago, I also told you how I'd seen you teary-eyed at work on several occasions. I mistakenly assumed it had something to do with Roger being a crossdresser. Instead you told me you were upset because of Doris, your mother, and how her dementia was effecting your relationship, how you didn't want to go home at night because she was so horrible to you."

"Yes," Brenda uttered, "yes, that's right."

"It's not right, Brenda. If your mother has dementia to the extent you claim, Roger would not have allowed her to drive your children across town to a birthday party, which is exactly what he did the night I met Stella for the first time."

Merry watched the blood drain from Brenda's face. She waited a moment then pushed forward. "You lied to me. I began to wonder why. I began to wonder if one lie was covering another."

"You must think I'm terrible, throwing my mother under the bus like that."

Merry's guffaw was humourless. "I think you're terrible for sending me those ridiculous notes. Why did you do it?"

The noise coming from Brenda was either disdain or discomfort, Merry wasn't sure which.

"I knew it was you. Can you believe it? Showing up in the office right next to mine, like it was nothing. Joseph. Joey Dzvonyk."

Merry recoiled at the sound of the name, her former name. No one had used it in such a long time she'd almost forgotten it, like you try to forget a bad memory.

"From the very first second I saw you, I knew. But you, you looked right at me," she spit out, "and saw nothing, nobody, just like always."

It was Merry's turn to carefully lower her wineglass. She placed it on the coffee table and pushed it aside. Brenda leaned forward and pushed hers aside too as if clearing the way for a battle royale.

"Brenda, I...how do you know that name? Who are you?"

"Of course you don't remember," she scoffed. "We went to high school together. Remember that place? Remember what happened there?"

"Yes, I remember high school, but…a lot of things happened, what exactly am I supposed to remember?"

"What about when you ripped out my heart and made a fool of me in front of everyone!"

"What…who…what are you talking about? I think you're mistaking me for someone else. It's been a few years, but I'd recognize you if we went to school together. The only Brenda I knew…" Merry stopped there. She moved in closer to stare at the other woman's face. *No, it wasn't her.* There may be similarities, but this was not the Brenda she knew in high school. But neither was the woman who sat in front of her now the Brenda she knew from 222 Craving Lane.

"You still don't see it?" Brenda challenged. "It's me. Brenda Reyes."

"No. Brenda Reyes was…different."

"Why don't you say it? I was fat. My face was so round I looked like the Pillsbury Doughboy. I fricking almost died working out in the gym because of you," she said with a bitter laugh.

If anyone should know about the power of transformation it was Merry. She once again, more slowly this time, studied the woman's features. Now that she knew what she was looking for, hints of teenage Brenda Reyes revealed themselves.

Sitting back, if for no other reason than to distance herself from the waves of pent-up rage finally freed from their cage now emanating from Brenda, Merry said, "We barely knew each other in high school. Why would you blame anything on me? Why are you so angry with me?"

Waving a perfectly manicured hand in front of her flushed face, Brenda also sat back in her seat, pulling in deep breaths as if fighting off a fit of hyperventilation. Merry watched with a mixture of curiosity and apprehension.

When she was ready, Brenda reached for her glass of wine, downed half of it, and continued. "You humiliated me. In front of everyone. The whole school watched you do it. Do you remember it now that you know who I am? I know you do."

Merry searched her memories but try as she might she could not find the one Brenda was looking for. "I'm sorry, I don't, I really don't. If you tell me what happened, maybe it will come back to me."

"You're right about us not being best friends or anything, but we knew each other. I thought we had a lot in common. I was big and not so pretty, I had zero confidence. You were small for a guy and really skinny, bad at sports. I know the other guys picked on you for that, called you names. They called me names too. I won't repeat any of them."

Merry remembered the name-calling. It was horrible. Painful. Even years later as a young adult she'd spent hours in therapy discussing ways to relinquish the power those brutal words had over her.

"We were kindred spirits," Brenda said, "going through the same lousy stuff day after day."

Merry shook her head. It was true she was miserable in high school, suffering from a near-crippling lack of confidence in herself, but not for the reasons Brenda thought.

"Girls in school talk about boys pretty much all of the time. I told my friends how I felt about you and they agreed we'd be perfect together. Our high school graduation dance was coming up. I thought we should go together. My friends convinced me to ask you."

Merry wondered what kind of "friends" these really were but said nothing.

"That day in the lunchroom you were sitting by yourself like you always did. I came up to you, in front of the whole school, and asked you to be my date for the dance. I thought it would make both of us feel good, to do it in front of everyone, show the world we weren't the losers they thought we were."

As if a floodgate had suddenly opened, Merry quivered as the scene came back to her. "I said no," she said in a hushed voice.

"You said no!" Brenda cried. "In front of everyone. You tore me apart. I already felt so bad about myself, but what you did made it so much worse. I was so excited that day. I thought it was my turn to be Cinderella, instead I was Carrie; fat Carrie!"

"But Brenda…"

"No buts," Brenda zapped back. "It happened. You did that to me. That night, when I got home, I felt like killing myself."

"Oh, Brenda, no, I…"

"If it wasn't for how angry I was at you, I might have done it too. Instead, I vowed to change myself. After grad, which I did not go to…"

"Neither did I."

"I began starving myself. I started working out, sometimes twice a day, for hours at a time. By the time I met Roger I was an entirely new person, the me I was always meant to be. By then you were long gone but I never forgot about you. Every time I look in the mirror and see this other Brenda, I think of you, Joey, and how you made me feel.

"Then suddenly you were back. I couldn't believe it. But you know what really peeved me off? You changed your entire body, you actually changed sexes, and I still recognized you, I recognized Joey Dzvonyk. But I was so invisible to you, then and now, you never for a moment saw me, never recognized Brenda Reyes."

Merry wished she'd brought something stronger than Sauvignon blanc. Her body felt as if it had been forcibly deflated, flattened until it was nothing but a one-dimensional version of itself. For several seconds the women sat there saying nothing, barely remembering to breathe.

Brenda refilled her glass but offered none to Merry. After downing half she continued. "I wanted you to know you couldn't just come marching back home and think no one was going to know you. I could tell you wanted to be incognito. I wanted you to know that…" Brenda stopped suddenly, a sob erupting from her throat. "Oh god."

"Brenda…"

Wiping away a tear she kept on. "Hearing myself saying this out loud I can't believe how horrible it sounds, how horrible what

I did was."

"Brenda, you don't have to do this…"

"No, I have to say this," she responded, her voice raw. "Merry, I slipped that note under your door because I wanted you to know that no matter how much you'd changed, how much you'd paid to transform your body, it wasn't good enough, because I still knew it was you, I saw right through you. Nothing you'd done was good enough to hide who you really are. I wanted you to suffer humiliation like I suffered humiliation. I wanted you to feel failure." She gulped another dose of wine and cried out: "Oh my god, I'm a terrible person!"

"Brenda," Merry began in a calm voice that belied how she was really feeling, "What I don't understand is that if you were feeling all of this, if you hated me so much, why would you invite me to your home that first day we met? You asked me to meet your husband, you gave me a makeover, for god's sake. It doesn't make sense."

"I know it doesn't. I was a moth drawn to a flame. Now that you were back in my life, I couldn't stay away. I suppose part of it is that after old Brenda became new Brenda, I began to think the improvements needed to be about more than just my physical appearance. New Brenda knows better, she tries to give people the benefit of the doubt. I wanted to give you a chance to see who I was, to recognize Brenda Reyes, to admit what you'd done and apologize, because teenage Brenda still needed that.

"And—this is hard to say—part of me loved the idea that Joey Dzvonyk, the terrible boy who made me feel so bad about myself, needed me. He was sitting in my makeup chair needing me, wanting my help to look better. I know how bad it sounds," Brenda said, sounding more and more like Designs by Brenda, "but there it is. When you still didn't recognize me that night, I kept thinking eventually you would if we just spent more time together."

Merry nodded. All those invitations for Sauvignon blanc time were about much more than she could have ever guessed.

"The longer it took for you to recognize me, the harder it got for me to keep my hate alive. I was forgetting Joey and coming to really like Merry. Not to mention how happy Roger was to have a real live private detective in our lives. By the time you came to my office to accuse me of sending the notes, I didn't know what to do. I was so conflicted. I didn't want to screw things up for Roger and I was too embarrassed to admit what I'd done. So when you outright accused me of sending the notes, I denied it to your face. The only person I told about who you really were and our past was my mother. She admonished me for how I was acting. She told me to 'buck up and get on with life.' So, when it came to blaming someone for the tears you saw, she was an easy target. I love my mother, but the one thing I did not lie about is that we do not have the easiest relationship.

"But teenage Brenda couldn't leave it there. I remember saying something to make you wonder who could possibly hate you enough to threaten you in this way. It was petty, I know, but I took joy from that. I really think I believed that if you thought about it hard enough, you'd realize that the only person who could hate you that much was Brenda Reyes, who you'd humiliated in high school."

"Brenda, the first thing I want you to know is how sorry I am that you went through what you did, and how it affected you for so many years. No one should have to go through that and for all the ways I played a part in that I am sorry."

Brenda began to speak but Merry held up a hand to stop her. "Please, let me finish. I know you believe what happened to you happened in the way you believe it did." Merry's brain was working overtime as she carefully chose her words. "I remember you and I remember that day. Memories are tricky. Things that happen in high school are tricky. People recall things from childhood with skewed perception, mostly because at that age you're too selfish to see it any other way than from your own limited, hormone-addled perspective. In high school I was going through things no one knew about, things I could barely understand myself. That's nobody's fault. You had every right to expect better from me that day. You had no way of knowing there was *no way* I could give you your Cinderella moment."

Yes, Brenda Reyes had come up to Joey Dzvonyk in the school

cafeteria that day and suggested they go to grad together. Yes, Joey said no. It was not, to Merry's recollection, in front of the whole school, or really anyone at all. The room was hardly full, most students preferring to eat outdoors at that time of year, and those who were there paid no attention to two nerdy kids they barely knew existed. There was no public humiliation, only a hushed rejection delivered for reasons that had nothing to do with Brenda.

Telling Brenda any of this would change nothing, Merry knew. It wouldn't make her feel better about herself, now or then. She might even think Merry was refusing to believe her to avoid having to admit she (as Joey) had done such a hurtful thing. And for Brenda to believe she was wrong, and had reacted in such an extreme way in response to such an insignificant moment, might quite possibly be disastrous to her mental health.

Merry cleared her throat and said: "I believe you, Brenda. What happened to you, what I did, was terrible. I know saying I'm sorry isn't enough, but for now it's all I've got."

By now Brenda was red-eyed, stuffed up with tears and surrounded by balls of wet Kleenex. "I'm sorry about the notes," she struggled to say between jagged breaths.

Merry nodded and wondered how new Brenda and new Merry could ever move on from this. What Brenda believed Joey Dzvonyk did to her was terrible. But so was what Brenda did to Merry. Designs by Brenda was a complicated, passive aggressive person. The question was, would the aggression remain passive, or would it rear its ugly head up one day and tear her apart?

"I think we've had enough for tonight," Merry said, standing up. "Leave the wine."

—

Back in her office, Merry collapsed on the chair behind her desk and swivelled it so she could stare at the graffiti mural outside the window. Instead of hashing over all the weirdness that had just occurred between her and Brenda, the scene that kept playing in her head was her first meeting with Stella, and the words she could not forget: *I think you're lonely.*

Merry didn't mind being alone. Lonely was another matter. She did need more people in her life. She needed a family, of one kind or another. She thought about who she had to pick from: a morally ambiguous, mullet-headed, flamingo-legged landlord; a prickly, serious-as-a-heart-attack cop; a true-crime-obsessed crossdresser, and a sickly-sweet interior designer who just might hate her guts.

Slim pickings.

Look what happened between Dustin Thomson and Calvin Wochiewski. Could she trust any of them not to kill her?

She looked down at the sound of a nasal whimper. She reached down and pulled Marco into her lap. "You're right," she said to the Lagotto Romagnolo whose wet brown nose was less than an inch from hers, "that's getting a bit dark, even for me."

In response, Marco licked her face.

"I guess it's you, buddy," Merry informed the dog. "You're officially my first friend in Livingsky, my number one. That okay with you?"

It seemed to be.

Before she could talk herself out of it, Merry pulled her phone from her pocket and dialed a number she hadn't used in years but never forgot. When the call was answered she replied, "Hi, Dad, it's me."

MORE ABOUT THE AUTHOR

Anthony Bidulka has dedicated his career to writing traditional genre novels in an untraditional way, developing a body of work that often features his Saskatchewan roots and underrepresented, diverse main characters. He tells serious stories in accessible, entertaining, often humorous ways.

Bidulka's books have been shortlisted for numerous awards including the Crime Writers of Canada Award of Excellence (three times), the Lambda Literary Award (three times), the Saskatchewan Book Award (five times). Flight of Aquavit was awarded the Lambda Literary Award for Best Men's Mystery, making Bidulka the first Canadian to win in that category. 2022's Going to Beautiful about a gay man rising from the depths of despair in search of joy on the Saskatchewan prairie won the Crime Writers of Canada Award of Excellence for Best Crime Novel and the Independent Publisher Book Award as the Canada West Best Fiction Gold Medalist. Most recently, Livingsky, the first book in a trilogy featuring the first Saskatchewan prairie-based transgender PI in Canadian literature was a double American Fiction Award finalist.

The University of Saskatchewan inducted Anthony into the College of Education Wall of Honour and presented him the College of Arts and Science Alumni of Influence Award. He received the Ukrainian Canadian Congress Nation Builders Award and was named, along with his husband Herb, Saskatoon Citizen of the Year. For his promotion of Saskatchewan through his writing, co-founding Camp fYrefly Saskatchewan (a leadership retreat for gender and sexually diverse and allied youth), and widespread volunteer and philanthropic efforts in the community, Anthony was honoured by the selection of a two-part park in Saskatoon named Bidulka Park and Bidulka Park North.

In his free time Bidulka loves to travel the world, collect art, walk his dogs, obsess over decorating Christmas trees (it's a thing) and throw a good party.

Website: www.anthonybidulka.com

ACKNOWLEDGEMENTS

I begin these acknowledgements with a huge shout-out to the readers, reviewers, booksellers and book promoters, the Beautiful Bunch, who have so enthusiastically welcomed Merry Bell P.I. into the mystery genre sphere. As an eternal optimist, I ultimately believe the world is a friendly place, even when at times it seems it isn't. When the world is on fire, I believe we must do what we can, when appropriate, to douse conflict, tragedy and negativity with togetherness, celebration, joy and hope. Reading books, sharing stories, recognizing diversity, promoting the idea that there is no THEM, only US, does exactly that. I hope, in some small way, Merry Bell is part of that. Thank you for being a part of it too.

From Sweetgrass Bridge is my third book with Stonehouse Publishing. I've enjoyed every minute working with the Stonehouse team and its authors. Thank you to Netta Johnson for her steadfast support and belief in these books, and for working tirelessly (and I'm sure often at great sacrifice) to make a difference in the Canadian literary landscape. Cheers to Elizabeth Friesen for her creativity and gift of time and talent in creating book covers that are not only eye-catching but meaningful.

As always, many thanks to my husband Herb for being the first to read anything I write (even when mysteries aren't really his thing.) He says he loves them. I believe him. Thank you to the readers who make a special effort to tell others about these books, either through online reviews, social media, commentaries, or simple shoulder-tapping.

Your support makes a HUGE difference.

Heartfelt gratitude to the people who've inspired certain characters and passages which have or will appear in the Merry Bell trilogy. You know who you are. I am in debt to you for your generosity in sharing your stories with me. I would also like to make special mention of three people who helped make this book better than I could have ever achieved on my own. First, Rhonda Sage for her expertise at finding errors in punctuation, grammar, and spelling that by some miracle always seem to evade the rest of us. Second, Dr. Robert Calder; oddly enough I did not consult with Dr. Calder for his prodigious accomplishments in the fields of literature and education (he is considered by many to be the world's leading authority on W. Somerset Maugham), but rather for his vast, at-the-ready knowledge of the Saskatchewan Roughriders football team which plays a vital role in this book. Third, I say thank you to Priscilla Settee, PhD, Professor Emerita, Department of Indigenous Studies, University of Saskatchewan. Dr. Settee generously agreed to read From Sweetgrass Bridge and provide guidance in areas where I have written about Indigenous characters or Indigenous experiences. Any remaining errors, omissions, insensitivities, or fumbles with football terms are mine to claim.